HOPE SPRINGS SERIES

Mistletoe and Wedding Bells

ASHLEY FARLEY

Scottie's Adventures

Breaking the Story

Merry Mary

1

STELLA

The sound of bells ringing in the distance silences the crowd. Families with young children migrate to the edge of the stone terrace, looking out into the inky darkness toward the mountains. Thousands of white lights blink on, outlining the barn and trees and sidewalk leading down to the lake. The spectators clap and cheer. A jolly voice echoes throughout the farm. "Ho, ho, ho!" More bells ring, and the night goes quiet again.

"Stella," Jazz says, tugging on my coat sleeve. She lifts her sweet face to me. "Do you believe in Santa Claus? Mommy says there's no such thing as Santa."

My heart goes out to my half sister. Only a callous woman like Naomi would tell her six-year-old daughter there's no such thing as Santa.

I bend over, eye level with Jazz. "I believe in the magic of Christmas, Jazzy." I touch my finger to her chest. "That magic lives inside of each of us. You get to decide whether you want to believe in Santa. No one else can decide that for you."

She drags her pink tongue over chocolate-smudged lips.

"But I'm living with you now. If there is a Santa, how will he find me?"

I cup her cheek, my thumb caressing her smooth caramel skin. "He'll find you, sweetheart. That's part of the magic."

"If you say so." Jazz trusts me, despite not being fully convinced.

Christmas is in three weeks. I have twenty-one days to turn her into a believer.

Jazz draws in a quick breath when she sees a golden retriever puppy on the leash of a little boy about her age. "Aw. Look. Isn't that puppy cute? Can I go pet him?" The puppy is obviously a male, fat with a boxy face and clunky paws.

"As long as you promise not to wander off." She skips away, and I call after her. "And ask the boy first before you pet his dog."

The little boy is as blond as his puppy. When Jazz approaches him, he smiles and sweeps his arm toward his dog.

Noticing Katherine and Presley standing at the edge of the crowd, I join them. "Congratulations on an amazing job with the lights and the illumination party. Once again, you two outdid yourselves."

Presley jabs an elbow at Katherine. "Our groundskeeper deserves the credit."

Rosy dots appear on Katherine's cheeks. "Only for the lights. Our event planner is responsible for the s'mores and the sound effects and getting all these people here. You should see Presley's calendar of events for December." Katherine snatches a flyer from the stack Presley is holding and hands it to me.

I scan the long list of events for hotel guests and local towns-people planned for the upcoming weeks at Hope Springs Farm. "You've added even more functions since our last meeting."

Presley takes back the flyer. "Only a few activities to keep the children busy during the week before Christmas. I thought the parents might appreciate an opportunity to enjoy themselves."

"Good thinking." Warmth floods my body despite the chilly night. Placing an arm around them, I draw Presley and Katherine in for half hugs. "Our hard work is paying off. For the first time since reopening after the renovations in September, I truly believe the inn will make it. I only wish Cecily could've been here tonight."

"Cecily's in the kitchen, overseeing our largest dinner crowd to date," Presley says. "She's as happy as a pig in the mud. She reports that reservations for Jameson's are filling up from now until after New Year's."

"That's amazing. And you're right. She's exactly where she wants to be. It'll be a miracle if we can drag her away from the kitchen long enough to get married on Christmas Day."

Presley's brow creases. "Now that you mention it, I admit I'm worried. She can't seem to spare me five minutes to talk about her reception."

"You know, Cecily. She's super driven. But I'll talk to her tomorrow. Now that our new sous chef has started, she can afford to take some time off."

I shift my gaze to Jazz, who is now sitting cross-legged with her new friend on the terrace while the puppy crawls all over them.

"He's a cutie," Presley says.

I smile. "Which one, the boy or the puppy?"

"Both," Presley says with a laugh.

"She looks happy," Katherine says. "How's she adjusting to her new circumstances?"

I flap my hand in the so-so gesture. "Mostly, she's doing okay. But she's terrified the judge will make her go back to Naomi."

A look of horror crosses Katherine's pretty face. "Is that a possibility?"

"Unfortunately," I say, an all-too-familiar dread weighing heavily on me. "The judge has given Naomi ninety days to prove herself. She's cleaned up her act before. There's nothing stopping her from doing it again."

"At least Jazz has *The Nutcracker* to look forward to," Katherine says. "She told me all about it earlier. Dancing Clara in the opening party scene is a huge deal."

Presley whips out her phone. "When is that again? I hope we're invited."

"Two weeks from tomorrow, on Saturday, December nineteenth, at seven o'clock. Put it in your calendar. Jazz would be disappointed if you don't come." I mentally increase the number of seats I need to save for the performance.

Presley's gray eyes glass over, and I can tell she's scheming. "Should we plan a reception for the dancers and their parents afterward?"

"I love that idea," I say. "But don't you already have enough events to organize this month?"

Presley consults her flyers. "We have nothing booked for that date. I'd like to do something special for Jazz. We'll host it in the solarium. Cake and punch for the dancers and champagne for their parents."

"As long as you keep it simple. Jazz will be thrilled. I'll talk to her instructor. We can encourage the families to stay for dinner in Jameson's afterward."

Arms engulf me from behind, and I smell the scent of Jack's sandalwood cologne. He plants a kiss on my neck and says to Presley and Katherine, "Evening, ladies. Sorry I'm late. I got tied up at the house. I recruited a few of my guys to help install wiring for the sound system."

"How are the renovations coming?" Katherine asks.

I feel Jack's body tense. "Slow. The kitchen contractor is

dragging his feet. I'd hoped to be in by Christmas, but I'm not sure that will happen."

"I know this is none of my business but . . ." Presley starts.

Jack groans, and I laugh. "You're going to say it, anyway."

"Ha ha." Presley plants a hand on jutted hip. "So, what's preventing the two of you from getting married? You're already engaged. Stella has admitted she doesn't want a big wedding. You could live together as a family in that big old house, and the judge will deem you better capable of giving Jazz a stable life than Naomi."

Jack drops his arms from around me. "Thank you, Presley. I've said that very thing a thousand times these past two weeks."

"And I've told Jack a thousand times that Jazz feels safe living in the cottage," I say in a harsher tone than intended. "I don't want to upset her apple cart until we have permanent custody."

Presley appears wounded. "I'm sorry, Stella. I didn't mean to touch on a sore nerve. Getting married and moving into that beautiful house seems like the obvious solution to me."

I soften. "If only it were that simple."

Katherine takes Presley by the wrist. "The crowd is dwindling. Let's go hand out your flyers before everyone leaves," she says, and leads Presley away.

Jack and I stand together in awkward silence. The marriage argument is old. I want nothing more than to be Jack's wife. But I have an obligation to my sister. I have to put her needs first. If there were a way to get married without the pomp and circumstance.

I sneak a glance at Jack, who is watching Jazz giggle with delight as the puppy licks her face.

As though sensing my eyes on him, he says, "We should get that kid a puppy."

I bark out a laugh. "As if our lives aren't complicated enough already."

A smirk appears on his lips. "If you tell me you're a cat person, the engagement is off."

I lean into him. The warmth of his body calms the anxiety that has taken up residence in the pit of my gut. "I don't know if I'm a cat or a dog person. I never had either."

"Seriously?" He draws his head back to look at me. "That's criminal."

"I grew up in New York City. Having a dog in an apartment is complicated."

Jack cocks his head to the side as he considers this. "I never thought about it, but I can see where it might present some challenges. Being a country boy, I grew up with dogs, and we have five acres at the manor house. I'd like to have as many as you'll let me."

"If you want dogs, we'll have dogs. You may have as many as you want," I say, thinking he's the most generous and selfless person I've ever met.

When the boy and his puppy leave the party with their parents, Jazz scrambles to her feet and waves them goodbye. For a split second, my sister appears as though she might cry. Glancing around, she sees Jack and rushes over to him.

"Jack! You're here." She throws her arms around him. "Did you see the lights?"

"Not yet. Wanna show me?"

Taking him by the hand, she drags him to the edge of the terrace. "How many lights do you think there are?" she asks.

"Thousands. Tens of thousands. Hundreds of thousands. Maybe even a million. Or tens of mil—"

"Jack! Stop! Please." Jazz lifts her arms to Jack, and he picks her up. "Guess what? Santa Claus was here. I heard him."

"Did you?" He holds his head back, his hazel eyes big. "What'd he say?"

Jazz deepens her voice. "Ho, ho, ho!"

"That definitely sounds like Santa."

She drops her head to his shoulder and closes her lovely golden eyes.

Jack takes in the festive landscape. "The lights are spectacular, Stella. Looks like you had a good turnout for the illumination ceremony."

"We had an excellent turnout. Our family-oriented events are proving to be popular. Both of our Saturday Santa Brunches are sold out already."

My phone's screen lights up with my head of security's caller ID. When I accept the call, Martin blurts, "Naomi's at the front entrance. She's causing a scene."

"I'm on my way." I end the call and return my attention to Jack. "We have a situation. Please take Jazz to the cottage and lock the door."

"I'm on it." He kisses my cheek. "Be careful."

Jack and I head off in opposite directions. Crossing the stone terrace to the veranda, I enter the main building and pass through reception to the wide front entry hall.

A handful of guests watch at a distance as Naomi squares off against Martin. My head of security is a mountain of a man, six and a half feet tall with broad shoulders and bulging biceps. But Naomi, with feet shoulder-width apart and fists balled at sides, appears unafraid.

When she sees me, she demands, "I want to see my daughter. Where is she?"

"Sorry, Naomi, but your supervised visitation isn't until next week."

"Forget about the visitation. I want to see Jazz this instant. Take me to her." She brushes past Martin, and as she draws nearer to me, I smell alcohol on her breath.

Still holding my phone, I click on the camera icon and begin videoing her.

Naomi stops in front of me. "What're you doing?" she asks, her stunningly beautiful face distorted by anger.

"Videoing you. Judge Marcum would want to know you've been drinking."

Naomi swats the phone out of my hand, sending it tumbling across the Oriental rug. Martin rushes her from behind, locking his muscular arms around her midsection. She sinks her teeth into his forearm, and when he hollers out in pain, she wrestles free of him. Losing her footing, she stumbles into the Christmas tree. The tree topples backward, into the corner of the room, and antique Radko ornaments shatter on hardwood floors. In disentangling herself from its branches, Naomi brings the tree forward with her. Martin dives for the tree, preventing it from landing on the eyewitnesses.

Naomi bolts for the front entrance. I scoop up my phone and run after her. "Naomi, wait! How did you get here? Let me call you an Uber."

As I burst through the double paned doors, I see her car speeding away from the curb. I dial nine-one-one. When the operator answers, I identify myself. "This is Stella Boor, general manager at the Inn at Hope Springs Farm. I'm reporting a drunk driver. Naomi Quinn. She's a disgruntled ex-employee, and the mother of my six-year-old half sister, whom I have temporary custody of. She left here seconds ago in a silver Honda sedan. Please! Contact the police before she kills someone."

"Do you know the license plate number?" the operator asks in a nasal tone.

"No! But she lives at Fifteen Bayberry Lane."

"I'm notifying the police now. Thank you, Miss Boor."

The line goes dead, and I click on the contact information for the detective who is handling Jazz's case. "I'm sorry to bother you at night, Detective," I say and explain the situation.

"Let me see what I can find out," Detective Sinclair says. "I'll call you right back."

I remain under the portico, watching guests come and go, while my breath steadies and heart rate lowers. Detective Sinclair has taken a special interest in our case. Two weeks ago, late on a Saturday afternoon, she found Jazz roaming around the neighborhood where Jazz lived with her mother. Naomi had gone on a date and left Jazz at home alone for hours. Jazz had been on her way to the inn to find me when she'd gotten lost.

My phone pings with an incoming text from Sinclair. *Naomi's car is parked in her driveway. We missed her but will keep an eye on her tonight. Will forward report to Judge Marcum.*

A shiver travels down my spine that has nothing to do with the dropping temperatures. Inside the entry hall, the nosy onlookers have cleared out and Martin is securing the tree in its stand while Katherine and Presley sweep up shards of glass from the broken ornaments. I wait for Martin to finish with the tree before pulling him aside, leading him out of the entry hall into reception.

"Naomi took off in her car," I explain. "I called the police, but she got home before they could pull her over."

He shakes his head in disgust. "She's gonna kill someone."

"I just hope it's not one of our guests." I start off toward the elevators, motioning for him to follow me. "Let's make a loop of the main floor, just in case."

As we stroll down the hall toward my office, I explain to Martin about my custody battle with Naomi. We stop outside of the game room and adjoining library, where clusters of guests are sipping cocktails by the fire and playing pool.

"I don't like what happened here tonight," I say. "Naomi is a loose cannon. You need to beef up your staff. I want every building on this farm secured at all times, most especially the main building and my cottage."

Martin gives me a solemn nod. "Understood."

We continue on our rounds. In the solarium at the end of the hall, a pair of lovebirds, their arms encircling each other's waists, stare up at a fifteen-foot tree that is shimmering with silver and white ornaments. We cross back through reception into the main lounge, which is teeming with people. Not only are our rooms booked to near capacity for the weekend, many of the locals stayed after the illumination ceremony for drinks at Billy's Bar—our cocktail lounge named after my late father, rock legend Billy Jameson—and dinner in Jameson's, our white-tablecloth restaurant.

"Everything appears in order," I say when we return to reception. "If anything happens tonight, I want you to call me immediately."

Martin two-finger salutes me. "I'll alert my staff to the potential danger."

Exiting the building, I jog across the terrace, down the stone steps, and over the narrow road to my cottage. Jack is waiting for me at the door. "I've been so worried. Is everything okay?"

"For the moment," I say and recount the events of the past hour. "I have a sick feeling that things with Naomi will get worse before they get better."

I slip off my coat and take a peek at my sister who is sleeping peacefully in the adjoining bedroom.

Standing beside me, Jack whispers, "She's only been asleep a few minutes. She woke up when I tried to put her to bed. I helped her change into her nightgown and brush her teeth. We read a few books, and she asked me a million questions about Santa Claus."

Turning away from the bedroom, I move over to the sofa, plopping down and kicking my feet onto the coffee table. "Can you believe Naomi told her there's no such thing as Santa?"

Jack sits down beside me. "Nothing about Naomi surprises

me anymore. Jazz grilled me pretty hard. I fumbled my way through a pitiful explanation about the magic of Christmas."

"Same. I want to give Jazz something special from Santa this year. Something that will help her believe in that magic." I grab my iPad off the coffee table and search for best toys for six-year-old girls.

"I don't think you'll find it on Amazon."

"You're right." I close the cover on my iPad. "Do you have any ideas?"

"I do actually." He grins and the lines at the corners of his eyes crinkle. "What about giving her a house?"

"Jazz isn't really into dolls, Jack."

"I'm not talking about a dollhouse, Stella." He angles his body toward me. "I'm talking about our new house. Jazz doesn't know I bought the manor house. If we make it a surprise from Santa, maybe she'll be more excited than intimidated to live in it."

I rest my head against the cushion and stare up at the ceiling while I contemplate his idea.

He goes on. "Think about it, Stella. We can come up with a fun way to present it to her, like putting a house key in the bottom of her stocking or something. And we'll decorate her bedroom with a ballerina theme. Not to mention the house has a state-of-the-art alarm system to keep Naomi out."

"That's a bonus, for sure." I close my eyes, imagining Jazz's face lighting up when she sees her new bedroom washed in shades of her favorite color, lavender. "Call me old-fashioned, but we'll need to have separate bedrooms until after the wedding."

"I'll insist on it. You'll have the master, and Jazz's room will be right next door. If she's afraid to be alone at first, she can sleep with you while she acclimates."

Eyes open, I sit up straight. "Okay. But why not let the house be from you, and the bedroom be from Santa?"

"Fine by me, if that's what you want."

I place my hand on this dear man's cheek. "Are you sure, Jack? This is asking a lot of you. Do you think you can even finish the renovations in three short weeks? Earlier, you told Presley and Katherine you weren't sure you'd be in by Christmas."

He kisses me lightly on the lips. "I'll move heaven and earth to make my girls happy."

"Then let's do it!" I snuggle in close to him. My excitement is tinged with trepidation. What if Jazz is no longer in my care come Christmas? What if I screw up somehow, and the judge takes her away from me? What if? What if? What if? The possibilities are endless. I'm grateful to my father for bequeathing me this seventy-acre farm and historic inn. I would never have discovered my family heritage if not for him. But, along with my inheritance comes the responsibility of protecting my half sister from his former mistress. Some days, the burden seems too great. But Jazz has stolen my heart and I'll do anything for her. Even if it means putting my marriage to Jack on hold while we continue our fight for custody.

2

PRESLEY

The Saturday Santa Brunch goes off without a hitch. Until a little boy projectile vomits all over the front of Presley's white wool dress as she hands out goody bags. Based on the size of the red stain, the kid consumed a gallon of fruit punch.

The odor makes Presley gag, and she abandons her few remaining guests to go home and change. She pulls her fur-lined wrap tight around her as she race-walks down the front drive toward Main Street. The temperature has fallen since she came to work this morning, and the dark clouds building in from the west threaten rain.

Presley lives above a lawyer's office in a renovated warehouse two blocks from the farm. Her spacious one-bedroom corner apartment, one of four occupying the second floor of the building, boasts heart pine floors, exposed brick walls, and floor-to-ceiling windows—two overlooking Main Street and the other pair offering a spectacular view of the mountains.

She strips off her soiled dress, fastens her thick auburn hair on top of her head, and steps into the shower. She scrubs her body with a soapy loofa until her skin is raw, but she can still smell the faint aroma of vomit when toweling off.

With hours to spare before she's due back at the inn, she slips on her short kimono robe and settles in at her desk with a cup of chai tea. She works until three thirty, putting the last touches on her schematic for Cecily's wedding reception. She's spent untold hours developing the rustic winter wonderland theme, and she can hardly wait to present it to Cecily.

Presley freshens her makeup, rearranges her hair into an elegant low bun, and dresses in a black silk wrap dress with knee-high boots. Leaving a lamp on in the living room in anticipation of her late return home, she grabs her black leather work tote and drives back to the inn, disheartened at the steady drizzle coating the windshield of her Volvo SUV. The art show is open to the public, but patrons paid three hundred dollars per plate for the wine dinner. At that price, the weather won't affect turnout. Or will it? They offer free valet parking under the portico. No one will even get wet.

Presley parks in the employee lot and enters the building through the kitchen door. Inside is a beehive of activity with waitstaff buzzing around and station chefs performing various assigned duties. Across the kitchen, Cecily appears to be having a heated discussion with an attractive guy dressed in chef's attire —double-breasted white coat with black-and-white checkered pants.

When Presley approaches, the guy cuts Cecily off in mid-sentence. In a swoon-worthy Italian accent, he says, "*Ciao, Bellissima.* Who are you?"

She extends her hand to him. "Presley Ingram, event planner. And you are?"

He takes her hand, bringing it to his lips. "Alessandro Ricci, your new sous chef." He is good-looking with a strong jawline, dark wavy hair, and black smoldering eyes. "Tell me, Presley, were you named after the King?"

He's teasing her, and she surprises him with her answer. "I

was, actually. My mother was a producer for one of Nashville's top country music record labels. Elvis was her hero."

"*Eccellente!* And when do I get to meet your mamma?"

Her throat thickens. *Will it ever get easier to talk about Renee?* "She passed away last summer." Before he can quiz her about Renee, Presley asks, "Where in Italy are you from?"

"Truth be told, I'm a born and bred New Yorker," he says without the Italian accent. "But I spent my summers growing up with my grandparents in Sorrento."

"Ah . . . the Amalfi Coast," Presley says in a dreamy tone. "My mother and I toured Italy one summer when I was in high school. The coastal regions were my favorite. I take it seafood is your specialty."

"Seafood is one of my specialties. My culinary skills are not limited. I can cook anything your beautiful heart desires, *mia cara.*"

Presley has an innate awareness of people's true characters, and the dial on her people reader tells her he's a good guy despite his theatrics.

Cecily clears her throat, making her presence known. "Excuse me, Presley. But Alessandro and I were in the middle of planning tonight's menu. Can I help you with something?"

"Nothing that can't wait." Presley removes a file folder from her tote and waves it at Cecily. "I've been working all afternoon on the plans for your wedding reception. When you get a free minute, I'd like to show them to you. I'm going to transform the barn into the wedding venue of your dreams."

"Oh." Cecily's expression goes blank. "I meant to tell you. I changed my mind about the reception. I know barn weddings are all the rage, but hay bales and blue grass bands aren't really my thing. I've decided to have my reception under a tent on the terrace with clear flaps so my family and friends can enjoy the lights. By the way, you and Katherine did an excellent job with them."

Presley thrusts the folder at Cecily. "Will you at least look at this before you make your final decision? My vision for the barn is simple elegance with white flowers, silver and gold accents, miles of satiny ribbon, and hundreds of creamy candles."

Cecily eyes the folder. "Save the simple elegance for another bride. I told you, my parents have given me a strict budget. We'll keep the decorations to a minimum—red poinsettias with some holly sprigs are fine—and spend the bulk of the budget on food and booze. Oh, and we may need to change the date to Christmas Eve. Lyle's sister is expecting her first baby on New Year's Day. His parents want to be there when it comes."

Presley jaw goes slack. "But haven't you already sent out your invitations?"

"We're not sending traditional invitations. There's no point when we're only inviting family and a few friends. Once we confirm the date, I'll do an Evite. My family makes up most of the guest list." Cecily snorts. "And knowing them, they wouldn't read it, anyway."

Cecily's family sounds like a classy bunch. "Tell me about your dress. That'll help give me some ideas about the theme."

Cecily's face turns red. "I haven't bought one yet."

Presley's brow hits her hairline. "Are you kidding me? Your wedding is in three weeks. Are you planning to get married in your chef's coat?" She risks a glance at Alessandro, who covers his mouth as he fights back a smile.

Cecily's honey-colored ponytail grazes her shoulders as she looks from Presley to Alessandro and back to Presley. "Don't worry about it. I'll find a dress online."

"Seriously, Cecily? Are you sure you're ready to get married? Why not wait until things slow down after the holidays? You can take your time in planning the wedding of your dreams."

"The wedding will be fine. You're the event planner. You take care of the decorations, and I'll plan the menu. Run along now." Cecily shoos Presley away. "Alessandro and I have a wine dinner to organize."

"Fine." Presley tosses her tote over her shoulder. "But I still need an idea of your budget for decorations. And you should be thinking about your seating chart."

Presley backs through the swinging doors to the dining room where she finds Lucy, their sommelier, busy at work organizing wine bottles in the dining room.

"There you are!" Lucy says when she sees Presley. "I've been looking all over for you. I'm freaking out here. The wine distributor who is helping with the dinner will be here any minute. We need to get the numbers on the tables. Do you have the seating diagram?"

"Right here." Presley plunks her tote on a chair to rummage for the wine dinner file.

"We need to hurry," Lucy says. "The artists will arrive soon to set up their paintings."

"Here it is." Removing the file from her bag, Presley waves the seating chart at Lucy. "And don't worry. We have plenty of time. The artists will set up their displays in the lounge. They won't be in our way."

Presley consults the chart before she begins placing the appropriate numbers on the corresponding tables.

Lucy holds a goblet up to the light, inspecting it for fingerprints and water droplets. She wipes a smudge off the glass before returning it to the table. "Where have you been, anyway? I thought you had that Santa Brunch earlier."

"I did. But I had to run home. A little boy puked all down the front of my winter-white dress." Presley sniffs her arm. "It's probably my imagination, but I can still smell vomit on my skin.

Makes me think twice about wanting children," she says with a snicker.

"We don't always have control over such things, Presley. You, of all people, should know that."

Lucy's bitter tone causes Presley's head to snap up. "I was joking, Lucy. Of course I want children one day. Everything I say offends you these days. Can we talk about this hostility between us?"

"I can't help how I feel, Presley. I wish I'd never . . ." Lucy's voice trails off.

"Never what, Lucy? Never found out I'm your biological daughter?"

Lucy averts her eyes, unable to meet Presley's intense gaze. "I just wish we could go back to being friends."

"Trust me, I wish for that as well," Presley says under her breath.

Staring at the floor, Lucy says, "We don't even know for certain you are my biological daughter."

"Why not get our DNA tested?" Presley suggests. "I'm sure we can find a lab here in town to do it. We can go together. Make a fun outing of it."

Her eyes still on the floor, Lucy says, "Not yet."

"Not yet? Or never?"

Lucy shakes her head. "I can't make any promises."

"Okay, then. I won't pressure you into doing something you're not comfortable doing." Presley gathers up her belongings. With tears stinging her eyes, she leaves the restaurant and enters the main lobby, a large but inviting room with plenty of seating and a wall of windows. Standing at the windows, she watches rain roll off the veranda roof in sheets. Fog shrouds the mountain range, and the landscape lights burn dimly through the gray haze.

Presley mentally replays her conversation with Lucy. *I can't help how I feel.* How exactly does Lucy feel? Does she resent Presley's intrusion in her life? By her own admission, Lucy yearned for years to find her biological daughter, and now that Presley is here, willing to pursue a relationship, Lucy wants nothing to do with her. Is Presley a disappointment to her? Was Lucy hoping for someone more successful or pretty or intelligent?

Presley never saw this dark side of Lucy when they were just friends. Before she discovered Lucy is her biological mother. Was her people reader that off about Lucy when they first met? Or is Lucy an expert at hiding her true self?

Presley's emotions now steady, she inhales a deep breath and faces the lounge. Artists are filing into the vast hall with works of art in all shapes and sizes. When she spots Stella's grandmother struggling under the weight of a large framed landscape, she rushes over to help her.

"Here. Let me take that." Presley eases the painting from Opal's hands. "Where would you like to set up?"

"Front and center," Opal says with a mischievous smile. "Where everyone can see my work."

Presley smiles back at her. She admires the older woman's spunk. The maxi dress Opal is wearing swallows her slight frame. She hasn't regained the weight she lost in a recent battle with leukemia. But her cheeks are rosy, her spiky silver hair shiny, and her skin glowing.

"What about outside of Jameson's?" Presley suggests. "That way, everyone will pass your exhibit on the way in to dinner."

Opal clasps her hands together. "That sounds perfect."

Stella and her uncle, Brian, their arms laden with easels and more paintings, round the corner from the entry hall. Stella looks festive in shiny black leggings and a red silk blouse, her dark curls pinned off her forehead with a rhinestone clip, but the dark circles under her eyes and the firm set of her mouth are telltale signs of her recent troubles.

Presley motions for them to follow her. "We're going down to Jameson's."

For the next hour, while Brian helps Opal arrange her exhibit, Presley and Stella bring the rest of the paintings in from Brian's SUV. They are just finishing up when the first patrons arrive.

Presley and Stella are standing off to the side, out of the way of the art viewers, when Lucy emerges from Jameson's. Presley experiences a pang of envy when Lucy strikes up a conversation with Brian. She wishes Lucy would talk to her with such enthusiasm.

"She has a crush on him," Stella says when she sees Presley watching them.

"Do you blame her? Your uncle is seriously hot for an old dude."

Stella smiles. "Lucy is no ugly duckling. I think he's into her. Maybe he'll ask her on a date. Love is in the air at Hope Springs Farm this holiday season."

"Speaking of love, Cecily doesn't seem very excited about her wedding."

Stella waves a dismissive hand. "Don't worry about Cecily. She's uni-focused on her career."

"I met Alessandro. He's over the top, but in a good way. Do you think there's enough room in the kitchen for two such large personalities?"

Worry lines appear on Stella's forehead. "Funny, that was my opinion when I interviewed him. And I warned Cecily about it. She doesn't always think things through. She has self-proclaimed impulse-control issues."

Presley bites down on her lip. "Which makes me even more worried she's rushing into marrying Lyle."

"Cecily loves Lyle, and he adores her. Being married means

more to her than the wedding itself. And I don't fault her for that. I feel the same way."

"Then we need to make this wedding happen for them," Presley says. "She hasn't bought her dress yet. Can you believe that? She's planning on buying one online."

Stella's navy eyes grow big. "No way! An intervention is definitely in order."

"I couldn't agree more. Let me tell you my plan." Presley leans in close to Stella and whispers in her ear.

3

CECILY

Alessandro's culinary skills live up to Cecily's expectations. As a bonus, he proves astute at solving the minor crises that arise behind the scenes in the kitchen throughout the evening. But Cecily finds certain things about him disturbing. He's a little too fresh for her liking. And the way Presley shamelessly flirts with him is embarrassing. But that's not it. There's something more. She wonders if he might be after her job. But then she tells herself she's being paranoid.

You've been working too hard, Cecily. You need to take some time off. But she can't take any time off, especially not during the holidays. This is her chance to shine. A golden opportunity has landed in her lap. The gig as head chef at the Inn at Hope Springs Farm will make her career. Or break it, if she's not careful.

A few minutes after midnight, she makes her final inspection of the kitchen and locks the door on her way out. She rarely drives to work and is relieved to see the rain has slowed to a drizzle. As she rounds the corner of the building, she spots Alessandro sitting alone on a wooden bench under the portico. The valet attendants have gone home, and no one else is in sight. He's bent over with elbows propped on knees, a cig dangling from his mouth and cell phone cradled between his ear and shoulder. Is he waiting for a ride? He doesn't notice her, and she inches closer, eavesdropping on his conversation.

"I miss you too, *il mio amore*. Have patience. I know what I'm doing. Once I get some experience under my belt, I can go after the big kahuna job."

Cecily freezes. *So, the bastard is after my job.*

When headlights approach, she steps backward, pressing herself against the building behind an enormous boxwood bush. A low-slung, two-door sedan with an Uber sign in the window sweeps Alessandro up and careens back down the long driveway.

Snapping open her umbrella, Cecily follows down the sidewalk on foot to Main Street. She walks two blocks to Marshall Street, takes a right, and travels another two hundred yards to her apartment complex, a row of generic beige buildings offering one, two, and three-bedroom units.

Changing out of her work clothes into her flannel pajamas, she brushes her teeth and washes her face. She's no sooner slid beneath the warm duvet when her fiancé calls.

"Cess-si-ly. Ba-by. I'm comin' over."

"Now? It's awfully late, Lyle."

"Aww. Come on. Don't turn me down. I'm dying to see you."

"You sound drunk. You're not driving, are you?"

"No, dude. I'll be there in one minute," he says and ends the call. She stares at her phone. Since when is she a *dude*.

Thirty seconds later, before she can slip on her robe, there's a loud pounding on the door. Lyle couldn't have gotten here that fast. Even if he sprinted all the way from Town Tavern, his favorite hangout on Main Street. Before opening the door, she peeks through the peephole to make certain it's him. In the hallway outside, Lyle sways back and forth as he holds onto a single wilted red rose.

When she opens the door for him, he presents the rose to her. "I brought you a flower." His eyes cross as he stares at the rose. "Oops. Flower's dead." He throws the flower on the floor.

"How did you get here so fast?"

"I called you from the Uber." He pins her against the wall, smothering her face with kisses. "You're so pretty. My beautiful bride to be. I'm one damn lucky man."

She shoves him off of her. "You're damn drunk is what you are. And you stink. Have you been smoking cigarettes?"

"Not cigarettes. Cigars. It's my bachelor party. Duh."

"Gross. That's disgusting. You will need to shower before you can sleep in my bed." Taking him by the arm, she marches him to the bathroom and turns on the shower. From the linen closet, she removes a clean towel and tosses it at him. "Don't drown."

Cecily returns to the warmth of her bed, and ten minutes later, Lyle joins her in his boxer shorts, his hair dripping and skin damp from the shower. "So . . . Cess . . . where are we gonna live after we get married?"

"Here, I guess."

"No way," he says, punching his pillow. "This place is a shoe box. Have you seen how much stuff I got? I'm an athlete, Cess-si-ly. I got a lot of gear. Bicycle and golf clubs. Lacrosse sticks and weights."

"Whatever, Lyle. I'm not moving in with you and your four roommates." Cecily rolls over on her side, placing her back to him.

He spoons her from behind. "What say we live on campus in faculty housing?"

Cecily has no interest in living on a college campus. "I think we should talk about it in the morning. When you're sober."

She hopes Lyle will forget this conversation in the morning.

But no such luck. The first words out of his mouth when they wake around nine on Sunday are, "So, I heard about a faculty house that's becoming available."

"Right. You mentioned that last night."

He scrunches up his face, as though trying to remember. "We probably won't get it, anyway. They'll let a professor rent it before they give it to an assistant lacrosse coach. But it's worth a try. Wanna check it out today?"

Cecily adds housing to the list of things involved with getting married that she hasn't considered and doesn't have the time to worry about. She swings her legs over the side of the bed, her feet hitting the floor with a loud thud. "Sure! But I'm not sold on living in a house. Who has time to keep up a yard?"

Lyle massages his temples. "I can take care of the yard. What else am I gonna do when you're at work? Which is all the time."

She goes into the bathroom and returns with two Advil. "Here," she says, handing him the pills.

He pops them in his mouth, swallowing them without water, and rolls over on his side.

She remains bedside, staring down at him. "You've never complained about my hours before. You're marrying a chef, Lyle. We'll never have a normal nine-to-five schedule like other people. If that's a problem for you, we should talk about it now."

Lyle covers his ear with her pillow. "Please, lower your voice. And it's not a problem. I promise. We'll deal with whatever life throws at us."

Moving to her chest of drawers, Cecily removes a pair of his running shorts and a T-shirt from the bottom drawer where Lyle keeps some of his clothes. "You need to exercise. You'll feel better after you sweat out all the alcohol you drank last night."

"Seriously, Cess? Can't we sleep a little longer?"

She rips back the covers. "No way. Sunday mornings are sacred. As you just pointed out, I have little time off."

Moaning and groaning, he rolls off the bed to his feet. "You're never gonna let me forget that, are you?"

"Not until I'm convinced you understand the demands of my career."

"I understand. Geez. Give me a break." Snatching his clothes from her hands, he stomps off to the bathroom.

After a five-mile run, Cecily and Lyle spend the rest of the morning sipping black dark roast coffee and catching up on the week's news at their favorite table by the fireplace at Caffeine on the Corner.

"What's on your mind?" Lyle asks when he catches her staring off into space.

"My new sous chef. I think he's trying to steal my job." When she tells him about overhearing Alessandro's conversation the night before, Lyle appears more interested in his phone. She listens to him when he talks about his problems at work. Does he not care? Or does he think her career is unimportant? "Did you hear anything I just said, Lyle?"

When he looks up from his phone, guilt is written on his face. "Um . . . yeah . . .someone is trying to steal your job. I'm sure you're just being paranoid."

Lyle has no sooner dropped his phone on the table when it vibrates again with an incoming text. He snatches up the phone and reads the text. "This is from Sean Baker, the guy currently living in that faculty house. He wants to know if we can come look at the house."

Cecily looks at him over the brim of her coffee mug. "You mean now?"

Lyle shrugs. "Sure! Why not?"

Be nice, Cess, she warns herself. *There's no harm in taking a tour.* "Okay. Cool. Let me get us some to-go cups."

They emerge from the coffee shop and head in the direction opposite Hope Springs Farm toward the Jefferson College campus. The sun is bright in a cloudless sky and the air unseasonably warm for December.

Lyle has a long gait for a man of average height, and Cecily increases her pace to keep up with him. "I have to be honest, Lyle. I'm not sure I want to live so far from the inn."

"Far?" Lyle glances over at her as he continues to walk at a fast pace down Main Street. "The entrance to the campus is exactly a mile from the farm. I know. I've clocked it. The extra distance will help you decompress after a long day. So what if you have to drive to work when it's raining or snowing? Would that kill you?"

"I guess not." Cecily can tell how excited he is about this house, and she doesn't protest when they walk an additional quarter of a mile past the stone entrance gates to the block of small houses where the faculty live.

Cecily is taken by the yellow Cape Cod. She envisions a bench swing hanging on the front porch where Sean is waiting for them with his two Labrador retrievers. Sean explains that he's accepted a job teaching American literature to first-year students at UVA and will move to Charlottesville as soon as exams are over.

The home's interior is basic with two dormer-windowed bedrooms upstairs, and a living room, dining room, and kitchen downstairs. A mud room off the kitchen and the screened-in back porch behind it would offer plenty of storage room for Lyle's vast collection of athletic equipment.

When Sean steps outside to take a call, Cecily pulls Lyle close to her and whispers, "His dogs have left their mark on this house. The place is filthy."

"Nothing a fresh coat of paint won't fix. We'll invite our friends over for a painting party!"

Like who has time to organize painting parties?

Exiting the house, they wave goodbye and mouth their thanks to Sean who is sitting on the porch steps, talking on the phone. Hand in hand, they retrace their steps through campus and down Main Street to Town Tavern.

"It's a long shot," Lyle says with a sigh, as though he's been thinking about the house this whole time. "We shouldn't get our hopes up."

"But it's worth putting your name in the lottery." Shielding her eyes against the bright sun, she stares at the building across the street. "Maybe there's something available in Presley's building. You've seen her apartment. It's gorgeous."

"Presley's is the largest unit in the building, but even it's not big enough for all our stuff. Besides, I want to live in a house. I like walking in the yard and having cookouts."

Cecily closes her eyes and imagines a warm summer evening in the yellow Cape Cod. A gentle breeze is blowing, and they've invited friends over for fruity cocktails and dinner. What will she serve? Scallops or shrimp? No, not everyone likes seafood. She'll have grass-fed flank steak. No. Barbecue ribs. Lyle isn't the greatest cook, but his grilled ribs are acceptable.

Lyle taps on her cheek. "Earth to Cecily. What're you thinking about?"

"What we will serve for dinner at our first cookout." She drops his hand and loops her arm through his. "We should keep looking for a rental house in case this one falls through. Why don't I look in town and you search the campus?"

"Deal." He kisses her forehead. "We need to talk about our honeymoon."

Cecily cocks an eyebrow. "Our honeymoon? I thought we agreed to wait."

"Only because we can't afford to take an expensive trip right now. But my parents have offered to treat us to a few nights at a local resort."

She shakes her head. "I'm sorry. There's no way I can take any time off until after New Year's. Besides, why would I want to go to a resort when I work at one?"

Disappointment crosses his face. "I didn't think of that."

They walk around to the small parking lot behind Town Tavern where he left his pickup truck. "So, what are your plans for this afternoon?" he asks.

They have spent every single Sunday together since they started dating last summer. Some of their favorite afternoon activities include going for rides through the mountains, or hiking on the wooded trails around Hope Springs Farm, or drinking beer and eating bar food while watching football at Town Tavern. But today, with Alessandro threatening to steal her job, she feels pressured to work. "I'm not sure. What about you?"

"Some of the guys invited me to a pickup basketball game," Lyle says, kicking at a pebble.

"That's cool. I was thinking I'd go into work for a while. With so many events coming up, I need to plan out my menus and experiment with a few new recipes."

"Really?" he says in an eager voice.

She flashes him her brightest smile. "Sure! How about if I cook dinner for you tonight?"

"That'd be awesome." He opens his car door. "Do you want a ride back to your apartment?"

"Thanks. But I'll walk."

She waves at him as he drives off. *Careful what you wish for, Cess.* Until a month ago, if faced with a choice between her career and Lyle, she would have chosen Lyle without hesitation. But everything seems so complicated now. Wedding plans. And a housing dilemma. He says he does, but Cecily doubts he truly understands the extent of her commitment to her career. Truth be told, she's only beginning to understand her inner drive to succeed. She doesn't doubt her love for him. She's had plenty of boyfriends in the past, but she's never felt the all-consuming love she feels for Lyle. He's her soul mate. They are destined to spend forever together. But, as the husband of a chef, he'll be responsible for taking care of their children in the evenings. With him being a lacrosse coach, their lives will get messy at times. *Chill, Cecily. You're not even married yet. Stop thinking about babies and start focusing on protecting your job from Alessandro.*

4

STELLA

Presley and I are waiting in ambush inside the kitchen door when Cecily arrives at work on Monday morning. I take one of Cecily's arms and Presley takes the other. "You're coming with us."

Cecily digs the heels of her black Birkenstock clogs into the sidewalk. "Wait! What are you doing?"

"We're kidnapping you," Presley says, and I add, "We're taking you shopping for your wedding dress."

Cecily twists and turns, trying to fight us off. "But I have work to do."

I tighten my grip on her arm. "You won't have a job unless you do as I say."

Cecily stares daggers at me. "Are you threatening to fire me?"

"If that's what it takes to get you into the wedding gown of your dreams."

"Fine." The tension leaves Cecily's body. "But can't I at least change first? I'd rather not go shopping in my work clothes."

"We have a change of clothes for you in the car," Presley says. "Lyle dropped a pair of jeans and a sweater off this morning."

"Great! So you got my fiancé in on your little conspiracy, too?"

"Like I said, whatever it takes." Opening the back door of Presley's Volvo, I give Cecily a gentle push inside. "Your clothes are in the bag." I gesture at the hunter-green duffle on the floorboard.

"Am I supposed to change in the car?"

"That's the idea." Snickering, I slam the door and climb into the front passenger seat.

"Where are we going shopping?" Cecily asks.

"To Richmond," Presley says, starting the engine.

"Richmond! You can't be serious. That's two hours away." Cecily reaches for the door handle.

"Go!" I shout at Presley, and she speeds off out of the parking lot. I crane my neck to look at Cecily in the back seat. "It's eight o'clock now. We'll be in Richmond by ten. I promise we'll start back no later than three this afternoon. You'll be here long before your first reservation arrives at six."

"What about breakfast and lunch? And I need time to prepare for tonight. Dinner doesn't just happen, you know."

"We only had a few guests in-house last night, so breakfast won't be a big deal. And Monday is a slow day for lunch. I've spoken with Alessandro. He has everything under control."

Under her breath, Cecily mumbles. "I bet he does." She slips her chef's coat off, revealing a black lacy bra, and I turn around to give her privacy.

Presley merges onto the interstate. Reaching her desired speed, she sets her cruise control and turns up the volume on the radio. My father's rich baritone fills the car.

"I approve of your taste in music," I say. "Did you choose it for my benefit or are you a fan?"

"A fan," she says. "I grew up listening to Billy. He reminds me of Van Morrison."

I press my hand against my heart. "I love Van Morrison."

Presley takes her eyes off the road for a split second to look at me. "You had big shoes to fill when you stepped into his role as general manager. I don't imagine it's been easy."

I think a minute before answering. "Honestly, I've felt overwhelmed at times. But I've learned so much about myself. And I thrive on the challenges."

"It must be bizarre, taking over the life of a virtual stranger."

"He doesn't feel like a stranger to me anymore, though. I'm living in his cottage, sitting at the desk where he once worked. Jack and I have bought the house where he grew up, the house my great-grandfather built. I've learned so much about my father, but I still have many unanswered questions. I wanna pick up the phone and call him. I guess everyone feels that way when they lose someone close to them."

"I know what you mean. I feel that way about my mother nearly every single day."

When tears well in Presley's eyes, I assume she's thinking about her mother. But something in her pained expression makes me think there's more. "Is there anything you want to talk about?" I ask in a low voice.

A tear escapes Presley's eyelid and slides down her cheek. "I'm not sure." She swipes at the tear. "I have a hard time opening up about myself."

I glance back at Cecily, who has finished changing her clothes and is now fiddling with her phone. "Whatever you say will stay between us. Sometimes it helps to get things off your chest."

Presley rummages one-handed in the center console for a travel pack of tissues to wipe her eyes. "I didn't come to Hope Springs in October for the fall foliage. I was on a mission. I was hoping to find out more about my biological mother. After Renee died, I found my adoption folder in her desk. Among the legal documents was a torn envelope with a Hope Springs address. Turns out Lucy is my biological mother."

"Whoa. That must have come as quite a shock to you."

Presley nods. "I wasn't looking for a new mother to replace Renee or anything like that. She had her share of problems, but she was a wonderful mother and role model. I wanted to know where I come from. Who my people are. I wanted to see my reflection in the faces of others, however corny that may sound."

I study her face. "I'll be honest. I don't see the resemblance."

Presley smiles. "Because there is none. I look nothing like Lucy. I haven't met Lucy's mother yet, but I've seen pictures. And I'm the spitting image of my biological grandmother."

"What a coincidence, when you and Lucy are such good friends."

"Not anymore. She shut me out." Presley pauses while she changes lanes. "Lucy told me herself, before either of us knew she was my birth mother, that she was desperate to find the child she gave up for adoption. I guess she's disappointed that that child turned out to be me."

"That's ridiculous, Presley. How could she possibly be disappointed in you? You're a rock star. She probably just needs time to adjust. Is this why you stayed in Hope Springs?"

Presley nods. "You offering me the job gave me the opportunity to get to know my family better. Anyway, that's my sob story for today." Presley points at a plastic shopping bag at my feet. "I picked up the latest edition of *Brides* magazine, to give us some ideas of what we're shopping for."

Removing the magazine from the bag, I thumb through the pages. "So, Cecily . . . tell us about your dream wedding dress."

Cecily runs her hand down her ponytail. "I haven't given it any thought."

"Here." I hand her the magazine. "You have ninety minutes to decide what you want."

Cecily snatches the magazine from me. "I'm on a budget, you know. Where exactly in Richmond are we shopping?"

"We have a ten-thirty appointment at a popular bridal boutique in downtown," Presley says. "If you don't find what you're looking for at Annalise, there are several other boutiques in Richmond we can check out."

"I can't afford any of these," Cecily says as she tears through the pages.

Presley looks at Cecily through the rearview mirror. "The aim is to get an idea of the style of dress you want to look for. What fabric? Sleeves or strapless? What kind of neckline?"

"I'll know it when I see it. But not in here." Cecily closes the magazine and shoves it back at me.

For the rest of the drive, over Afton Mountain and past Charlottesville, Presley and I discuss the dinner dance planned for this coming weekend. Cecily stares out the window, her face set in stone. Why is she being so difficult? Is she still angry at us for kidnapping her?

The bridal salon is washed in white—walls, lacquered console tables, a pair of matching leather sofas. Even the flowers on the acrylic coffee table are white. Surrounding the sitting area, headless mannequins display flowing white gowns while the adjacent small room features a freestanding brass rack housing more dresses.

Ginger, our designated stylist, greets us at the door. She's our age with blonde wavy hair and a soft smile. "You'll make a lovely bride." She spins me around, assessing me. "Your hair style is . . . um, interesting. Can you take vitamins to make it grow?"

I laugh out loud. "Considering I shaved it all off in June, I'd say it's growing pretty fast."

A look of horror crosses Ginger's face. "You shaved your head? Why would you do such a thing?"

"My grandmother has . . . had leukemia. The cancer is in

remission now. I wanted to cheer her up when her hair started falling out."

"That is so badass." Ginger musses my dark curls. "You have such striking features. You don't need much of a veil anyway. An old-fashioned clip with a poof of tulle."

"That sounds lovely. But I'm not the bride."

Ginger's gaze travels to my left hand. "But . . ."

"I'm engaged, but I haven't set the date for my wedding. We're shopping for Cecily today." Grabbing Cecily by the arm, I yank her forward.

Ginger focuses her attention on Cecily. "And you're every bit as gorgeous. What did you have in mind for a dress?"

"Something cheap," Cecily mumbles.

"Ignore her," I say to Ginger. "She's in a mood."

Presley tugs on Cecily's ponytail. "The sooner you cooperate, the sooner we can return you to your beloved kitchen."

"Some brides know exactly what they want. While others don't have a clue. It's a process." Ginger taps on the screen of an iPad. "And when is your wedding?"

"Christmas Day," Cecily says.

"Hmm. That's soon. With so little time, I wouldn't recommend ordering anything." Ginger motions them into the showroom. "Please, make yourselves at home. Have a look around at the dresses we have on display, while I pull a few from the back."

Presley waits for Ginger to leave. "I thought you decided to get married Christmas Eve."

Cecily rolls her eyes. "Lyle's parents keep changing their minds."

"That's not fair to you," Presley says. "Or me. We need to lock in a date by Wednesday, at the very latest."

"Fine. I'll talk to Lyle tonight." Cecily crosses the room and begins flipping through the rack of dresses.

A wedding gown on one of the mannequins catches my

attention. The bodice and skirt are made of creamy satin, while the high neck and long sleeves are stretch tulle. Reminding myself that we're shopping for Cecily, I turn away from the mannequin.

When Ginger summons Cecily to a fitting room, Presley and I sit down side-by-side on one of the white leather sofas. As we thumb through magazines, I say, "About what you told me earlier in the car . . . if you ever wanna talk about Lucy, I'm here for you."

Presley closes the magazine she's looking at and tosses it on the coffee table. "I probably shouldn't have told you. You're Lucy's employer. I wouldn't want you to think badly of her."

"And I don't. She's doing an excellent job as sommelier. Because we're a small team, it's difficult to keep our personal and professional lives separate. But I promise, anything you ever tell me, I will keep in the strictest confidence."

Presley inhales a deep breath. "Thanks."

I settle back on the sofa, "So, how are things going with Everett? Do you think he's the one?"

Presley's lips part in a smile that lights up her face. "He could be. I love him enough to last a lifetime through thick and thin. I miss him like crazy. Being in a long-distance relationship is so much harder than I thought it would be."

"Don't take this the wrong way, Presley. I don't know what the inn would do without you. But, if you have a chance to be with the man you love, you should be together. Life is short. Don't waste a single solitary day."

"This, coming from the woman who's too busy to pick a wedding date," Presley says in a teasing tone.

"Jack and I are taking baby steps. We're moving in together. We haven't told Jazz about the manor house yet. We've decided to let it be Jazz's Christmas present. But it's a secret." I bring my finger to my lips.

Presley clasps her hands together. "I absolutely love it. I promise not to say a word."

Cecily tries on no fewer than twenty dresses. She hates every single one. Presley and I are whispering, discussing what we'll do if Cecily can't find a suitable dress, when she emerges from the fitting room in a white satin gown with a sweetheart neckline and lace sleeves and bodice overlay. She is radiant, and her beaming face tells us she thinks so too.

Presley nudges me. "She's smiling."

"Finally," I respond under my breath.

Cecily admires herself in the tall antique gold-leaf mirror. "This is it."

Ginger stands behind her, fluffing the long train. "It's a perfect fit, aside from the hem."

Cecily angles her body so she can see the back of the dress in the mirror. "Do you think Lyle will like it?"

"Lyle will love you in that dress," I say, surprised at the sudden lump in my throat.

"All right then," Ginger says. "Let me grab my alterations person."

When Ginger starts off, Presley calls her back. "Before you go, Stella would like to try on that dress." She points at the mannequin with the creamy satin dress. "She's been drooling over it the whole time we've been sitting here."

My face warms. "I have not."

"You have too. And I see why. Simple elegance is perfect for you."

I throw up my hands. "Okay. Fine. I love the dress. But I'm not trying it on. We're here for Cecily."

Ginger carefully removes the dress from the mannequin. "If

you like the dress, you try it on. If you love it, you buy it. If you hate it, you can put it out of your mind. But if you don't try it on, you'll keep thinking about it. Then I'll have to ship it to you."

I laugh. "You make a valid point."

The three of us follow Ginger to Cecily's fitting room, which easily accommodates all of us amidst comfortable seating, an alterations platform, and racks of dresses and veils. The alterations lady arrives, and while she pins Cecily's hem, I strip off my clothes and Ginger helps me into the satin dress.

I stare at my reflection in the three-way mirror. My eyes fill with tears as I imagine gliding down the aisle to where Jack awaits me at the altar. Four sets of eyes are on me, but no one says a word.

Presley is the one to break the silence. "You look positively stunning. You have to buy that."

"Don't be ridiculous. Jack and I are talking about getting married next summer. This dress is all wrong for a warm weather wedding."

Ginger fastens the fabric-covered buttons on the back. "You wouldn't be the first bride to plan her wedding around a dress."

"That would mean next winter, and I don't want to wait that long to marry Jack. Anyway, I should be looking for a bridesmaid's dress for Cecily's wedding."

"We have plenty of those." Ginger disappears out of the fitting room, returning a minute later with a rolling rack of bridesmaid's dresses.

Ginger pops a cork on a bottle of champagne and fills three plastic tumblers. While I model dresses, Cecily guzzles champagne, but Presley takes only a few sips since she's driving.

Presley's eyes light up when I try on a scrumptious emerald-green velvet gown with flutter sleeves and an open back. "That's the one."

Cecily stands beside me on the alterations block, studying my reflection in the mirror. "Right dress. Wrong color."

Presley's jaw drops. "What are you talking about? Green is perfect for a Christmas wedding."

"It's too dramatic. Does it come in any other colors?" Cecily asks Ginger.

"Several. Let me see what we have in her size." Ginger leaves the fitting room and comes back with the same dress in dark gray.

"Ooh. So pretty," Cecily says, tipsy from the champagne. "That color will be elegant against red poinsettias."

The dress makes me look washed out, but I don't argue with Cecily. It's her wedding. She gets to pick. I drain the last of my champagne and hand Ginger my credit card.

When we get to the car, feeling the onset of a headache, I claim the back seat, letting Cecily have the front.

"Mission accomplished," Presley says, starting the engine. "Let's celebrate with lunch, my treat. There are many excellent choices for restaurants in Richmond. Bateau. Sam Miller's. The Hard Shell."

"Why don't we eat on the way back to Hope Springs?" Cecily suggests. "I know just the place in Charlottesville. Lyle and I pick up sandwiches there for picnics at UVA lacrosse games."

Leaning my head against the back of the seat, I close my eyes, and I'm asleep before we hit the interstate. When I wake an hour later, we're pulling into an Exxon station.

"This is it?" Presley is saying to Cecily. "We're eating lunch at a gas station?"

"Bellair Market is inside the building," Cecily says. "Trust me, you will thank me for this."

We follow Cecily inside and place orders for sandwiches with location-specific names like Farmington and Jefferson and Hooville. Despite Presley's original offer, Cecily insists on paying for our lunch. When we're seated at a small table by the window, she says, "I owe you guys an apology. You went to all this trouble for me, and I've been a straight-up bitch. I had a lot I was hoping to accomplish in the kitchen today. Our impromptu shopping trip threw me off. I need to learn to be more flexible."

I take a sip of my sweet tea. "I applaud your commitment to your job, Cecily. The next few weeks will be stressful for all of us with the holidays and wedding planning. But this is a special time for you. Enjoy it as much as you can."

"I promise, I'll try," Cecily says in a soft tone.

"We have a lot to accomplish to pull this wedding off," Presley says. "We absolutely must lock in your date by Wednesday. Understand?"

Cecily gives an affirmative nod. "Understood."

For the rest of the drive back to Hope Springs, Cecily and Presley discuss plans for her wedding and reception while I stare out the back window, daydreaming about the dress I left behind. The truth is, I'm more than a little envious of Cecily. I'm eager to enter this next stage in my life. Who says Jack and I have to wait until Jazz's custody is settled to get married? Not Detective Sinclair. She encouraged me to get married. I'm the one who's holding back, wanting everything to be perfect when I start my life with Jack. But I'm beginning to understand that there will never be a perfect time. We'll always have one crisis or another complicating our lives. Being together is the most important thing. While we can't get married until after the holidays, why not plan a wedding for late January or February? A small affair with Jazz as my flower girl and only our families plus a few friends in attendance. Next chance I get, I'll sit down with Jack and we'll set a date.

5

PRESLEY

The idea comes to Presley during her morning Peloton cardio workout. She's come up with some crazy schemes before, but this one wins the prize. She tries to imagine how the involved parties . . . how the primary person in said party might react? She envisions it going either way. The person would either be thrilled or furious.

Presley dismisses the idea as preposterous, but as she moves through her morning, she can't stop plotting the event. Could she pull it off? Could she plan a person's major life event without her knowing about it? She couldn't do it alone. She would need a lot of help.

On her way back from eating lunch in Jameson's, Presley stops by the reception desk to welcome Rita to the team. Rita is Lucy's sister. When Lucy found out Rita had applied for a leading position at the inn, she'd said to Presley, "Rita isn't qualified to be guest services manager. Aside from being a housewife for most of her adult life, her job experience is limited to a year of working as an administrative assistant in the principal's office at the high school."

Presley had thought this an unsupportive thing for one sister to say about another.

Presley is drawn to Rita's easygoing personality, her kind hazel eyes and the hint of mischief in her smile. As she watches Rita, with her head close to Stella's as they stare at a computer screen, she wishes Rita had turned out to be her biological mother, as Presley had originally thought when she first arrived in Hope Springs.

"How's it going?" Presley asks and both women look up.

"Great!" Stella says.

Rita blows a strand of blonde hair out of her face. "Stella's being kind. She may very well fire me by the end of the day. Mine may be the shortest career as guest services manager in history."

Stella laughs. "You're doing fine. I'm throwing a lot of information at you, and you're handling it extremely well. I fully expected it to take you awhile to get acclimated, since you lack experience in hotel management. But you have other qualities that make you the ideal candidate for the job. You're a hard worker, and a people pleaser, and you have amazing organizational skills."

A smile spreads across Rita's face. "I appreciate the vote of confidence. I'll do everything in my power not to let you down."

The elevator dings down the hallway, and Lucy emerges. Her smile fades when she sees them. "Afternoon, ladies." She runs her hand across the reception desk as she hurries past. "Gotta run. I'm late for a meeting."

Rita's smile fades and she returns her attention to the computer screen.

Does Lucy have issues with everyone in her life? Presley wonders.

She steps away from the desk. "I'll let you two get back to

work. If you need anything, Rita, I'm right across the hall," she says, aiming her thumb over her shoulder.

Presley retreats to her office. Leaning against the closed door, she replays the scene that just transpired. Presley shares Stella's confidence in Rita for all the reasons Stella cited. Even if Rita struggles at first with technical issues, her special way of communicating with people will make her popular with their guests. Stella doesn't care about resumes. Neither Presley nor Cecily have much experience in their fields. Stella, herself, only worked for a year as a desk services agent in New York before inheriting the inn and taking over as general manager. When Stella believes in a person, she gives them a chance. She's done a lot of good for others. It's time for someone to do something special for her.

Seated at her desk, Presley opens Cecily's wedding file and begins jotting notes from their conversations yesterday. But her mind keeps drifting back to the barn reception she'd originally planned. She engages her computer and accesses Pinterest. The board she created for the event features photographs of barn holiday weddings. Birch bark wedding cakes and glass geometric terrariums with creamy candles on tables with simple arrangements of white flowers. Pine garlands and fairy lights wrapped around wooden support pillars. Large wreaths of seeded eucalyptus with white and gold ornaments and mini white lights hanging from the ceiling. Sprigs of greenery tied with satin ribbon around backs of gold Chiavari chairs.

She thinks back to her conversation with Cecily in the kitchen. *Red poinsettias with some holly sprigs.* Cecily wants simple decorations with more emphasis on food and alcohol. While this barn theme may be all wrong for Cecily, it has Stella's name written all over it.

Tossing her bag over her shoulder, she exits the main building via the back door and strolls down to the Summer

House Wellness Center. Warm sunshine and temperatures in the fifties remind her of the extended forecast she heard on the local news this morning. The long-term prediction calls for a colder and snowier than normal winter, which she finds hard to believe on a gorgeous day like today.

During the inn's heyday, the summer house was an oversized screened porch where guests played bingo and danced to live bands during warmer months. The original building is undergoing an extensive expansion and remodeling. Much progress has taken place since Presley last toured the facility two weeks ago. Jack's crew of workmen tackle various tasks throughout. They lay subway tile in the spa treatment rooms on the third floor, finish the interior surface of the lap pool in the fitness center on the second floor, and install cabinetry in the health food restaurant on the first floor.

She inquires of Jack's whereabouts of everyone she sees and finally finds a foreman who informs her that Jack had left an hour ago for a meeting with his kitchen contractor at the manor house. When she emerges from the building, Presley spots Opal painting at an easel under her favorite cherry blossom tree, which is now bare of leaves. With no time for a visit, she waves at Opal and hurries up the sidewalk. She skirts the main building, continues down the front drive, and crosses over Main Street.

Presley sees the manor house every day on her way to and from work. But as she draws nearer, she realizes the home is a mini replica of the inn with a stone facade, dormer windows, and expansive lawns. A long line of pickup trucks occupies the driveway, but when she knocks on the front door, no one answers. The door is unlocked, and she steps tentatively inside.

Tall ceilings, random-width hardwoods, and a sweeping staircase greet her in the wide center hallway. Presley follows the loud whining of an electric saw to a solarium-style room at the rear of the house. Jack is in the adjacent kitchen with a crew of workmen installing a navy cabinet base she assumes will be the island. She waves at him, and he crosses the room, kissing her cheek in greeting.

"The house is fabulous," she says.

He massages the back of his neck. "The house is a work in progress that isn't going very well at the moment. We're having some issues with the cabinets. I had to pull my most skilled carpenters over from the wellness center."

"I went there first, looking for you. It's really taking shape."

"Thank you. We're on target to finish in March." He drops his hand from his neck. "So, what can I do for you?"

Presley is suddenly at a loss for words. Has she made a mistake in coming here? Jack will think she's lost her mind when she tells him her plan. "I . . . um—"

The annoying whirl of the saw saves her from having to answer.

"Let's step outside." Taking her by the elbow, he leads her out french doors to a stone terrace, much like the one at the inn, only smaller. "Is there something I can help you with? I trust nothing has happened to Stella."

"No. It's nothing like that." Presley's eyes dart about as she considers escaping, around the side of the house and back across the street to the safety of her office at the inn. But she'll never rest until she tells him her idea. If he hates it, she'll be satisfied that she tried and can stop obsessing about it. "So . . ." She takes in a deep breath. "I have an idea for a surprise for Stella. It's a bit . . . um . . . unconventional. Promise you'll be honest if you think it's crazy. I mean, it is crazy. But—"

"Spit it out, Presley," he says with a chuckle. "I'm sure I'll love it. I'm all for surprising Stella."

"I think we should plan a surprise wedding for Stella." She holds her hand out, preventing him from reacting. "Hear me out.

You may or may not know that Stella and I took Cecily to Richmond yesterday to shop for her wedding dress. While we were there, Stella tried on a gorgeous gown and looked positively stunning. I sense she's ready to be married. But coupling Jazz's custody suit with the fact that she's been working so hard at the inn, she doesn't have time to plan a wedding. So, I thought, why not plan it for her?"

She pauses, giving Jack a chance to shut her down. Instead, to her surprise, he says, "I'm intrigued. Go on."

"Okay," she says, feeling more confident. "So, you see, I designed a winter wonderland barn theme for Cecily. But Cecily changed her mind. She wants to get married under a tent on the terrace instead. Pulling off a surprise like this would take an enormous amount of coordinating. I would do most of the work. But I would definitely want your input. Now, with the house and the wellness center, might not be the best time."

"When would this wedding take place?"

"Either Christmas Eve or Christmas night. Whichever Cecily doesn't choose. She promised to let me know by Wednesday."

Jack moves to the edge of the terrace and stares out across the back lawn. She gives him a minute before going to stand beside him. "I realize it's a crazy idea. You should probably take a couple of days to think about it."

"I don't need to think about it." He turns to face Presley. "I've been ready to marry Stella since I put a ring on her finger. And I agree, I think she's ready. We would need to call her mothers, to make certain they can come." He smiles at her. "Count on me to help."

"Yay!" Presley throws her hands in the air and dances in a circle. "This will be so much fun."

"But . . ."

Presley freezes. "There's a but?"

"We should talk to Opal first. I'd feel better if we had her blessing. We can trust her to tell us if it's a bad idea."

"I agree. Do you want to talk to her or should I?"

"Why don't you? This is your brainchild."

"Okay. I'll go do that now. I just saw her over at the farm, painting." Presley removes her phone from her tote. "I'll let you know what she says. What's your cell number?"

He gives her the number, and she enters it in her contacts. When she looks up from her phone, she spots clumps of greenery high up in the branches of the trees in his backyard. Shielding her eyes against the bright sun, she asks, "Is that mistletoe?"

"Lord, yes. We have a crop like you wouldn't believe. Would you like some for the inn?"

She looks at him and then back up at the trees. "I would love some. We can hang a ball in the entryway to welcome guests. How do you get it down?"

"Shoot it with a shotgun. Several of my guys are hunters. I'll have one of them get some for you."

"That would be awesome. Thank you, Jack!" she says, and hugs his neck.

"I should thank you. What you're doing for Stella . . . for us . . . is an amazingly thoughtful gesture and greatly appreciated."

"Stella is a special person. I want to show her how much we all care about her." She presses her palms together under her chin. "Say a prayer that Opal approves of the idea."

Presley descends the stone stairs and retraces her steps to the inn's back lawn where Opal is still painting under her tree. Presley peers over the woman's shoulder at the canvas. "Is that the original summer house?" she asks of the low-slung building with verdigris copper roof.

"Mm-hmm. I'm painting from memory." She drags her brush

across the canvas, adding a streak of silvery paint that gives the illusion of light shimmering off the surface of the lake. "Stella commissioned this piece for the lobby in the new wellness center. We had some wonderful times in the summer house back in the day."

"I'd like to hear about them sometime," Presley says. "Can you spare a minute now? I have an idea for a surprise for Stella, and I want your honest opinion about it."

"Sure. Let's sit a spell." Opal sets down her paintbrush and they walk together to a nearby park bench.

Presley explains about the wedding dress and her schematic for the barn wedding. "Jack has tentatively agreed to the plan. But we want your blessing before we proceed."

"It's a bold move." Opal removes a small rag from the pocket of her smock and wipes at the paint smudges on her fingers. "Most brides these days micromanage their weddings. But Stella's not like that. Sweet girl has so much on her plate. I imagine she'd welcome the opportunity to marry Jack without the trouble of planning a wedding. I think your idea is brilliant." Stuffing the rag back in her pocket, Opal shifts toward Presley. "You're a dear child for wanting to do this for Stella. Count on me to help in any way. And I insist on paying for the reception."

Presley hasn't gotten that far in her thinking. "That's generous of you. I'm sure Stella will appreciate it."

"I never had the chance to do it for my own daughter, and I would consider it an honor to do it for Stella. She means a lot to me." Opal holds up a finger in warning. "But we must clear all this with Stella's mothers first. We can't have a wedding without them."

"Jack mentioned that. Do you want to call them, or should I?"

"If you don't mind, I'll leave that task to you. My daughter and I are not on the best of terms. I've never even met her partner, Marnie."

Presley averts her eyes. "Maybe this is a bad idea. I'd hate to cause more friction in your family."

Opal slowly gets to her feet. "A family reunion is way overdue. A surprise wedding will bring out the best in everyone."

Presley stands to face her. Staring into Opal's olive eyes, she asks, "You're sure about this?"

Opal smiles. "I'm positive. I will forward you Hannah's contact information."

"Great. And as soon as I talk to Hannah, I'll be in touch about the next steps."

Too excited and on edge to return to her office, Presley strolls back to her apartment. Her mind racing with ideas for the wedding, she brews a cup of peppermint tea and paces the room while she records her thoughts via audio text transcription into her Notes app.

Summoning the nerve, she places the call to Hannah, who is not only receptive to the surprise but insists on paying for the wedding. "Opal has already staked that claim. However, if you want to buy her wedding dress—"

"Yes! Please! I would love that." Hannah's enthusiasm is genuine, and Presley wonders what has driven this family apart in the past.

"Be sure to have tissues handy when you see your daughter in the dress." They discuss logistics of having the dress shipped to Presley for safekeeping and talk for a minute about dates and room reservations before ending the call.

Presley collapses on her blue velvet sofa. The plan is in motion. No turning back now. Despite having the support of Stella's fiancé and family, Presley has a nervous feeling in the pit of her stomach. She's interfering with Stella's life on the most personal level.

6

CECILY

Cecily is on her way home from buying lettuce at her favorite farmer's market on Tuesday afternoon, when she spots a sign advertising a guest house for rent. She slams on the brakes in the middle of the road, and making certain no one is behind her, she backs up. She pulls into the driveway of a grand, although slightly rundown, brick Georgian. When she calls the number scrawled on the sign, a chipper-sounding woman answers, identifying herself as Beverly McKinney.

"I'm Cecily Weber. I'm calling about the guest house for rent. Is it still available?"

"Indeed. I just put the sign out today. The guest house has two bedrooms and one bath. Would you like to see it?"

"Yes! Is now too soon? I'm in your driveway. I was just driving by when I saw the sign."

"Pull around back. I'll be out in a few minutes."

Cecily drives forward past the main house and a swimming pool to the detached building at the rear of the property. Getting out of her car, she takes in her surroundings. The location is ideal, directly across the street from the inn. And next door to

Stella's manor house. Wouldn't it be fun for them to be neighbors?

A gray-haired woman with more lines in her face than a Chinese Shar-Pei shuffles down the concrete driveway toward her. The woman smells like kitty litter and white cat fur covers her navy housecoat.

Beverly taps her walking cane at Cecily's feet. "Are you single, dear? I was hoping for a bachelor or a young couple, someone who can help me with odd jobs around the house. The rent reflects these ... uh ... favors."

Cecily works hard to keep a straight face when Beverly tells her the rent. For that amount of money, Cecily will volunteer Lyle to do whatever Beverly needs. "I'm getting married in a few weeks. My fiancé is a lacrosse coach at Jefferson College, and I'm the head chef at Hope Springs Farm."

Beverly perks up. "How nice." She removes a set of keys from her pocket and unlocks the paned door. "Come on in and have a look around."

Cecily enters a large living room with a stone fireplace and hardwood floors. The appliances in the adjoining kitchen are outdated but not ancient. Two ample-size bedrooms share a pink-tiled bath. Cecily giggles to herself at the vision of her manly fiancé surrounded by so much pink.

"You'll have free use of the pool in the summers. But you'll have to clean it. That's one of the odd jobs. I'm too old for swimming, but there's a fountain in the center of the pool, and I enjoy listening to the water sounds while sipping my gin and tonics on the porch in the evenings."

Gin and tonics? Go granny. "What other odd jobs can we expect?" Cecily asks.

"Stacking firewood. Helping bring in groceries. Changing light bulbs in ceiling fixtures. That kind of thing. I promise not to take advantage of you. My children live in New York and California. I need someone nearby in case of an emergency. You can contact my previous tenant. He lived here for going on eight years."

"That won't be necessary." Cecily is tempted to pay the deposit, but that wouldn't be fair to Lyle when he has his heart set on the campus house. "I need to talk to my fiancé. Is there any chance you would hold it for me until tomorrow?"

"Sure! Why not? You seem like a nice gal. I'll give you until noon tomorrow."

"Thank you so much, Mrs. McKinney! I really love the house. I'm sure my fiancé will too."

"You're welcome, dear. And please, call me Beverly."

Cecily glides on air back to her car. How did she get so lucky? Removing her phone from her bag on the passenger seat, she clicks on Lyle's number. His phone rings once before going to voicemail. At the beep, she says, "I found an adorable guest house for us to rent across from the main entrance to the inn. There's a sign in the front yard. You can't miss it. Drive by and let me know what you think."

She starts her engine and is backing out of the driveway when she notices Jack on his terrace next door. He's embracing someone. Must be Stella. Cecily places her hand on the horn. Is it too soon to tell her they might be neighbors? When the couple pulls apart, Cecily sees a shock of auburn hair. That isn't Stella. That's Presley.

Cecily speeds off. Did she misinterpret what she saw? Jack and Presley were off in the distance. At least a football field away. While Cecily has always had perfect vision, it's been a few years since she's been to the eye doctor for a checkup. Jack loves Stella. He would never cheat on her. Would he?

She's pulling into the employee parking lot when her mom calls. She's been avoiding her mom for days. Might as well get this over with. "Hi, Mom."

"Cecily! Finally. I've been trying to reach you."

"I know. And I'm sorry. It's crazy busy here. What's up?"

"What's up is that you're getting married in a couple of weeks, and we need to finalize plans. I hope you're sticking to your budget. We're paying for your aunt and uncle and their kids to fly down for the wedding. That fancy hotel of yours ain't cheap."

Cecily grabs her bag and opens her car door. "I don't understand. Why are you paying for their trip? Are they having financial problems?"

"Don't be ridiculous, Cecily. You know Harold's auto parts store is a gold mine. I just think it's the right thing to do."

"When Jerry married Nicole, Uncle Harold and Aunt Paulette didn't pay for our airline tickets to Arizona. But whatever, it's your money." Cecily walks toward the kitchen door. "They're not coming until Tuesday, right? We have that dinner with Lyle's parents on Monday night."

"Now, honey, what fun would that be? We wanna travel together."

There's no point in arguing with her mother. Her mother goes nowhere without her sister.

"Don't worry about the dinner, sweetheart. Everything's gonna be fine. Paulette and I will charm the pants off of Lyle's parents."

Charm? Winnie and Paulette? I don't think so.

She reaches the building. "I need to go, Mom. I'm at work. I'll call you later." She ends the call before her mother can argue.

Cecily goes to her office and closes the door. The room is closet-size with no windows and room enough for only a desk and two chairs. A wall of shelves behind the desk houses the inn's extensive collection of cookbooks, contributed by various chefs and guests over the decades.

Seated in her chair with her feet propped on the desk, she contemplates the dinner with Lyle's parents. Cecily has never met his parents, nor has he met hers. She considers hosting the dinner at Jameson's. Then decides she'll be way too nervous to cook for them. There is only one other place in town worthy of the gathering. She calls Elmo's Bistro and speaks with Elmo himself.

"I would be honored to help you arrange this special occasion," Elmo says. "I'll reserve our private room in the back and email you a few of our sample menus."

After a lengthy discussion about his food offerings, Cecily promises to be in touch and ends the call. She spends the next two hours poring over cookbooks, planning menus for several big events coming up at the inn.

It's after eight o'clock and dinner is in full swing when she emerges from her office. As she makes her way through the various stations, she notices something odd about the evening's mountain trout special.

"What is that on my trout?" she asks the station chef.

Bruce snickers. "Um . . . Capers?"

Cecily gives him the death stare. "I realize they are capers, Bruce. But the dish is Trout Almondine. Those capers should be almonds. Is that rosemary?" She touches her pinky finger to the sauce at the edge of the plate and brings it to her tongue. "It's supposed to be parsley. Who approved these changes?"

Bruce glances nervously at Alessandro, who is hovering nearby with a guilty expression. Her arm shoots out, finger pointed at her office door. "My office! Now!"

She follows him into the office and closes the door. "You have some explaining to do, Alessandro. Either you failed to learn it, or your professors at culinary school forgot to teach you the code of ethics for the kitchen. Never, under any circumstances, alter a head chef's recipe without consulting him or her first."

"But, Cess-i-ly, my version of the fish is delicious. Did you try it?"

"What I just saw is not a different version of Trout Almondine. It is a different dish altogether. I'm a fan of the rosemary, lemon, and caper sauce on trout. But that is not what's on the menu tonight, and not what our customers are expecting. I'm surprised no one has complained yet."

He grins sheepishly.

Cecily pins him against the wall with her glare. "So, we have had complaints."

Alessandro holds up one finger first and then two.

"And no one bothered to tell me? I've been in my office all evening."

"I handled it myself."

"By telling them what?"

Alessandro stares down at his feet. "That we had a last-minute change in menus."

"This is so not cool, Alessandro. You are way out of line. You are never to change a recipe without my permission. And, if we ever have a guest complain, I want you to notify me immediately."

"I'm sorry, Cess-i-ly." The tone in his Italian accent sounds genuinely apologetic and makes her slightly less angry. "I was trying to help. You seemed distracted when you came in. I thought maybe you didn't want to be disturbed."

"I am distracted, Alessandro. It's the holidays. I've been holed up in here working on menus." She gestures at the cookbooks covering her desk. "Consider this your first warning. Three strikes and you're out. Understand?"

"Yes, ma'am. I'm really, truly sorry."

"Just don't let it happen again." They leave the office

together, and she spends the rest of the night monitoring operations in the kitchen.

She's so engrossed in her work, she forgets about the guest house until the last patron finishes dessert and she's preparing to go home. She checks her phone. Lyle never texted back. When she tries to call him, the line rings four times before going to voicemail. She leaves Alessandro to lock up. The heavy lifting is done. There's nothing he can do to undermine her at eleven o'clock at night.

She drives through town to Jefferson College. The farmhouse Lyle rents with three other young guys—one professor and two coaches—is adorable. Too bad she and Lyle can't live here. They could fix it up. Paint the walls and plant flowers in the beds in the spring. But first they would need to clean it up. The front porch is littered with folding stadium chairs, coolers, and a mountain of firewood cresting above the sill of the living room window.

When Cecily knocks on the door, someone from inside calls out for her to enter. Inside smells like a locker room and is trashed like a fraternity house. She's never asked Lyle which of the furniture is his. She hopes none. She doesn't want any of it in her house. She passes through the living room to the dining room where Lyle and his roommates are playing poker. She says a silent prayer that the round oak table with its heavy carved pedestal belongs to one of the other guys.

Lyle looks up, but he doesn't bother getting up. "Hey, babe. What're you doing here?"

"I tried to call you," she says, deadpan.

"Did you?" He checks his phone on the table beside him. "Oops."

She flashes the table a smile. "Sorry guys. I need to borrow Lyle for a minute. Wedding business," she says as if it's the most annoying thing ever. To them, she's sure it is.

Cards in hand, Lyle leaves the table and follows her into the living room. Turning to face him, she asks, "Did you talk to your parents? I'm supposed to confirm our wedding date with Presley tomorrow."

"Um . . . sorry. No. I've been busy."

"Right," she says, eyeing the playing cards. "Seriously, Lyle, Christmas Day is important to my family. We always get together on Christmas afternoon. If it's really that big of a deal, we'll change it to Christmas Eve, but the least you can do is have a discussion with your parents about it."

He stuffs his hand of cards in his back pocket. "I'll call my dad in the morning. He's not as worked up about my sister's baby as Mom is."

"Thanks. I also need for you to talk to him about this dinner we're putting together for our parents. I've decided to host it at Elmo's Bistro. According to Google, the groom's parents should pay when the bride's and groom's parents meet for the first time. And since we're not having a rehearsal dinner, and my parents are paying for the reception, it seems only fair your parents should pay."

He shrugs. "That's fine. I'm sure they won't mind."

"Will you confirm it with your dad? I want it settled in advance, so there aren't any awkward moments when the bill comes."

"Chill, Cecily. This is weeks away. Why are we stressing out about it now?"

Irritation crawls across her skin. "Because I am. Did you ride by the house?"

"I did." His gaze shifting to the right of her, he looks longingly at his friends in the dining room. Is he eager to return to his game? Or get away from her? "Do we really wanna live in someone's backyard?"

"When that backyard has a pool that will be all ours? Heck, yes!"

"But that woman is old. I can see it now. She'll drive me crazy, wanting me to trim her hedges and clean her gutters."

She squints at him. "How do you know she's old? I didn't tell you that in my text."

"I saw her when I drove by. She was showing the guest house to another couple."

Cecily tosses her hands in the air. "Great. She promised to hold it for me until noon tomorrow. Think about it, Lyle. The location is convenient."

"It's convenient for you, which shouldn't matter when you go to work in the morning and come home late at night. I'm in and out of my house all day long. It makes more sense for me to be near the college." He softens his tone. "Can't we wait a few more days, Cess? I should hear about the campus house by early next week."

"The guest house will be gone by then. But whatever. We'll wait. I've notified my landlord that I'm not renewing my lease. I have to move somewhere."

"Understood. If the campus house doesn't work out, we will find somewhere else to live." Placing his hand on the small of her back, he nudges her toward the door. "Let me walk you out."

He's trying to get rid of her, so he can return to his buddies. But she doesn't care. She's tired and ready for bed. When they reach her car, she gives him a peck on the lips. "By the way, is that dining room table yours?"

"That heinous thing? No way! Give me some credit, Cecily. I have some taste."

"Just checking." She thumbs her lipstick off his lips. "I'll talk to you tomorrow."

Cecily keeps one eye on Lyle in the rearview mirror as she drives off. What just happened? She senses a seismic shift in their relationship on the horizon. But where are these feelings coming from? Because they don't agree on where they should live? Because he seems more interesting in playing cards with his friends than talking to her about their wedding? She dismisses her concern. Growing pains are only natural. That's what this is, right? Growing pains?

7

STELLA

On Tuesday afternoon, I strike up a conversation in the checkout line at Target with the woman in front of me who is purchasing the same denim jumper I'm buying for Jazz. I smile when she tells me her name—Erma Duncan, an old-fashioned name for a hip young woman. Her daughter, Elena, is in Jazz's first-grade class. When Erma tells me she's a residential interior designer, I make an appointment with her at her studio for the next day to talk about Jazz's Christmas surprise.

I've been working with a top commercial interior design firm for months in renovating the inn and building the wellness center. But I want more of a personal relationship with the person who helps me decorate my home. Erma understands my vision for a ballerina bedroom with lavender being the primary color. We order a white upholstered bed with fluted posts and turned legs, a tufted lavender comforter, and ballerina printed sheets. Erma's seamstress will fashion the bed skirt and drapes out of white tulle embroidered with white flowers to resemble a ballerina tutu.

"Do you think your seamstress can have them ready in time?" I ask.

"As long as the fabric is available. I'll get on her calendar for a rush order. She's never let me down. That's not to say it can't happen, though." Erma fans out her Benjamin Moore color wheel. "For the walls, I would suggest Dreamy Cloud." She shows me a color swatch that is mostly neutral with a hint of dusky lavender.

I study the color. "I love it. So soft and feminine." I add Dreamy Cloud to my list of colors on the Excel spreadsheet on my laptop. I'd previously taken a stab at picking out paint colors for the other rooms, but Erma fine-tuned those choices with tried-and-true hues.

I close my laptop. "I'd love to do something in Jazz's room that really makes a statement, something that makes Jazz gasp when she sees it."

"Hmm." Sitting back in her chair, Erma stares up at the ceiling and twirls a blonde lock of hair while she thinks. "What about a painting above the bed? A ballerina doing a flying leap or whatever they call those dance moves in ballet."

"A grand jeté." When Erma stares at me, as though surprised I know this, I add, "I've been a fan of ballet all my life. Never a student, though. I have two left feet. Growing up in New York, I attended some outstanding performances of both the American Ballet Theatre and the New York City Ballet."

"I admit I know little about dance," Erma says. "I was a tomboy. And Elena is following in my footsteps. She has ideas of becoming the first female NFL player."

I burst out laughing. "She'll outgrow that when she becomes interested in boys."

Erma appears genuinely worried. "I hope you're right," she says.

I return my attention to the fabric swatches, carpet samples, and furniture catalogues spread out on the table in front of us.

"Your idea of ballerina artwork is brilliant. My grandmother is an artist. She could paint Jazz in her leotard and tutu. It would be Opal's Christmas present to her."

"That makes it even more special. Jazz will treasure her first masterpiece forever."

I check my phone for the time. "I'm supposed to pick Jazz up from ballet in a few minutes. If I get there before class ends, I can snap a few pics of her in action for Opal to use for composition."

Erma stands. "Then you'd better get going. I'll get everything ordered and let you know when we have an install date. We'll be down to the wire on this, but I'll do everything in my power to make it happen."

"You're the best, Erma." I gather my things and Erma walks me to the door.

"I know you're in a hurry, and it's probably not my place to say this. But Hope Springs is a small town and word travels fast around here. I know about your custody battle. I had a run-in with Naomi last year, when the girls were in kindergarten. We were on a class field trip to the farmer's market. When I saw Naomi sneaking sips from a flask, I called her out on it, and she turned on me. She has quite a nasty temper. Jazz is much better off with you."

"Let's hope the judge thinks so as well," I say past the lump in my throat. I hate that everyone in town knows about Jazz's problems. Children can be cruel. Are the kids in her class saying things to hurt her feelings?

I race down Main Street to the ballet studio five blocks away, arriving in time to catch the end of the rehearsal for the opening scene of *The Nutcracker*. Jazz is among the youngest chosen for the production. I've seen my sister dance countless times, but I've never seen her move with such grace and competence as she does today. I snap a dozen photographs before the dance instructor announces the rehearsal over.

I am snapping more photographs of Jazz stretching in front of the mirror at the barre when Tasha glides toward me with toes pointed outward. She's a Russian immigrant and retired professional ballerina, a lovely woman with strawberry hair, high cheekbones, and a faint accent.

"In all my years of teaching ballet, I've never taught a child with such aptitude for dance. Jazz took her talent to a new level today." Tasha places her hand on her chest. "Brings tears to my eyes when I think of what's ahead of her."

"Really? She's good, but . . ."

"*If* she stays focused, the sky is the limit. She'll easily have her choice of ballet companies in the states. But she could go international to London or Paris or even Russia."

"Wow. That's hard for me to wrap my mind around."

"I've known for some time that your sister has raw talent, but the confidence I've seen in her today is something new. Moving back in with you is the best thing that could have happened to that little girl. I'm praying you get permanent custody."

"Thank you. That means a lot." Choked up for the second time in an hour, I pause until the emotion passes. "My event planner had the marvelous idea of hosting a reception at the inn for the dancers and their families after the performance. We would keep it simple with cake for the kids and champagne for the adults. But you may already have something planned."

Tasha shakes her head. "Not at all. I haven't even thought that far. This is kind of you, Stella. On behalf of the Hope Springs Ballet Company, I accept. How can I help?"

"We should have the flyer invitation ready by the end of the week. If I forward it to you, will you please email to the parents and dancers?"

"Yes. I'd be happy to."

Jazz, with pink gym bag and ballerina backpack slung over her shoulder, dances on her toes across the room toward us. "Stella! Did you see the rehearsal?"

"I caught the end." I offer her a high five. "Miss Tasha and I were just talking about your performance. You were brilliant."

Jazz pivots on her heels to face Tasha. "Do you really think so?"

A smile spreads across Tasha's lips, lighting up her brilliant blue eyes. "I think your performance was superb."

Jazz looks over at me. "What does *su-burb* mean?"

Tasha bows to Jazz's eye level. "It means you danced beautifully today. And I'm very proud of you. From now until the performance, I want you to eat healthy, do your homework, and go to bed early so you'll be prepared for your big day. Can you do that?"

"Yes, ma'am!" Jazz says and executes a graceful pirouette.

Bidding Tasha goodbye, Jazz and I walk hand-in-hand to the Wrangler. Jazz is quiet on the way home, and when I risk a peek at her in the rearview mirror, she's chewing on her lip.

"What're you thinking about, kiddo?"

"Miss Tasha said for me to eat healthy. I had grilled chicken strips for lunch today. Do you think that's why I danced so good?"

"You danced well," I say, correcting her. "The food we eat fuels our body and our bodies respond accordingly. If we eat a lot of sugar, we have short bursts of energy and then we crash. But if we feed our bodies a well-balanced diet, our energy levels will last longer, and our muscles will be stronger and leaner. Does that make sense?"

"I think so." But she narrows her golden eyes, and I'm not entirely sure she understands.

When we reach the farm, I drive up the front driveway and around the main building to the cottage. Putting the car in gear, I turn around to face my sister in the back seat. "Properly fueling our bodies is very important, but the drive I saw in you today comes from within. Every time you dance, I want you to think back on today and try to summon that same determination. You have natural talent, Jazzy. You can take your ballet a long way, if you so choose."

"Yay!" She tugs on the car seat strap. "Can we go to Jameson's for dinner? I wanna eat a salad."

I check the time on the clock. Almost six o'clock. "Sure! If we go now before it gets too crowded. Do you want to put your things inside first?"

"Only my gym bag. I'll take my backpack with me so I can start on my homework."

"All right, then. Let's do it," I say, and help my sister out of the car.

Dropping her gym bag on the front porch, we race each other across the street. As always, I let Jazz win. She's faster than me by far, but my stride is longer.

When we enter the building, Jazz hurries ahead of me to the entry hall to see her favorite of all the seven Christmas trees in the main building. I stop at the reception desk to speak to Rita. "How's it going?"

Rita looks up from the computer. "Great! I'm finally getting the hang of the reservation system. Not only are we booked to capacity for New Year's Eve, we only have a few more rooms left for the long Christmas weekend. Even the themed weekends Presley is planning for January are filling up."

A tingle of excitement dances across my chest. "That's excellent news."

We talk for a few minutes about minor issues until Jazz

appears at my side, tugging on my Barbour coat. "Come on, Stella. I'm hungry."

"All right, already. I'm coming." I smile at Rita in parting. "We'll be down at Jameson's if you need me."

As we exit reception and enter the lounge, Jazz sheds her coat, tossing it at me, and takes off across the room in a series of leaps and spins. She's so immersed in her dancing, she doesn't see Naomi emerge from Billy's Bar. Jazz crashes into her mother and they both fall to the floor.

A man I've never seen before rushes to Naomi's rescue, helping her up. As I sprint across the lounge, Jazz gets to her feet and runs toward me.

Naomi smooths out her short black skirt and teeters toward us on spiked heels. "Jasmine! You could have seriously injured me just now. You need to watch where you're going. I've told you a thousand times. No good will ever come from ballet. You're a bright girl. You should be a doctor or a lawyer."

At the sound of her mother's harsh tone, Jazz darts behind me and clings to me, her arms around my waist and face planted in the small of my back.

"What're you doing here, Naomi? Have you been drinking again?" I whip out my phone and start videotaping her.

Naomi flashes her brightest smile at the phone. "Orlando and I are here on a date. I was giving him a tour of the inn before we go to dinner at Jameson's."

"Sorry. Jameson's is closed for a private party tonight."

Naomi glances at the nearly empty dining room and back at me. "I don't believe you, but whatever. We'll go somewhere else. I just wanted to set eyes on my daughter. Can't I talk to her for a minute? Please, Stella. I miss her so much."

I'm not sure whether the show is for Orlando or Jazz. Either way, I'm not buying it. "Sorry. You'll have to wait for your supervised visitation with the social worker. Now, excuse us."

I pick Jazz up, and she buries her face in my neck as I carry her to the hostess stand where we wait for Julie, the hostess, to escort an elderly couple to their table.

I nuzzle Jazz's ear. "Hey, kiddo. Why don't we go back to the cottage? I can make pasta. Or we can order our food and have a server bring it over."

Jazz lifts her head. "No! Please. I wanna eat here."

"Are you sure?"

She gives me a definitive nod. "Positive."

"Then we'll eat here."

Julie returns and shows us to a table by the window. We order southwestern salads and lemonades from Elsa, our server. Jazz removes a math worksheet from her backpack and begins scribbling the answers while I scroll through my email on my phone.

After a few minutes, I set my phone on the table. "Do you want to talk about your mom?"

Jazz doesn't look up from her worksheet. "Miss Tasha says I have to do my homework."

I take the pencil from her. "You can finish that in a minute. We need to talk about what happened. Did it upset you to see your mom?"

Jazz ignores my question. "Do I have to live with her again?"

"Not if I have my way about it. I'll do everything in my power to keep you with me."

Jazz scrunches her brow. "Do you think ballet is bad, Stella? Should I be a doctor or a lawyer?"

"I think you have years before you need to worry about what you want to be when you grow up. For sure, you should keep your grades up, do the best you can in school in case one day you decide you want to be a doctor or a lawyer or even an astronaut. As for ballet, I believe it is a wonderful extracurricular activity for you. You're getting your exercise and making friends and learning a discipline that will serve you well when you're an adult."

"What's a *dis-a-pline*?"

I laugh. "Never mind. You may one day outgrow your love for ballet, or you may make a career out of it. These are decisions you make along the way, not something you decide overnight. And definitely not something you decide when you're six."

Jazz gives me a sassy head bob. "I'll be seven in March."

I palm my forehead. "How could I forget?" I hand her back the pencil. "You can always talk to me about anything, Jazzy. If you're ever afraid or sad or lonely, you come to me, your big sister."

Jazz tilts her head to the side. "How are you my sister when your skin is white and mine is brown?"

"Families come in all sizes and colors."

"Huh? What's that supposed to mean?"

"Well, let's see." I pause while I decide how best to explain this to her. "Do you remember Billy?"

"Of course. He was my friend." No one ever told Jazz that Billy was her father, and I never considered it my place to tell her. Until now.

"Billy was my father. And he was your father too."

Those golden eyes grow wide. "Billy was my father? Not Derrick?" Derrick is her stepfather, who has shown no interest in Jazz since his separation from Naomi last summer.

"Nope. Billy was your father. And, even though you and I have different mothers, we each carry parts of Billy with us. You have his eyes, and I have his hair. But we both have some of his blood, which makes us blood kin regardless of the color of our skin."

"That's cool! I loved Billy." I envy her the memories she has of him. With any luck, she will always carry them in her heart.

Jazz returns her attention to her worksheet and is soon

absorbed in her math problems. I wish I could forget about
Naomi. Why was she here, anyway? To threaten me? To prove
she can get close to Jazz? As best I could tell, she hadn't been
drinking. And she was about as pleasant as I've ever seen her.
Which tells me she's up to something. She's making a show for
the judge. I lost my sister to her once. I won't let it happen again.

8

PRESLEY

Presley arranges a meeting with Opal and Jack for Thursday morning. Opal and Presley arrive a few minutes past nine, and Jack greets them at the front door.

"Let's go to the second floor where it's quieter," Jack yells over the sounds of loud banging and sawing in the kitchen.

They follow him up the grand staircase and down a wide hallway to the master bedroom at the front of the house. The enormous room features a gas fireplace and windows over-looking the inn. Presley stands by a window. "What a wonderful spot for Stella to watch over her inn."

"As did her ancestors before her," Jack says.

Presley turns away from the window. "Let's get you two married, so you can enjoy your dream home together." She removes her iPad from her bag and drops the bag on the floor. "Here's where we stand so far. Cecily has chosen Christmas Eve, which means your wedding date is officially set for Christmas night. The more desired date, in my opinion. Christmas will be over, and things will have settled down, but not too much since it falls on a Friday night. We could always have it on Saturday, the most common day for weddings."

Jack doesn't hesitate. "Let's stick with Christmas Day."

"Christmas Day it is." Presley's gaze shifts to Opal. "Hannah and Marnie are fully on board. Just so you know, they offered to foot the bill for the reception, but I told them you already beat them to it. They are paying for her wedding gown instead. Which is being shipped to me for safekeeping until the big day. I think I remember seeing a mannequin in the basement storage closet at the inn. There's at least one of everything else in that closet."

"Where are Hannah and Marnie staying?" Opal asks. "I would offer my guest room, but . . ."

"You're not on great terms," Presley says. "No worries. I completely understand. I'm currently holding a suite for them in the main building, but I'm hoping to work things out for them to stay in the carriage house. I've encouraged Stella's mothers to fly in on Christmas Eve. I'd feel better if they arrive early in case of bad weather or flight cancellations due to holiday travel. The negative side of that is we'll have longer to keep them hidden."

"We'll figure something out," Opal says. "If push comes to shove, I'll have Brian put them up."

"How many people are you inviting to this shindig?" Jack asks.

"That's entirely up to the two of you," Presley says. "If you supply the list, I'll reach out to the guests individually, to explain about the surprise."

Presley accesses her Pinterest account on her iPad and shows the barn wedding boards to Opal. "I'd love your input. Especially since you're paying for it."

Opal quickly scrolls through the photographs. "Elegantly rustic. Stella will love this."

When Presley tries to hand Jack the iPad, he waves his hand, refusing to take it. "I prefer to be surprised, along with Stella."

"Then surprised you'll be." She snaps the cover shut on her iPad. "What about the ceremony? I know Stella attends church regularly."

Jack thinks a minute before responding. "She attends two churches, but she prefers the chapel at Jefferson College over the Hope Springs Episcopal Church in town. And she's become friends with Melissa Malone, the minister at the chapel. I'd be happy to talk to Melissa about officiating a small ceremony at the chapel."

"That would be great," Presley says. "We'll keep the decorations in the chapel simple. A few white poinsettias on the alter."

The slamming of the front door reverberates throughout the house. Footfalls on the hardwoods grow closer, and Brian appears in the doorway. "Why are the three of you hiding out up here? If I didn't know better, I'd think you were conspiring."

Brian crosses the room to Opal and kisses her cheek. "You look awfully guilty, Mom. What're you up to?"

A flush travels up Opal's neck to her face. "If you must know, we're planning a surprise wedding for Stella."

Brian raises an eyebrow. "You mean a surprise birthday party?"

"No," Jack says. "Her birthday is July Fourth. We're surprising Stella with a wedding on Christmas night."

Brian stares at Jack as if he's lost his mind.

Jack hunches his shoulders. "What can I say? I'm desperate to marry her."

"It was my idea, actually," Presley says, and explains how Stella's dream wedding gown inspired the surprise.

"Have you given any thought to the marriage license?" Brian asks.

Three faces fall at once.

Presley smacks her forehead. "I can't believe I didn't think of

73

that." Instead of googling it on her iPad, she asks the attorney, "What's involved with getting a wedding license in Virginia?"

"Not much, fortunately," Brian says. "You don't need a blood test, and there's no waiting period. And I know the clerk of court personally. I can probably convince him to make a house call on the day of the wedding."

A wave of relief washes over Presley. "Do you mind checking with him right away? This is a game changer if we can't work this out. Feel free to bribe him with dinner on the house for him and his wife in Jameson's. Heck, tell him to bring his entire family."

Brian nods. "I'll call him as soon as I get to my office."

Presley consults the notes on her iPad. "The fewer people who know about this, the better. I'll enlist Katherine to help with the flowers and Alessandro to coordinate the food. What do you think, Jack? Should we tell Jazz?"

"No way!" Jack says, vehemently shaking his head. "Keeping a secret like that is asking too much of a six-year-old."

"But won't her feelings be hurt?" Opal asks.

"Not if we buy her a pretty dress and let her be the flower girl," Brian says.

Opal's hand shoots up. "I'll take care of that!"

"Perfect. Thank you." Presley hugs her iPad to her chest. "Speaking of hurt feelings, I spent a sleepless night worrying about whether to let Cecily in on the surprise. On the one hand, Cecily is Stella's best friend. On the other, Cecily is so distracted right now with work and planning her own wedding, I worry she'll accidentally let something slip to Stella. Besides, I wouldn't want to steal her thunder."

"There's no need to tell Cecily," Jack says. "She'll be on her honeymoon, anyway."

Presley looks first at Opal and then Brian, who both nod their agreement.

"All right, then. To recap." Pointing at each of them in turn, Presley says, "Opal, you're getting a dress for Jazz. Brian, you're arranging the marriage license. Jack, you're coordinating the ceremony at the chapel. And you can all three collaborate on the guest list."

"Done," Jack says. "Let me know what else I can do, as long as it doesn't involve flowers or wedding cakes or anything I might screw up."

Presley laughs. "There is one big issue we need to sort out. The surprise element. I'm thinking the ceremony will begin around six thirty. Can you keep Stella preoccupied and away from the proximity of the barn during the day while we decorate?"

"Piece of cake," Jack says. "We'll be preoccupied with giving Jazz the Christmas of her dreams."

Presley grins. "Stella told me. You may have trouble dragging them out of here when the time comes for the wedding." She slides her iPad into her bag and slips on her coat. "Okay then! Full steam ahead on the planning."

With Jack leading the charge, they file out of the room. At the bottom of the stairs, Brian and Opal peel off to explore the rest of the house while Jack sees Presley out.

When they step outside, onto the covered stoop, she wraps her coat tighter against the frigid air. "The temperature has dropped since I arrived," Presley says.

Jack, wearing a flannel shirt with no coat, shivers. "I'm afraid the unseasonably warm weather we've been having is a thing of the past. I think we're in for a cold winter."

"Not only that, we may get our first storm at the beginning of next week. You and Stella may have a white wedding."

Jack squishes his brow together. "Wait. Isn't that a song?"

Presley laughs. "Yes. An awful one by Billy Idol."

Jack leans down and kisses Presley's cheek. "Thanks again for everything you're doing."

In a soft tone, she says, "It's my pleasure, Jack."

Presley is halfway to her car when Jack calls her back. "I almost forgot. I have a bag of mistletoe for you. It's on the terrace. I'll go grab it."

When he starts down the steps, she says, "I'll get it, Jack. You go back inside. It's freezing out here."

She retrieves the black trash bag of mistletoe and tosses it into the back of her SUV. *Mistletoe and wedding bells.* Presley thinks about what Stella said the other night at the wine dinner. *Love is in the air at Hope Springs Farm this holiday season.*

Presley drives around the main building and down to the lakefront. Bag of mistletoe in hand, she enters the maintenance shed. She checks the office and the storage rooms, but no one is in sight. She's about to leave when Katherine emerges from the restroom. Sweat is dotting her forehead and her skin has a greenish tint to it.

"You don't look well," Presley says. "Are you sick?"

One hand on her tummy, Katherine removes a red bandana from the back pocket of her jeans. "I think I may have the stomach flu."

Presley takes a giant step backward. She can't afford to get sick with so much going on. "You should be in bed."

Katherine blots her forehead with the bandana. "Actually, I'm feeling a little better now that I've emptied my stomach. What can I do for you?"

Presley holds up the trash bag. "I brought you some mistletoe. Jack has quite the crop at the manor house. He had one of his workers shoot it down for us. I thought we could make a ball for the entry hall."

Katherine takes the bag from her and tosses it into the corner. "Thanks," she says, less than her usual enthusiastic self.

"I have a secret, and I'm dying to tell you."

This perks Katherine up. "Ooh. What is it?"

Presley tells Katherine about the surprise wedding.

Frowning, Katherine says, "But isn't Cecily's wedding Christmas Eve?"

"Yes. I realize it's a lot."

"It's not only a lot. It's insane." Katherine leans heavily against the riding tractor. "I don't know if I can pull off two weddings, Presley."

"I can help. And we'll have an intern working here the two weeks over Christmas. But, if you think we need more hands, we can always hire your friend who owns the flower shop on the outskirts of town."

Katherine shakes her head. "That won't work. Claire's going to Colorado skiing for Christmas."

"I've already done the schematic. If you order the flowers for me, I'll figure out the rest. Emma, our intern, is impressive. She'll probably show me a thing or two about flowers."

Katherine pushes off the tractor. "I'm sorry, Presley. I just don't feel well today. We'll make it work. I want to do the flowers for Stella's wedding. This is a wonderful thing you're doing for her."

"We'll talk more about this later. You need to go home to bed."

"I'm headed there now. Let me get my stuff, and I'll walk out with you." Shoulders slumped, Katherine goes into her office and returns seconds later with her bag and coat.

Exiting the building together, they part in the parking lot.

"Feel better," Presley calls to Katherine as she climbs in her white pickup truck. "Let me know if I can do anything for you."

She watches Katherine drive away. Is it more than a stomach virus? Presley wouldn't blame Katherine if she resents having to work on the holidays. Christmas is family time. While Presley loves Christmas as much as anyone, this year is her first year without her mother, and she's grateful for the distraction of work. Staying busy will help keep her mind off her loss.

9

CECILY

Cecily drives by the guest house on her way to work on Thursday morning. The sign is still in the front yard. Does that mean Beverly hasn't found a tenant yet? She called Beverly yesterday to notify her she wouldn't be renting the house, explaining that her fiancé needs to be nearer to campus. But Cecily can't stop thinking about it. She imagines good times together as couples with Stella and Jack. Cookouts and late-night swims. Maybe the old lady will one day move to a retirement home, and Cecily and Lyle can buy the house. Then Cecily's children will grow up best friends with Stella's. Lyle won't admit it, but he would totally enjoy the pool during the summer. Why is he being so stubborn? Is he trying to prove he has the upper hand in their relationship?

Just as well, she thinks as she turns around in Beverly's driveway. Cecily wants Lyle to be happy. This is what marriage will be like. She might as well get used to compromising. She doesn't mind the sacrifice. She loves Lyle and she wants to please him.

In front of the manor house, she spots Jack and Presley under the covered stoop. When Jack kisses her, Cecily nearly runs off the road. While the kiss is an innocent peck on the cheek, that's the second time in three days she's seen them together. Jack and Presley are cheating on two of Cecily's closest friends—Stella and Everett. What should she do about it? Racking her brain, she concludes that she needs proof of their affair before ratting them out.

At the inn, she sequesters herself in her office and spends two hours catching up on paperwork. Late morning, she emerges to find the station chefs scurrying about as they prepare for lunch, but Alessandro isn't among them.

Cecily calls out, "Has anyone seen Alessandro?"

Lou, the grill chef, answers, "He's around here somewhere. Check the dining room. I saw him go in there a few minutes ago with Presley."

"Thanks." She leaves the kitchen for the dining room, where the first table of lunchers is being seated. Through the windows, she sees Alessandro and Presley on the veranda. They are seated on the same side of a four-top table with shoulders touching and heads bent over papers strewn about the table. A space heater near the table keeps them warm. How cozy.

Cecily wanders out onto the veranda. Sounding casual, she asks, "What're the two of you up to?"

Both heads jerk up at once. Presley shuffles her papers together and closes the file. "Planning an event for Christmas night. Alessandro is helping me since you'll be on your honeymoon."

Cecily glares down at her. "Who says I'm taking a honeymoon?"

Presley's gray eyes narrow. "But you're getting married. Aren't you going away with Lyle after the wedding?"

"Not until later. Maybe next summer. I'm too busy with work to leave during the holidays."

"But surely you'll take one or two days off to spend with Lyle," Presley says.

"Hadn't planned on it." Cecily turns off the space heater. "Alessandro, you're needed in the kitchen."

"I'm on my way," he says and flees the porch.

Is he suddenly scared of me? wonders Cecily. *Or is he hiding something?*

Cecily sits down opposite Presley. "I saw you with Jack at the manor house. Twice. On Tuesday, you were hugging him on his patio, and today I saw you kissing him on the front stoop. What gives, Presley?"

"I . . . um . . ." Presley's face beams red as she busies herself with gathering her things. "Jack was getting some mistletoe for me to use for decorating."

Cecily points her finger at Presley. "You're lying. Your face is as red as Santa's suit. Everett and Stella are my friends. You and Jack better not be cheating on them."

Presley pushes back from the table, knocking her chair over. "You are way out of line, Cecily. I love Everett with all my heart. I would never cheat on him, any more than Jack would cheat on Stella."

Cecily folds her arms over her chest. "I'm not buying your little mistletoe story. I know you're up to something. And I intend to find out what it is."

"Whatever." Presley slings her bag over her shoulder. "I don't have to justify myself to you."

Cecily watches Presley storm off. For Stella's and Everett's sakes, she hopes Presley is telling the truth.

Throughout the afternoon and evening, Cecily grills Alessandro about the Christmas night event he's planning with Presley. But all he'll say is that it's a small cocktail buffet for a guest.

Cecily is on her way to her car around midnight, when she

receives a text from Lyle. *I have a surprise for you. Meet me in Billy's Bar.*

A surprise? Intriguing. She could use some good news. She returns to the building.

Billy's Bar is hopping with locals and hotel guests. A month ago, the lounge would've been deserted at this late hour. Cecily approves of the atmosphere inside the bar. The paneled walls are painted a high-gloss indigo blue, and the carpet yields an abstract pattern in red, white, and blue. Lyle is seated at a table under the former owner's impressive collection of rock and roll memorabilia—electric guitars in acrylic cases and framed record albums signed by greats like Lynyrd Skynyrd and Mick Jagger.

Cecily slides onto the banquette next to Lyle and gives him a soft kiss on the lips.

"How was your day?" he asks.

"Chaotic."

"You look tired, Cecily. You work too hard."

"That's an insult, Lyle. Tired is not a good look for a woman, regardless of her age. I'm almost thirty-one years old, and my career is just getting started. What is wrong with giving it every-thing I've got?"

His hands shoot up. "Easy. I didn't mean to touch on a nerve. I've come in peace."

Kristi, the bartender, appears with a brown liquor drink for Lyle and a flute of champagne for Cecily.

"Champagne!" Cecily takes a sip, and when the bubbles tickle her nose, she licks her lips. "What're we celebrating?"

"Our honeymoon. I made the reservations today."

"But—"

He presses his finger to her lips. "Shh! Listen, before you object. I booked a cabin at a fly-fishing camp. To quote from the brochure, 'We offer luxury accommodations in a rustic setting.' It sounds perfect for us."

It sounds like a prison sentence, she thinks. "I like fishing, Lyle. I don't love fishing. And I definitely don't want to do it when it's freezing outside or when I'm on my honeymoon."

He hangs his head like a scolded child. "God, Cess. I try to do something nice for you, and all you do is bitch."

"You went behind my back, after we decided not to take a honeymoon until later."

"You decided that. This is our wedding. We should spend at least a few nights alone together. If we stay in town, you'll work the whole time."

"Look around you, Lyle. The inn is crazy busy, and, as I mentioned before, I'm worried Alessandro is after my job. Now is not the best time for me to get away. I'll be worried sick the whole time we're gone. Next summer will be better when we can both relax. And we can go somewhere warm."

"Next summer will be the same thing. You'll come up with another excuse. You can't marry me, Cecily. Not when you're already married to your job." Lyle gets up from the table and disappears into the crowd.

Cecily gathers her belongings and goes after him. By the time she fights her way through to the lounge, he's disappearing around the corner toward the main entrance. With tears blurring her vision, she slinks off in the opposite direction.

On the short drive to her apartment, she thinks back to a conversation she had with Stella a few weeks ago, when they were terrified the inn would close due to lack of business. Stella had been questioning whether her love for Jack would be enough if she no longer had a career. "I'm not sure I'd be happy scooping ice cream at the Dairy Deli," Stella had said.

And Cecily had responded, "But you'll still have Jack. Isn't that enough? I'd be happy scooping ice cream as long as I have Lyle."

"I know you, Cecily," Stella had said. "You might be happy for a while. But you would grow bored quickly, and then what would you do?"

Now, all these weeks later, given the choice between her career and Lyle, Cecily's uncertain she would pick Lyle. What's changed since October? Has the newness of their engagement worn off? With the big decisions they've been forced to make for the wedding, Cecily has seen a different side of Lyle. She loves him with all her heart, but he's immature in some ways. She doesn't want to wear the pants in their family. She wants a strong male figure to father her children and take care of her needs.

Entering her apartment, Cecily drops her coat and bag on the floor and wanders over to the sliding glass door that leads to a standing-room-only balcony. Two years ago, she'd landed in Hope Springs after escaping a relationship gone bad with the head chef at the restaurant where she was working in DC. Enamored by the small town, she'd gotten a job at Caffeine on the Corner and rented this dreary apartment, never dreaming she'd end up staying.

She's tired of these tan walls and matching carpet. She's ready for a real home, a place she looks forward to returning to at the end of a long day.

Headlights approach from Main Street. As the vehicle grows closer, she sees Lyle at the wheel of his truck. When he knocks on her door a minute later, she drags him inside to her bedroom where she makes love to him with all the burning passion she feels for him. The only thing that really matters is her love for him. All the other issues will work themselves out.

Afterward, as they lay sweaty and satisfied in each other's arms, Lyle says, "Did we just have our first fight?"

"I think so. And we survived."

He plants a trail of kisses in the crook of her neck. "Coincidentally, you don't look tired. You look gorgeous."

Cecily rolls over to face him. "About the honeymoon. I appreciate the gesture. But the restaurant is so new, and now that we finally have some business, I need to give it my undivided attention." She brushes a hank of sandy hair off his forehead. "Besides, I can't get excited about taking a honeymoon when we don't even know where we will live. We might very well be spending our honeymoon unpacking boxes."

His blue eyes narrow. "I hadn't thought about that. But I'll have an entire month off for winter break. I can do most of the moving."

"Why don't we wait and see how our house hunting goes before we make the final decision about the honeymoon?"

He perks up at the suggestion. "Great idea! We can cancel the cabin seventy-two hours out without penalty."

Who knows? Maybe by Christmas week, she'll feel differently about taking a honeymoon. A rustic cabin sounds cozy. She'll pack her suitcase with sexy lingerie. She can think of plenty of ways to entice him into staying with her by the fire instead of going fishing.

10

PRESLEY

A fter the lunch crowd clears out of Jameson's on Saturday afternoon, Presley oversees the transformation of the main lounge into a ballroom. The maintenance staff clears out furniture while the rental company installs the stage for the band and a black-and-white checkered dance floor. Presley instructs the crew to create several groupings of chairs and love seats off to the sides of the dance floor for guests lounging during the party. They take the leftover furniture to an off-sight warehouse for overnight storage. Once they finish moving furniture, her men turn their attention to tenting the terrace. With nearly six hundred guests expected, they need all the space they can get.

Hope Springs Farm hasn't hosted the once famous annual Christmas formal in twenty-five years. Not only is the inn booked to capacity for the weekend, the town is buzzing with excitement. People have come from all over Virginia and more than four hundred locals have purchased tickets. Presley has hired Liquid Pleasure—an R and B band popular with all ages who never fails to bring down the house. The entire first floor will be open with every room in the inn featuring specialty drinks and themed foods, much like the grand reopening party they hosted back in early November.

Satisfied with the progress in the lounge, Presley enters Jameson's where Cecily's staff is setting up for a cocktail buffet. Presley, covering for Katherine who is still feeling under the weather, spent much of the morning refreshing greens and poinsettias and fashioning a large ball of mistletoe now hanging in the entryway. She's particularly proud of the enormous arrangement of red and white fresh flowers—roses and lilies and hydrangeas—she created for the main food table.

Over near the windows, Lucy wears a faraway expression as she prepares for the wine tasting.

"Impressive display," Presley says of the local wines and chocolate truffles shipped in from Stella's favorite chocolatier in New York.

Lucy's head jerks back, as though startled to see her standing there. "Sorry. My mind is a million miles away."

"Is something wrong?" Presley asks.

Lucy lets out a sigh. "Yes. No. I'm not sure. Brian asked me to be his date to the dance tonight."

"That's exciting. You said yes, right?"

She nods. "But now I wish I hadn't."

Presley narrows her eyes. "Why? If it's because of the wine tasting, I can cover for you."

"It's not that. Brian knows I have to work. The tasting won't last but an hour, anyway." Lucy absently moves wine bottles around on the table. "The problem is, I have nothing to wear. I haven't been shopping for new clothes in years."

"But you always look so nice." And she does, although on the frumpy side sometimes.

"I have a closet full of clothes," Lucy explains. "I just don't have any fashion sense. I don't know what's hip and what's not."

"Do you want me to help you pick something out?"

Lucy's face lights up. "Would you? You have excellent taste."

"I don't know about that, "Presley says with a laugh. "But I'll make certain you look stunning for your big date." She checks her phone for the time. "It's almost five now. I'd like to be back by six thirty. If we leave soon, I'll have enough time to stop by my apartment to change on my way back."

"Then let's go." Lucy gathers up her trash and stuffs it into an empty wine box. "Let me take this to the wine cellar and grab my bag. I'll text you my address, and we can meet at my house."

Presley retrieves her coat from her office, and she's walking out to her car when the text comes in from Lucy. She's never been to Lucy's house, and she's surprised when her Maps app directs her to a street two blocks away from Rita. She and Lucy arrive at the same time, and while Lucy is unlocking the front door, Presley says, "You and Rita are practically neighbors."

"We are. Our parents gave Rita the house where we grew up. Would've been nice if they'd offered it to me."

Why would their parents have offered it to Lucy when she already has a home nearly identical in size and style? Rita was desperate when she moved back to Hope Springs from Charlotte after her husband mismanaged their chain of high-end restaurants into bankruptcy. Wouldn't Lucy want her sister to have a nice home to live in? Lucy's glass is always half-empty.

The home's interior is dreary with drab wall colors and dim lighting. While the house is orderly, the rooms have very little furniture. With no rugs on the floors, Lucy's voice reverberates throughout the downstairs. "As you can see, my husband took more than half of everything, all the good furniture, art, and rugs. I can't wait to get out of here. This place holds nothing but bad memories of dark years. Once Chris goes off to college, I plan to sell it and get a place of my own."

What about the happy times from Chris's childhood, before Lucy was diagnosed with cervical cancer and things went wrong in her marriage? Once again, half-empty glass. Presley makes a mental reminder to find out whether depression is heredity.

"Why wait, if you're unhappy living here?" Presley asks.

Lucy shrugs. "This is Chris's home."

Presley remembers Lucy telling her that Chris had asked to live with his father a few years back. Presley doesn't blame him. This house is sending off some seriously dismal vibes. "Have you talked to Chris about moving? Maybe he feels the same way."

"You've never met my son, Presley. Don't assume you know how he feels about anything."

Lucy's words sting. Why is she even here? Lucy is using her. The sooner she can get out of this depressing house, the better. "Right. Let's find you something to wear tonight."

Presley follows Lucy upstairs to the master bedroom where a king-size bed and single chest of drawers are swallowed up by gray walls and bare floors. One side of the walk-in closet is empty, while the other side houses neatly organized pants, skirts, blouses, and dresses. Lucy gestures for Presley to have a look.

Peering over her shoulder as Presley flips through the hanging clothes, Lucy asks, "Where do you shop for clothes?"

"I've found some cute things at Fiona's Fashions on Main Street." Presley holds a silk print dress up to Lucy, but the ruffles at the neck and on the sleeves are too much, and she quickly returns it to the rod.

"I'm too old for cute," Lucy says in a clipped tone.

"I use the word loosely. The things I've purchased from the boutique are surprisingly stylish for a small town. You should stop in there sometime. Fiona is very adept at matching clothes to body styles."

"Maybe I will."

Presley comes to the end of the rack of clothes. Only one

dress is suited for a black-tie formal—a sleeveless burgundy velvet sheath that dips low in the back. She removes the dress from the rack. "Do you have any dressy heels?"

Lucy scans the shoe boxes on the shelf above. She finds the box she's looking for and pulls it down. Inside are a pair of black suede sandals with a thick strap across the bridge of the foot and another around the ankle. "This is all I have."

"Then they'll have to do," Presley says, even though she would never wear them.

Lucy takes the dress to the full-length mirror on the back of the closet door. "But it's so plain."

"You can dress it up with some clunky earrings. Be sure to wear your contacts." Presley removes Lucy's heavy black-framed glasses. "And put your hair up."

Lucy gathers her hair back. "You mean like in a ponytail?"

"Like in a chignon," Presley says to Lucy's reflection.

Doubt crosses Lucy's face. "How do you do that?"

"I'll show you. Do you have any bobby pins?"

"I think so." They move to the en suite bathroom. Lucy opens and closes drawers until she finds an unopened package of bobby pins.

Brushing her hair back into a smooth ponytail, Presley twists and pins Lucy's mahogany hair into a low chignon.

Lucy admires her reflection in the mirror. "It's sophisticated."

Presley nods. "Where's your costume jewelry?"

Lucy opens another drawer, revealing a tangled mass of necklaces, bracelets, and earrings. Presley rummages through until she locates a pair of teardrop pearl and rhinestone earrings.

"These are perfect. You'll be the belle of the ball." She hands Lucy the earrings. "I really need to get going."

"I'll walk you out," Lucy says, as she fastens the earrings to her ears.

They're descending the stairs when a teenage boy barges through the front door. He looks up at them, and Presley gasps. This is the moment she's dreamed of. There is no doubt he's her half brother. Gripping the bannister, she continues the rest of the way down the stairs.

When they're face-to-face, she sees that Chris's hair is more brown than auburn, and his eyes are stormy whereas hers are a lighter gray. Their jawlines are the same, although his is stronger, more pronounced, more masculine.

Lucy is at her side in an instant. "Chris, this is my . . . my coworker, Presley Ingram."

"It's nice to meet you, Chris. I've heard a lot about you."

Chris's gaze narrows as he studies her. He would have to be blind not to notice the resemblance. "Who did you say you are?"

As slow seconds tick off the clock while Presley waits for Lucy to explain, she risks a glance at Lucy, whose expression is impassive. *She's not going to tell him.* "I'm Presley Ingram. The event planner at the inn. I was helping your mom pick out a dress for the party tonight."

"Oh. Okay. Well, nice to meet you." Is that disappointment in his tone?

Presley's eyes lock with Chris's as he continues down the hall to the back of the house. When he's out of sight, she jerks her head back toward Lucy. "Why didn't you tell him about me?" she asks in a loud whisper.

Lucy's face is set in stone. "I don't want my son to know what happened to me in college."

"Why not? Are you protecting him from the unpleasant reality that not all guys are good guys? Learning his mother was date-raped could be a lesson well learned about how he shouldn't treat girls."

"My son would never do something like that." Lucy swings the door open. "I'll see you at the party."

Presley remains glued to the floor. "Chris would be proud to know that you made the most of a difficult situation."

Lucy white-knuckles the doorknob. "I gave my child away. That's not exactly making the most of it."

"You gave your child the life you couldn't provide." As understanding sets in, anger surges through her. "You're never going to tell Chris, are you? You're never going to claim me as your daughter. All these years you've been desperate to find the child you gave up for adoption, but now that I'm here, you want nothing to do with me. It's because of my biological father, isn't it? Every time you look at me, you think of him."

Lucy lowers her gaze to the floor. "Maybe. I don't know. I'm confused about a lot of things."

"Then I'll make it easy for you. I'll get out of your life." Presley storms past her. "Enjoy your date."

Presley wills herself not to cry. Why be miserable over something she can do nothing about? Lucy has more problems than Presley has patience for. Presley's real parents are dead. She's on her own now. Everett is the closest thing to family she has left.

She starts her car and heads toward her apartment. She's stopped at a red light on Main Street when her phone vibrates in the console, and Everett's face appears on the screen. She snatches up the phone. "I was just thinking about you."

"Only good thoughts, I hope," he says in a sexy voice.

The tears she's been holding back fill her eyes and trickle down her cheeks. "I wish you were here. Being apart is harder than I expected."

"I know, babe. I'm missing you too. What if I told you I can come early for Christmas?"

"Really, Everett? That'd be awesome." Presley turns into the small parking lot behind her building. "But what about your mom?"

"Looks like her family reunion is going to happen. After thirty years, she's going to Texas to see her family."

"That's wonderful! Please tell her how happy I am for her." Presley puts the car in park and leaves the engine running. "Are you sure you shouldn't go with her?"

Everett sighs. "I've offered a dozen times. She really wants to do this alone. The situation will be awkward enough without me around."

"That makes sense. I'll cancel the room I'm holding for her in the carriage house. When are you coming? Soon, I hope."

"Mom's flight leaves Thursday morning. I'll get on the highway as soon as I drop her at the airport. Stella is counting on me to work through New Year's, which means I'll be staying with you for two weeks. If that's too long . . ."

"Are you kidding me? I wish you could stay forever." Silence fills the line, and Presley worries she's overstepped. They've been dating only a short time. "I don't mean forever, forever. I just mean, stay as long as you like."

"As much as I'd like to stay with you forever, forever, my music career is waiting for me here. *However,* if you move back to Nashville, we can be together forever, forever."

Yes! She palms the steering wheel. Everett wants forever, forever as much as she does.

"I wish I could. I miss Nashville more than I thought I would. But I can't. Not yet. I promised Stella I'd stay at the inn for at least six months. Besides, I love my job."

But Presley loves Everett more. She can't think about leaving Stella until she finds and trains her replacement. Which means June at the earliest. How can she possibly live apart from Everett for that long?

11

STELLA

I speak with each of my team members as I make my final rounds through the main rooms. I confirm that their staff has arrived and confirm that their bars are fully stocked. While everything appears in order, my heart remains heavy. I'm the general manager. I should attend the event. But I can't leave Jazz with a babysitter. Not with Naomi on the loose. Jazz wouldn't go for it anyway. She's been clinging to me since her run-in with Naomi on Wednesday night.

With Jazz skipping along beside me, I'm returning from my progress check on the library and solarium, when I spot Opal talking animatedly to Rita in the reception lobby.

I join them at the check-in desk. "I didn't realize the two of you know each other."

Opal grins. "Rita is my new bestie. She was just telling me her daughter, Emma, got accepted early to Cornell."

I clap my hands. "Bravo. That's excellent news, Rita. Congratulations to you both. I'm looking forward to having Emma intern with us over the holidays. She'll learn a lot from Presley."

"She can hardly talk of anything else," Rita says. "Now that she's been accepted to the school of her choice, I'm worried I'll have a hard time keeping her focused on exams."

"I wouldn't worry too much," I say. "I only met her the once, when she came in for an interview, but she's a smart girl. She knows how important it is to keep her grades up."

A guest approaches the desk with a question, and Rita turns her attention to him.

Opal eyes my jeans and sweater. "The party starts soon. Why aren't you dressed?"

"Because I'm not going."

Opal follows my gaze to Jazz, who is intrigued by the stream of arriving guests.

"Why don't you let her spend the night with me?" Opal suggests.

"I doubt she will. You know how apprehensive she's been lately."

Opal's lips part in a toothy grin. "Can I ask her?"

I give her a one-shoulder shrug. "Go for it."

Opal taps Jazz on the shoulder, and Jazz drags her attention away from the guests. "Wanna spend the night with me? I'll make your favorite chicken fajitas, and I have a drawer full of old Christmas movies we can watch."

Jazz bounces on her toes. "Really? Can I, really? I haven't spent the night with you in for-ever."

Opal winks at me, an I-told-you-so-expression on her face. "Yes, you really can. Are you ready to go now? We'll need to stop by the cottage for your nightgown and toothbrush."

Jazz holds up a finger. "One minute. I wanna look at the Christmas tree first." She hurries off toward the entryway.

I cock an eyebrow at Opal. "You've been holding out on me. You never told me you and Jazz are sleepover buddies."

Opal's expression turns serious. "She stayed with me a lot

when Billy was sick. On his worst days when Naomi refused to leave him."

I stare at my grandmother. "But Naomi despises you."

"Now she does. She didn't back then. After your daddy died and Naomi started drinking heavily, I told her she needed to get her life together for the sake of her child. She's hated me ever since."

"That makes me almost feel sorry for Naomi."

"Don't!" Opal says in an adamant tone. "Brian and I made that mistake. We felt indebted to her for taking such good care of Billy on his deathbed. That's why we insisted you give Naomi the benefit of the doubt for so long. *If*, and that's a very big if, Naomi ever had an ounce of compassion in her, it died with your father."

I shake my head at the sad story. "She must have really loved him."

"Love? I don't think Naomi is capable of loving another human being. She was obsessed with Billy. She wanted to control him. When he became ill, she got her wish, however pathetic that may sound."

"I don't understand, Opal. Why haven't you told me any of this before now?"

"Because I didn't want to sway your opinion of Naomi. I kept hoping she'd come around. I now know that's never going to happen." Opal grips my arm. "Don't let your guard down, sweet girl. Naomi isn't evil. She's mentally ill, and that makes her extremely dangerous."

Jazz wanders back over to us. She's chewing on her lower lip, like she does when something's bothering her. Has she changed her mind about spending the night with Opal?

Opal asks, "Are you ready to get your things?"

Jazz nods, her earlier enthusiasm for the sleepover gone.

Opal gestures in the direction of the back entrance. "Then what're we waiting for?"

Filing out the door, Opal and I each take one of Jazz's hands as we walk under the tent on the terrace. We're crossing the street to the cottage when Jazz asks, "Where do angels come from?" and I know she's thinking about the angel on top of the tree.

"God sends them down from heaven to watch over us." I unlock my red front door and step out of the way for Opal and Jazz to enter.

The conversation continues in the bedroom, as we gather her belongings for the sleepover. "Are angels people who have died and gone to heaven?" Jazz asks.

"That's right."

Jazz stuffs a change of clothes for tomorrow into her backpack. "Is Billy an angel?"

Opal and I lock eyes over the top of the child's head. Jazz has been talking about Billy a lot since I told her he was her father.

Lowering myself to the bed, I pull Jazz onto my lap. "I can't say for sure. Nobody really knows who the angels are. Heaven and God and angels are all a great mystery. But it makes me feel safe knowing our daddy is watching over us from heaven."

Jazz's chin quivers, and tears pool in her eyes.

"Maybe this sleepover isn't such a good idea," I say to Opal.

"No!" Jazz accidentally kicks my shin as she leaps off my lap. "I wanna go to Opal's!

I grimace at the pain in my leg. "Can you try to forget about the angels for tonight and have fun?"

"Yes! I promise!" She slings her backpack over her shoulder and dashes to the front door.

Opal and I follow. "Are you sure you want to do this?" I ask.

"I'm positive. You and Jack need a night to yourselves. Now, call your fiancé and get yourself dolled up." Opal takes Jazz's backpack from her and opens the door. "Ready, kiddo?"

With an affirmative nod, Jazz repeats, "Ready, kiddo."

"Be good for Opal." I kiss Jazz's cheek and then Opal's. "Call me if you need anything."

From the porch, I watch them pile into Opal's yellow Mini Cooper, and as they speed off, I say a silent prayer Opal doesn't kill them with her erratic driving.

I don't blame Jazz for being confused. The kid has been through so much in the past twelve months. Billy was her friend. She was distraught when he died. Then, Naomi divorced Derrick and he disappeared from their lives. And now she's living with me, her long-lost sister, because the court temporarily deemed Naomi unfit. She needs some normalcy in her life, but I fear none of us will get it until Naomi's out of the picture for good.

———

"I'll put on my tuxedo and be right over," Jack says when I call him about the party. He's thrilled at the prospect of a night out, even more so about the prospect of a private celebration afterward at my cottage. We haven't been together since Jazz came to live with me before Thanksgiving.

With no time to shower, I freshen my makeup and straighten my brown curls with a flat iron. I've been waiting for the right opportunity to wear the red satin strapless gown I bought on a whim at Fiona's last month. But as I stare at my reflection in the mirror, I worry the slit up the thigh is too risqué. The gleam in Jack's eye when he comes to pick me up is confirmation.

"It's too much," I say, a statement, not a question.

"It's fine as long as you don't leave my side. Every man at the party will drool over you."

"That's it. I'm wearing something else." I spin around, heading for my bedroom.

He comes after me, grabbing hold of my hips. "Don't you dare change. It's not the dress. It's you in the dress. You're drop-dead gorgeous." He plants a trail of kisses on my neck. "Please. Wear it for me."

"Seriously, Jack. I don't want my guests to think the new general manager is a slut."

"No one will think you're a slut. They'll think you're elegant." His breath is warm near my ear. "But you may not dance with anyone but me."

I turn around to face him. "Why would I do that when you're the best-looking guy at the party?" I straighten his red tartan bow tie. "I've never seen you in your tuxedo. You look hot."

"That's it. We're skipping the party." Pinning me against the wall, he crushes his lips to mine.

I push him away. "Stop, Jack! You're messing up my makeup. We have to at least make an appearance." I reapply lipstick from the tube in my bag. "The sooner we get going, the sooner we can come home."

"If you insist," he says, and helps me into my black velvet coat.

Guests have already begun to arrive when we enter the main building. When Jack gives my coat to the attendant at the makeshift coat check, a chill sends goose bumps crawling over my flesh. I should have thought to bring a shawl.

Grabbing cranberry champagne cocktails from a tuxedo-clad server, we stroll about throughout the main floor, mingling with our guests, catching up with old friends and meeting new ones. We make our way down to Jameson's where we load small plates with traditional cocktail foods like tenderloin rolls, miniature crab cakes, and oysters on the half shell as well as some of

Cecily's more contemporary hors d'oeuvres, including an extensive array of sushi items.

We mosey over to the wine tasting where Lucy is pairing wines from local vineyards with truffles from my favorite chocolate shop in New York. Brian hovers nearby, wearing an expression of unadulterated infatuation as he watches her.

When Jack strikes up a conversation with a gentleman about table saws, I excuse myself and make my way over to Brian. "Our sommelier is looking especially lovely this evening," I say in a teasing tone. "Are you two on a date?"

Brian's handsome face glows bright red. "I . . . um . . . yes. As a matter of fact, we are."

I laugh out loud. "You've got it bad."

He casts me a warning look. "Easy, Stella. I'm an old man. My self-confidence is fragile. I haven't been on a date in decades."

"Neither has she from what I hear. I think the two of you make a wonderful couple. And you deserve happiness."

He offers me a shy smile. "Thank you for saying that."

"With any luck, the chocolate will run out soon, and you can ask her to dance."

Brian grunts. "If I remember how."

"You'll remember. It's like riding a bicycle." In the brief few minutes I've been talking to Brian, I've lost sight of Jack. "I'm itching to dance myself. I'd better go find my date. If I don't see you again, I hope you enjoy your evening."

I kiss his cheek and head off to search for Jack. After checking all the rooms on the first floor, I finally find him on the terrace with a group of guys his age, none of whom I recognize. "There you are. You ditched me."

"Sorry, babe. I would never ditch you." Jack drapes one arm around my neck. "I want you to meet an old high school buddy.

Lennie, this is my fiancé, Stella. When I heard Lennie was in town for the weekend, I had to come find him."

Glancing around, I recognize several of Jack's best friends in the small groups clustered on the terrace. He's in his element with these people. I don't want to interrupt his fun. "I need to run across to my cottage for a minute. I'll be right back."

His hand slides down my back. "Is everything okay?"

"Everything's fine." I hug myself. "I'm just cold. I'm going to get a shawl."

"You'll freeze on the way over. Wear this." Shrugging off his tuxedo jacket, he holds it open while I slip my arms into the sleeves.

I hurry across the stone terrace and down the steps as fast as my stiletto heels will carry me. At the cottage, I remove the key from my clutch and unlock the door, leaving it open as I hurry through the living room. I don't notice that someone is lying on my sofa until she sits bolt upright and says, "Stella!"

My hands fly up, my clutch tumbling across the floor, and I stumble backward into the bookcase. I grab onto a shelf, preventing myself from falling. Straightening, I stare over at the sofa. "Naomi! What the heck? You scared me to death. What're you doing here?"

"I wanna see Jazz. Where is she?"

I smooth out my dress. "You'll see her at your visitation on Monday. She's at a sleepover tonight."

"Did the court approve this sleepover?"

Heat flushes through me. "I don't need permission from the judge. I'm not the one who has to prove myself. You're trespassing. How did you get in, anyway? I specifically remember locking the door on my way out."

She dangles a key in front of her face. "It's not considered trespassing if you have a key."

"But you gave me your keys when I fire . . . when I terminated you."

"I gave you one set of my keys, Stella. I have copies."

I march in my spiked heels to the door, yanking it open. "You need to leave."

Naomi barks out a laugh. "Or else what?"

"Or else I'm calling the police."

Her eyes travel to my clutch on the floor. "I'm guessing your phone is in there." Sitting back on the sofa, she crosses her legs, as though she's planning to stay awhile.

I glare at Naomi. She has that now-familiar maniacal look in her eyes. She's here to cause trouble. I stare out the open door. I should make a run for it. But if I show Naomi my fear, she'll continue to torment me until she wears me down.

"You can see for yourself that Jazz isn't here. I need to get back to the party." I realize my mistake the minute the words leave my lips.

"The party, huh? You're such a hypocrite, Stella. You rat me out to your detective friend every time I try to have a little fun. Meanwhile, you're out getting drunk and whoring around in an obscene-looking dress."

My heart pounds in my ears. This is the first time I've been out in weeks. I've sacrificed my social life and sex life for her child. But I won't argue with her. I refuse to stoop to her level. But I need a way out. I'm not leaving her in my house alone.

I feel a heavy object against my right hip. I pat the pocket of Jack's tuxedo. His phone.

When I slip my hand into the pocket, Naomi sits up straight on the couch. "What're you doing?"

Tugging the phone out of the pocket, I use Jack's password to unlock the screen. "I'm calling the police."

Naomi rests her hand on her purse at her side. "Don't do it."

I freeze, my finger poised over keypad. "Why? Do you have a gun in there?"

"I do. If you don't put the phone away, I'll splatter your blood all over your red door." Her sadistic tone of voice causes the hairs on the back of my neck to stand to attention.

From outside comes the sound of footsteps, leather souls against pavement and then wooden porch steps. Jack and Martin appear in the doorway. I hold my hand out to them. "Stop! She has a gun."

Naomi jumps up off the sofa. "Stella, you're ridiculous. I don't own a gun."

My arm shoots out, finger pointed at Naomi. "She broke into my house and ambushed me. She threatened to splatter my blood all over the door. I had no way of knowing whether she had a gun."

Naomi dangles the key. "I didn't break in. I let myself in." When she tries to brush past Jack, Martin grabs her by the arm with one hand and takes her bag from her with the other.

I place the call to nine-one-one. "This is Stella Boor at the Inn at Hope Springs Farm. I'm reporting an intruder. My head of security is currently detaining her. Send the police immediately. Have them come around to the caretaker's cottage. No sirens, please. I'm hosting a dinner dance for six hundred guests."

"I understand, Miss Boor. I'll send the police right away."

I end the call and hand the phone to Jack. When my body trembles, Jack puts his arm around me, pulling me close.

We watch Martin handcuff Naomi and drag her back inside. When he searches her bag, he finds a flask of vodka but no gun. "Have you been drinking?"

She shakes her head.

He leans in close to her face, smelling her breath.

Naomi glares at him. "Breathalyze me, asshole. I have had nothing to drink tonight."

Two police officers arrive in a patrol car followed by an unmarked gray Charger with Detective Kathy Sinclair behind the wheel. "I heard the dispatch on the radio," Sinclair says. "What happened?"

I recount the events of the past thirty minutes.

"Take her to the station," Sinclair instructs the officers.

"On what grounds?" Naomi demands.

Sinclair ticks them off her fingers. "Criminal trespassing and assault with a deadly weapon."

"But I didn't break in. I have a key. And I don't own a gun."

"You entered Miss Boor's private property without her permission. That is criminal trespassing, a misdemeanor. And you threatened Miss Boor with a deadly weapon, regardless of whether you actually own one." Sinclair tosses her thumb over her shoulder. "Get her outta here."

I wait for the officers to escort Naomi out of the cottage. "Will any of those charges stick?" I ask Sinclair.

"Enough to keep her overnight. I'll report this to the judge as soon as possible. In the meantime, get every lock on the premises changed."

12

STELLA

Jack and I return to the party, but we don't stay long. We go to his house instead of my cottage, where the memory of Naomi is still vivid. Our tender lovemaking serves as a reminder of how we're meant to be together and the sacrifices we're making for Jazz. I apologize for ruining our evening and for complicating our lives to the point of making Jack angry.

"Please! Stella, none of this is your fault. I love you. And I love Jazz. We'll get through this together. And Naomi will eventually get what's coming to her."

An incoming text from Detective Sinclair wakes me at dawn. *FYI, Naomi has been released from jail on bond.*

Jack goes with me to pick Jazz up from Opal's. We find my grandmother and sister eating large stacks of pancakes at the small round table in Opal's sunny yellow kitchen. Jazz seems so happy and relaxed with Opal. If I could guarantee her safety, I'd let her stay. But I can't guarantee her safety. Not at Opal's. Not at my cottage. Not anywhere, as long as Naomi is free to roam the planet.

Opal pushes back from the table. "Sit down, and I'll make you some flapjacks."

My stomach is in knots. The smells of butter and syrup make me nauseous. "Thanks, but we can't stay."

Jack adds, "But we won't say no to coffee."

While Jazz finishes her breakfast, Jack and I lean against the counter, sipping coffee and answering Opal's many questions about the party. We don't tell her what happened with Naomi. No sense in worrying her unnecessarily.

On the way back to the farm in Jack's truck, Jazz says, "We're going to Sunday school, right?"

"Not today, sweetheart. I have something important I need to take care of at the farm." I shift in my seat so I can see her in the back. "The forecast is calling for snow tonight. Isn't that exciting? I think I remember seeing sleds in the barn. We can get them out and have them ready."

"But I wanna go to Sunday school. My teacher is telling us about angels and baby Jesus's birth. Please don't make me miss it."

Jack and I exchange a look. "I'll take her."

"Do you mind?"

"Not at all. It would be my pleasure." Jack looks at Jazz in the rearview mirror. "What say, Jazz? Do you think your Sunday school teacher will let me sit in on your class today?"

"Yes! And afterward, can we go to Lucky's for lunch?"

Jack snickers. "If you're hungry after eating all those pancakes."

I see Jazz off to Sunday school and then contact our locksmith, who understands the urgency of the situation and graciously agrees to work on a Sunday. By midafternoon, he's changed the locks on all the buildings on the farm. He leaves me with five copies of the master key. I keep one. Give one to Martin. And store the remaining three in my office safe. Martin and I create a schedule for his staff to lock and unlock each of the buildings at dawn and dusk until further notice.

At four o'clock, Detective Sinclair stops by the cottage to see me. Jack has gone to his office to catch up on some paperwork, and Jazz is curled in a ball with pillows and a blanket on the sofa, watching Rudolph on television.

"Would you like to come in?" I ask Sinclair.

"No, I think it's best for little ears not to hear what I have to say." We lean against the front porch railing with our backs to the main building. Sinclair gestures at the three plastic sleds standing against the house. "All ready for the storm?"

I smile. "I'm trying to keep Jazz preoccupied. She's dreading her visitation with Naomi tomorrow. Maybe we'll have to cancel due to snow."

"Unless we have blizzard conditions, I encourage you to see this visitation through. To postpone would be to postpone the court's decision on permanent custody. I've spoken with Judge Marcum and Cynthia Green, the social worker, today. They are both aware of what happened last night. Naomi's reckless behavior is not helping her case. I realize this is hard on you, Stella, but Naomi's actions play in our favor."

A chill travels down my spine, and I fold my arms around me. "Naomi really got to me last night, Detective. She scared the life out of me, sneaking into my house like that. And I honestly thought she had a gun. I've been looking over my shoulder all day. I have this creepy feeling she's watching me. Do you think I should get a handgun?"

Detective Sinclair lets out a sigh. "You could request a temporary protection order. It would be a long shot, but something to consider."

"A long shot? That's ridiculous. She scared the life out of me last night. Forget the protective order. So you don't think I should get a gun?"

Detective Sinclair pushes off the railing and stands before me. "Have you ever shot one before?"

I shake my head. "I'm not even a fan of guns, yet I'm considering buying one, if that tells you how afraid I am of Naomi. She's mentally unstable, out to get me at all costs."

Sinclair stares out toward the lake. "I believe in the Second Amendment, Stella. Every citizen of the United States has a right to bear arms. *However*, it is your responsibility to learn how to properly use and care for your weapon. Before you do anything rash, consider the danger associated with having a gun in the house with a young child. A better option might be to have Jack move in here with you. Or you and Jazz move in with him."

"In other words, let my man take care of us. I'm surprised at you, Detective. I didn't take you for an old-fashioned girl."

Sinclair tugs her phone out of her coat pocket. "I'm texting you the contact information for the local shooting range. You'll want to speak with Debbie. She'll help you pick out the right handgun and teach you how to use it."

"Thank you! I feel relieved already." Seconds later, my phone pings with her text.

"You're a good person with a big heart, Stella. I trust you not to let anything happen to your little sister."

Six inches of snow fall during the night. Cynthia Green calls first thing on Monday morning. "I heard what happened Saturday night. Normally I would suggest rescheduling due to the weather. But I think it's important for Naomi to see her child."

Taking Detective Sinclair's advice, I agree.

"Wonderful. How does two o'clock sound? I have a four-wheel drive. I'll bring Naomi over myself."

"We'll see you then," I say.

Jazz, Jack, and I spend the morning sledding down the hill to the lake. I don't remember when I've had so much fun. For a few brief hours, I forget about my troubles with Naomi.

Back at the cottage, I fix grilled cheeses and heat a can of tomato soup for our lunch. After we eat and Jack heads into work, I insist that Jazz rest to prepare for her visitation with her mother.

We climb into my bed with the covers piled high and a stack of books beside us. We're four books in when Jazz asks, "What if Mommy makes me go home with her?"

I set the book down. "We're a long way away from that happening, Jazz. If all goes well, it will never happen. The judge would have to order it, and if he ever has reason to do so, we'll have plenty of advance notice. The process is complicated. You need to trust the adults to handle it."

"Okay," she says begrudgingly. "Do I have to be nice to Mommy?"

I hug her close. "Yes, sweetheart. You should always try your best to be kind to everyone. Especially your mommy. She's going through a rough time and we should support her."

As much as it kills me, I know this is the right thing to tell Jazz. But it doesn't appear to ease her apprehension. At ten minutes until two, when we put our snow boots back on and trudge across the street to the main building, she grips my hand so tight it hurts. Naomi is waiting with Cynthia in the game room. She greets me with a friendly smile and embraces Jazz in a warm hug. She's as cool as an icicle hanging from the eaves outside the window.

"I'll be in my office down the hall if you need me." Turning my sister over to Cynthia, I walk backward into the hallway, but instead of going to my office, I head in the opposite direction, slipping into the adjacent library. I ease up to the doorway and eavesdrop on the threesome in the next room.

"Look at this wonderful assortment of games," Cynthia says

of the collection of board games we keep on the shelves for our guests. "Would you like to play one?"

I hear Naomi and Cynthia whispering, but I can't make out their words.

The room goes quiet, and Cynthia peeks around the door-jamb at me. "Go wait in your office. I'll find you, if I need you."

"But—"

"Stella," Cynthia says in a warning tone.

"Fine." I retreat to my office where I pace the floors. The visitation is scheduled to last an hour, but forty-five minutes later, Jazz comes flying into my office, her face wet with tears and Cynthia on her heels. I scoop Jazz into my arms.

"I take it that didn't go well," I say, kissing the top of Jazz's head.

"Not at all. Naomi took off on foot. She can walk home as far as I'm concerned. We need to talk. Is there somewhere we can go?" Cynthia's eyes are on Jazz, letting me know that whatever she has to say she doesn't want my sister to hear.

I set Jazz down and lift her chin up so I can see her golden eyes. "How would you like some of Cecily's hot chocolate?"

She nods, sniffling. I take her hand and the three of us leave my office. Cynthia and I don't speak on our way through the main lounge to Jameson's. The restaurant is empty, and I motion Cynthia to have a seat. "I'll be right back. Would you like some tea or coffee?"

"I'm fine. I won't take but a minute of your time."

The kitchen is relatively quiet, and we find Cecily taking a sheet of sugar cookies out of the oven.

"I need to talk to the social worker. Can Jazz hang out with you for a few minutes?"

"Of course." Cecily sets the cookie sheet down and bends over to Jazz's level. "Wanna help me decorate these sugar cookies?"

A smile tugs at Jazz's lips. "Can I eat one?"

Cecily holds up two fingers. "You can eat two."

"Can I have some hot chocolate too?"

"You drive a hard bargain," Cecily says, tickling Jazz.

I join Cynthia in the dining room, sliding into the banquette opposite her. "Tell me what happened?"

Cynthia folds her hands on the table. "On the way here, I explained to Naomi that the purpose of this visitation was to break the ice. And she appeared to understand. Things were going well. The three of us were playing a game. Then, out of the blue, Naomi went on a rant about you. She told Jazz not to trust you. She said that you don't love her, and that once you and Jack get married, you will have your own children, and Jazz won't matter to you anymore."

I feel a stabbing pain in my chest for my little sister. She must be so confused and hurt. "Only a monster would say such things to a child. Especially her own daughter."

Cynthia shakes her head in bewilderment. "I don't understand Naomi's motivations. She's certainly not trying to impress me, which means she doesn't care what Judge Marcum thinks either. She's wasting our time."

"I agree. It makes no sense." I fold my arms across my chest. "Where do we go from here?"

"I'm not sure. I'll be in touch after I talk to the judge." When Cynthia pushes back from the table, I move to get up. "Stay where you are," she says. "I can show myself out."

I remain seated at the banquette, staring out across the empty tables in the dining room through the windows to the snowy mountain landscape beyond. What is Naomi up to? She has a plan. I'm certain of that. We are her puppets, and she's controlling our strings. But why would she deliberately sabotage her chance to get custody? What will she gain by turning Jazz against me? Why would she intentionally hurt her daughter?

Then it suddenly *does* make sense. She was tormenting Jazz today. Like she tormented me on Saturday night when she sneak-attacked me in my cottage. Her point is obvious—custody or not, she's never going away until she gets what she wants. Judge Marcum can't give that to her. But I can. She will wear me down and then offer me a deal.

13

CECILY

Late Monday afternoon, as the last bands of light snow are moving out of the area, Cecily is in her office placing food orders for the coming week when Lyle calls with the news that someone else won the lottery for the campus house. She tries to sound upbeat, despite the panic that has recently taken up residence in her chest. "Then it wasn't meant to be. Don't worry, Lyle. We'll find somewhere to live. Let's divide and conquer. You search the campus, and I'll look in town."

"Okay," he says, and she imagines him hanging his head like a dejected puppy. "But I'd rather live in a house than an apartment."

Cecily grips her phone. "You've made that clear. But I have seventeen days before I have to move out of my apartment. Unless we want to risk being homeless, we should explore all our options."

"Way to be melodramatic, Cecily. We won't be homeless."

"Melodramatic?" She jumps to her feet and begins pacing in the small space in front of her desk. "You haven't seen melodramatic. Have you picked out your suit for the wedding? No. Have you sent me the list of friends you want to invite to the wedding?

No. Have you talked to your dad about paying for the dinner we're hosting for our parents the first night? No."

"Stop! You're giving me a headache, Cecily. You're like a Chihuahua going after a neighbor's cat. Arf. Arf. Arf."

She stares at her phone. *Did he just bark at me?* "I can't talk to you right now," she yells into the phone without returning it to her ear. She jabs the red end call button and slams the phone down on the desk.

What is wrong with him? Why can't he get his stuff done? He can make time to play poker and pickup basketball, but he can't do these few things to prepare for their wedding?

Lyle is waiting at her apartment when she gets home from work around eleven. He apologizes. Then she apologizes. And they have sex. But the makeup sex is nowhere near as passionate as the last time they fought. What is happening to them?

As they lie in bed afterward, she says, "I hate being a pest, but we really need to tick these items off our task lists."

"I know, babe. And I promise, I'll get them done." He runs his hands through his sandy hair. "What am I supposed to do again?"

As she lists his responsibilities, she holds one finger up at a time. "Suit for the wedding. List of friends you want to invite. Talk to your father about paying for the dinner."

Lyle draws a check mark in the air. "Got it. You don't have to ask me about them again."

Cecily looks at him from under a furrowed brow. "Are you sure?"

"I'm positive."

She has a bad feeling about this. She suspects these three things won't get done if she doesn't hound him about them. But she's willing to let this be a lesson to him. In order for their marriage to succeed, she needs to be able to count on him to do his part.

Cecily spends the first part of her day on Tuesday searching the internet for houses and apartments for rent in Hope Springs. Her choices are few. Apparently, no one moves in December. Which is surprising since it's the end of the year, but also understandable considering everyone is busy during the holidays.

She sneaks out after lunch to tour her handful of options. But none of them are suitable. They're either too small or rundown. The one she really likes—a three-bedroom apartment that occupies the whole third floor of a renovated warehouse building—is too expensive, even with their combined income.

On the drive back to the inn, she calls Lyle to report her lack of success. "Have you had any luck?"

"Not yet. All the apartment buildings on campus are designated for students. I've asked around. No one knows of any houses coming available anytime soon."

Cecily says, "I even called my landlord, to see if I can stay another month, but he's already rented the apartment."

"You could move in here with me." Lyle sounds almost eager about this suggestion.

"No thanks. I refuse to share a bathroom with three other guys."

Cecily drums her fingers on the steering wheel while she considers whether to mention Everett's old apartment. She isn't keen on living next door to Presley, who Cecily's growing less fond of every day, but it is a viable option. "I spoke to the gentleman who owns Presley's building. Everett's apartment is still available. Mr. Sanders will rent it month-to-month until we find something more permanent. It's a studio, though, and we'd have to store most of our stuff."

"Hmm. At least it's something. Let's keep looking."

Cecily is wound as tight as a guitar string. Could that funny feeling in her chest be heart palpitations? She needs to stop stressing about their living situation and focus on her job. Starting with tonight's specials, which she needs to discuss with Alessandro. But when she arrives back at the inn, he's not in the kitchen or the dining room. She glimpses him at a table at the way back of Billy's Bar, and as she approaches, Cecily sees that he's with Presley. The two are so intent on the notes in front of them they don't hear her until she's looming over them. "Why are the two of you hiding out in here?"

Presley turns her legal pad over so Cecily can't see her notes. "Alessandro is helping me with that event, the one I told you about on Christmas night."

"And I told you I'm not taking a honeymoon, so your event is my responsibility." Cecily thinks about the fishing cabin Lyle has on hold. He'll have to get over it. Her career comes first.

"Even if you don't go on a trip," Presley says, "you should take a few days off to spend with Lyle."

Cecily glares at Presley. "And you shouldn't tell me what I should do."

"Ooh! Cat fight!" Alessandro swipes his fingers at her, imitating a cat clawing the air.

Cecily points at the doorway. "Alessandro. In the kitchen. Now."

"Yes, ma'am." Alessandro climbs out from behind the table and scurries off.

Presley stands to face Cecily. "Now that you're back, will you unlock your office? I want to borrow some cookbooks."

She's tempted to say no, but the cookbooks belong to the inn. "As long as you return them tomorrow."

"Of course." Presley gathers her notes and they start off together toward the kitchen. "By the way, are you making any progress on your seating chart?"

"Not yet. I don't even know who's coming. I haven't emailed the invitations."

Presley stops in her tracks. "Wait. What? Do you realize your wedding is next week? On Christmas Eve. People typically have family plans for Christmas Eve. You better get on it."

"I've already designed the Evite. Once I get Lyle's list, all I have to do is press send." Cecily starts walking again, and Presley catches up with her. "Besides, other than a few friends and Lyle's parents, my family makes up most of the guest list. And I know they're all coming. They've already booked their flights and rooms."

"That's a start," Presley says. "You can create the seating chart for your family and plug the others in later."

Cecily waves away her concern. "There's no rush. My family thrives on drama. You never know who's speaking to whom at any given moment. It's best to wait until the last minute."

They reach Cecily's office, and she unlocks the door. She motions for Presley to enter ahead of her. Presley, her eyes on the bookshelves, doesn't see the large cardboard box on the floor beside Cecily's desk until she trips over it. She catches herself on the desk. "Geez, Cecily. That's a hazardous place to keep a box that size. What is it?"

"My wedding dress. I don't have anywhere else to keep it. If I take it to my apartment, Lyle will see it. I figured I'd leave it here until my mom arrives on Sunday. Then she can deal with it."

Presley picks up the box and places it in a chair, as though the dress is safer there. "It'll be a wrinkled mess by then. Why don't I take it home with me? If I hang it up tonight, most of the wrinkles will fall out by next week."

Softening toward her, Cecily offers her a smile of gratitude. "That'd be great, if you don't mind."

Presley sets her phone on the desk while she peruses the cookbooks. An incoming text catches Cecily's attention. While she can't read the actual message, she can see the text is from Jack. Cecily has seen Presley and Jack together twice, and now the text. Why are they suddenly so tight? Whatever is going on between them is about more than mistletoe. Poor Stella. How could Presley do this to her? And Everett, oblivious to his girlfriend's extracurricular activities. And where is Alessandro in all this? Cecily isn't entirely convinced Presley isn't doing the naughty with him as well. Cecily has to do something. She can't sit by and watch her friends get hurt. But she can't go pointing fingers until she has concrete proof.

Anger replaces the anxiousness she's been feeling in recent days. Which is fine with Cecily. She's better equipped to cope with anger than those squirrelly feelings of apprehension. Anger supplies her the energy to accomplish tasks she's been putting off. Lyle's guest list is waiting in her inbox, and she finally sends out her wedding invitations. She's rewarded with immediate responses. Lyle's roommates and plus ones are coming, as are the few friends Cecily has made in town outside of her coworkers.

In the days ahead, Cecily can't get away from Presley. On Wednesday afternoon, when setting up the dining room for the evening's event, Presley's incessant flirting with Alessandro makes Cecily retreat to her office. But Cecily is capable of giving credit where credit is due, and Presley is a genius when it comes to party planning. The event—a large private fiftieth wedding anniversary party for a local couple—is a tremendous success. Cecily pats herself on the back as well for the meticulously designed and executed seven-course menu.

After the last guests leave, Cecily claims two nearly full left-over bottles of Veuve Clicquot and summons Presley and Alessandro to the kitchen. "Well done, team! We deserve a cele-bratory drink." She hands each of them a flute of champagne.

Presley holds up her glass to toast. "Cecily, the food was amazing. Your best dinner yet."

Cecily feels guilty for having been so annoyed with Presley lately. "I couldn't have done it without my sous chef." She clinks Alessandro's glass and then Presley's. "You did an outstanding job on the decorations. The dining room has never looked lovelier. The gold accents were elegant without being overbearing."

Cecily refills their glasses, and Alessandro sets funk music to play over his Bluetooth speaker. An hour later, the threesome is dancing in a conga line around the islands when Everett bursts through the back door, bringing with him a wave of frigid air.

Presley flings herself into his arms, pulling his head down and kissing him. "You made it! I've been so worried about you on the highway alone at night."

Cecily's irritation comes crashing back. Everett is her friend. She texts with him constantly. Why didn't he mention to her that he was coming today? And why did Presley keep his sudden return a secret?

She holds her glass up to him. "Welcome back, Everett."

"Hey, Cecily." He bestows a warm smile upon her before returning his attention to Presley.

"I didn't think you were coming until this weekend," Cecily presses.

"I was able to get away early." His eyes are on Presley. He looks as though he might devour her, the way he once devoured Cecily's baked Alaska.

Cecily's stomach turns, and she downs the last of her champagne. "I'm glad to see the two of you getting along so well. I was worried there might be trouble in paradise."

Presley pulls away from Everett. "What do you mean?"

"You know, the way you and Alessandro have been carrying on lately . . ." Cecily waves her empty glass back and forth between Presley and Alessandro. "I thought maybe you two were . . ."

Presley and Alessandro bust out laughing. Presley looks at Alessandro. "Do you want to tell her or should I?"

"I'll let you do the honor," Alessandro says.

"Alessandro is gay, Cecily. He's in love with Mateo."

Cecily's mouth drops open. "I never would've guessed. You seem so . . ."

"Normal?" Alessandro says with a smirk on his lips.

Cecily stiffens. "I don't believe you. Why haven't I met Mateo?"

"Because he still lives in New York."

Presley leans against Everett. "By the way, Everett, this is Alessandro."

The men shake hands. "I've heard a lot about you," Alessandro says, and Everett responds, "Likewise."

Cecily is mortified. How did she get this so wrong? She falls back against the counter. "I admit I'm relieved. The way you two flirt with each other is shameful. While we're clearing the air . . . Presley, why don't you tell us what's going on between you and Jack. And don't give me that line about him getting mistletoe for you. I've seen you together, in each other's arms. Twice. And I saw a text from him on your phone."

Everett looks at Presley with eyes narrowed. "Presley?"

"Not that it's any of your business, Cecily, but Jack and I are working on a surprise for Stella for Christmas. And we weren't in each other's arms. I hugged him once, and he gave me a goodbye peck on the cheek the other time."

Cecily's face warms. "What surprise? Why didn't anyone tell me about it? I'm Stella's best friend."

Presley holds her chin high. "To be honest, we were worried you might blow it. You haven't exactly been yourself lately." She turns to Everett. "I'm ready to go. Let me get my bag."

Presley disappears into Cecily's office and returns with her work tote. Cecily follows Everett and Presley to the door. "I can keep a secret better than any of you. Tell me the surprise."

Presley shakes her head. "Sorry. I can't. Too many people already know about it."

When Everett and Presley run hand-in-hand off toward the parking lot, Cecily slams the door behind them. She resents being left out of the surprise. Instead of being hurt, she's angry, an emotion that is becoming a little too familiar for her liking.

14

PRESLEY

Presley and Everett barely make it to her apartment before they tear at each other's clothes. He unties her wrap dress, and she shrugs it off, letting it drop in a puddle of black silk on the floor. She unfastens her bra and stands before him, naked except for her black thong and thigh-high boots.

"You're so beautiful." With hands on her breasts, he walks her backward into the living room. They drop to the floor and make love on her antelope rug.

Afterward, Presley rolls onto her back, and with arms spread wide at her sides, she stares up at the ceiling. "That was incredible. God, I missed you so much."

"I missed you so much. And I missed this place. Our little love nest." Everett looks around the room, as though reacquainting himself with his surroundings. When he spots the mannequins in the corner, he says, "What's up with the wedding dresses, Presley? Are you opening a bridal boutique?"

"Ha. I should! One of those belongs to Cecily. I'm keeping it for her so Lyle doesn't see it. The other is Stella's Christmas surprise."

"Wait a minute." He flips over on his belly, propping elbows on the floor. "You and Jack are giving Stella a wedding gown for Christmas?"

Presley flashes him a grin. "We're actually surprising her with the whole wedding."

Everett's electric blue eyes grow wide. "I've never heard of such a thing. How's that gonna work?"

Snatching a cashmere throw off the sofa, Presley drapes it over them and snuggles close to him as she explains her plan.

"That's insane," he says when she finishes. "What about the marriage license?"

"A blood test isn't necessary in Virginia. And the state doesn't require a waiting period. Brian has arranged for the clerk of court to issue the marriage certificates right before the wedding."

"Is her family coming from New York?" he asks.

Presley nods. "Her mothers will arrive on Christmas Eve. I gave them the suite I was holding for your mother in the carriage house. Fingers crossed we can keep them hidden."

"This seems risky to me, babe. I mean, you're planning another woman's wedding with no input from her. What if Stella isn't ready to get married?"

Presley rolls onto her side toward him. "You should have seen Stella's face when she tried on that dress. She's ready to marry Jack. But Naomi is causing so much trouble for her and Jazz right now."

"Naomi! What a witch," Everett says, shaking his head and rolling his eyes. "Who else knows about this surprise?"

"Pretty much everyone except Cecily and Jazz. We told as few people as possible, but we need everyone's help to pull this off. Including yours. Will you design a signature cocktail for the happy couple?"

"Sure. I promised Cecily I'd mix one for her. She wants something with Christmas spices." He taps his chin. "I'm thinking Stella's will be a dessert drink. Something sugary sweet."

"We should probably tell Cecily about the surprise," Presley says. "I thought she'd be on her honeymoon. But now, she says she and Lyle aren't taking a honeymoon until next summer. Do you think she'll freak out that Stella's wedding is stealing her show?"

"Probably. She's freaking out about everything these days. Don't worry about it. I'll talk to her." Everett slips out from beneath the blanket and gathers up his clothes. "I need to run down to my truck for the rest of my stuff. I'll be back in a minute. I'm starving. Do you have any ice cream?"

Presley laughs. He's always hungry. "Not only do I have ice cream. I have a very special brand of ice cream for you. Do you want any help unloading your truck?"

"I've got it. But thanks." He gives her a lingering kiss. "After our snack, we'll move to the bed," he says, his breath a whisper against her lips.

Wrapped in the blanket, Presley goes to the bathroom for her robe and then to the kitchen. She loves its minimalist design with black base cabinets and open shelves above. The counter-tops are fake marble—white with grey veining—and the appliances stainless steel. She retrieves a plastic container from the freezer and two spoons from the utensil drawer.

She hears the door open, and Jack's footsteps in her bedroom. When he enters the kitchen a minute later, his expression is somber. "What's wrong? Did something happen on the way to the parking lot?"

He shakes his head. "Everything's fine," he says, but she can tell it isn't.

He plops down on the barstool beside her, and she hands him a spoon. "This is Cecily's homemade rum raisin ice cream. Wait until you try it. It's the best I've ever had."

He digs the spoon into the ice cream and shoves it in his mouth. "That's good," he says, not nearly as impressed as Presley thought he'd be, connoisseur of ice cream that he is.

"Cecily may be a pain in the butt sometimes, but she's an amazing cook."

He jabs at the ice cream as though angry at it. "I have to admit, I felt like she'd kicked me in the gut when she accused you of sleeping with Jack."

Her jaw goes slack. "Seriously, Ev. Do you really think I would do something like that?"

Everett hangs his head. "I *hope* you wouldn't cheat on me. But I'm not gonna lie. For a split second, I considered the possibility. We've only been in a relationship for six weeks, and most of those we've spent apart. There's still so much we don't know about each other."

Presley spreads her arms wide. "I'm an open book. What do you want to know?"

He refuses to meet her gaze. "Whose wedding dress is in your closet? I wasn't snooping. I saw it when I put away my hanging clothes. Is it yours? Were you married before, Presley?"

She stares at him, dumbfounded. Does he seriously think she would keep something as important as a previous marriage from him? "That's my debutante dress, Everett."

Presley slides down off her barstool and leaves the kitchen. She stands at the living room window, looking down Main Street toward the inn, which is lit up despite the late hour. Everett is right. There's so much they don't know about each other. She already found out about one secret he was keeping, about his old lover, his *friend* with benefits who is having his baby in March. What else is he hiding? She loves him with her whole heart. But is it enough to overcome all obstacles? Can she forgive him whatever skeletons remain in his closet?

He joins her at the window. "I'm sorry. I didn't mean to

offend you. I come from a poor family, Presley. I've never met a debutante before."

"The night Mom presented me at my debutante ball nearly ten years ago, she was on her best behavior. For once, she didn't drink too much. We danced and sang on stage with the band. When we got home, we stayed up late talking about the future. I brought the dress with me from Nashville to remind me of the few good times Mom and I had together." A tear spills over her eyelid and trickles down her cheek.

Everett fingers away the tear. "This is a difficult time for you, your first holidays without your mom. I know you miss her."

"I do. But I'm grateful to have you and my job to keep my mind occupied. This isn't an easy Christmas for you either, your first without your dad."

"That's not exactly the same. God may strike me dead, but I don't miss my dad. I'm thankful he's no longer around to beat up on my mom."

Presley smiles. "And your mom has reunited with her family."

"And I'm here with you." He slips his arm around her waist and draws her near. "And there's nowhere else I'd rather be."

She leans against him. "I meant what I said, Everett. I'm an open book. I'm not keeping any secrets. I have more reason not to trust you than you have not to trust me."

"That's fair. But I promised you no more secrets, and I meant it. Cross my heart." He draws an *X* on his chest. "It's not that I don't trust you, Pres. This long-distance relationship is messing with my mind. I imagine all kinds of crazy scenarios when I'm lying in bed alone at night, and your gorgeous self is hosting some event with good-looking studs fawning all over you."

"I haven't so much as looked at another guy since we met." It's Presley's turn to cross her heart. "You're the one who's going to be a country music star. Beautiful girls will throw themselves at you every night."

He hip-bumps her. "I'll need you to protect me from them. All the more reason for you to move back to Nashville." He lets out a deep breath. "Seriously though, being away from you is way harder than I thought it would be. This isn't a normal life. If we're meant to be together, and I believe we are, what are we doing apart?"

"I do miss Nashville. And I miss being with you. As much as I love my job, I'd give it up in a second if not for Stella. I promised her I'd stay at least six months. There's no reason for me to stay. I took this job to be closer to Lucy, but since she's made it clear she's not interested in having a relationship with me, I might as well leave."

"Give her a little more time, babe. Maybe she'll come around."

"I'm not holding my breath. I don't know what's eating her up inside, whether it's her divorce or she's genetically predisposed to living a glass-half-empty life. But I find her bitterness off-putting. I would love to know my half brother better. But it doesn't look like that will happen either." Presley turns her body into his. "Anyway, let's talk about something more pleasant. Would you be willing to sing in Billy's Bar on Friday and Saturday nights?"

"Sure. I wanna try out some new songs I've been working on. Do you think Stella needs me to bartend this weekend?"

"You'll have to ask her. We're only booked at 50 percent capacity for the weekend. But starting on Monday, we'll need you every night through New Year's. You won't believe the lineup of events I'm organizing. Gingerbread house contests and scavenger hunts for the children. Cooking demonstrations and wine tastings for the adults. Sleigh rides for all, if it snows again, and it's supposed to. Early morning yoga classes in the solarium and nature walks. Opal is teaching painting classes for adults and children in the barn."

"I'm willing to host a mixology demonstration, if you think our guests would be interested," Everett says.

"They would love it. Thanks."

He presses his body against hers. "I'm looking forward to two weeks of working with you during the day and making love to you every night."

"Hm. I like the sound of that. Can we start now?"

"You bet," Everett says, sweeping Presley off her feet and carrying her into the bedroom.

15

STELLA

Every time I turn around, I run into Naomi. Coming out of Jameson's or Billy's Bar or wandering aimlessly around the main floor of the inn. Sometimes she's alone, but usually she's with a man who, I assume, is her new boyfriend and who looks enough like Denzel Washington to be his twin. My mind plays tricks on me. I imagine her peeking at me from behind trees, and when the wind rattles my windows, I'm certain Naomi is trying to break in. Worst of all are the vivid nightmares that force me awake in a cold sweat at all hours of the night.

On Tuesday, I go down to the police station and fill out the forms to place a protection order against Naomi. On Wednesday, the judge, claiming my half sister's mother isn't posing any threats, denies my request. By Thursday, I'm such a nervous wreck, I call the local shooting range and schedule a session with Debbie for the next morning.

Debbie is in her mid-fifties, and she knows her stuff when it comes to guns. She helps me pick out a pistol, a Sig Sauer that nestles perfectly in my small hands, and shows me how to load, cock, and shoot it. Debbie heaps praise on me when I shoot up the paper target's torso. I purchase a lock for the gun's safe box and store it on the top shelf of my closet. I feel a sense of relief, not only that it's there but that I'm competent to use it to protect myself and my family.

I've no sooner arrived home from the shooting range, when I receive an unexpected visit from Brian, who is still dressed from court in a charcoal gray suit. I take his overcoat, and we go into the kitchen for coffee.

"They're calling for more snow tonight," he says as the Keurig brews. "Four to six inches."

"I heard." I remove a container of cream from the refrigerator and the sugar shaker from the cabinet about the coffee machine. "Jazz will be crushed if it interferes with her dance recital."

He takes the coffee from me and adds a stream of cream. "About the performance. Is it okay if I bring a date? Lucy loves *The Nutcracker*. She'd like to come."

I put a new K-cup in the coffeemaker and push the button to brew. "Lucy is more than welcome."

"We'll arrive early. No need to save us seats."

"No need to do that. I've lost track of the number of our friends who are coming. I figured I'd save an entire row." We sit down across from one another at the pine farm table. "We're having a reception in the solarium afterward if you'd like to drop by for champagne and cake."

"Yes, to the champagne. No to the cake. We have late dinner reservations at Jameson's."

I grin at him. "So you and Lucy are a thing?"

"We've seen each other nearly every night. I haven't had a romantic interest in decades, and I'm not sure how to act. I enjoy her company. She's smart and easy to talk to. I hope she feels the same."

"I'm sure she does, handsome and intelligent attorney that you are."

Brian places his hands on the table, fingers entwined. "We have a situation. I'm not overly concerned about it, but you need to be aware of it. Naomi is suing Billy's estate."

"Of course she is. She cares nothing about her daughter. She wants the inn. And she won't stop until she gets it. I assume she's hired an attorney."

"Not only did she hire an attorney, she's dating him."

"So that's who he is," I say. "I've seen them together around the inn. She's using him."

Brian gives my hand a squeeze. "There's no need for you to worry, Stella. Your father and I expected something like this might happen. Frankly, I'm surprised it's taken Naomi this long to sue. We made certain Billy's will is ironclad. There's no way Naomi can take the inn away from you."

I slump back in my chair. "I trust you, Brian. I just wish Naomi would go away for good."

When five inches of snow fall during the night, Jazz becomes frantic with worry they'll cancel *The Nutcracker*. She stands by the window, staring out at the white landscape with a gloomy expression, as though willing the snow to disappear. She asks me a dozen times if I've heard from Tasha, and we're both relieved when I receive an email from her midmorning.

"Tasha writes that the roads are clear, and the performance is on!"

Jazz's mood does an about-face, and for the next two hours, she dances around our small living room, practicing her techniques.

Around noon, she says, "Can we go to Jameson's for lunch, Stella? Please!"

I can't risk running into Naomi. The last thing we need is for

Naomi to upset Jazz before her big night. "I have a better idea. Why don't we eat a bowl of chili and then go sledding?"

"But I can't go sledding, Stella. Duh. What if I crash and hurt myself?"

I laugh. "How old are you? Only adults are supposed to worry about such things."

"We need to do something today," Jazz says. "It's Saturday, the first day of my Christmas break. Where's Jack? He always comes up with fun ideas."

I can't tell Jazz that Jack is at the manor house overseeing the painters who are working overtime to finish her Christmas surprise. "Jack has to work today. But hold on. I have an idea." I text Presley. *Is sleigh riding on for today?*

She responds immediately. *Yes! My guys are bringing the horses over around one. Meet us at the maintenance shed if you want the first ride. But dress warmly. It's freezing outside.*

I look up from my phone at Jazz. "Guess what, kiddo? We're going for a sleigh ride!"

"Yippee!" Jazz leaps onto the sofa and begins jumping up and down.

"Careful. You might fall. Let's go fix lunch." I throw her over my shoulders like a sack of potatoes and carry her into the kitchen.

I reheat a container of Cecily's chili and toss a small green salad. But Jazz is too excited to eat and only picks at her food.

"We can't go on a sleigh ride until you finish your lunch, Jazzy. Remember what Tasha said about eating healthy. You need energy for tonight."

"Oh, right," Jazz says and shovels the food into her mouth until every morsel is gone.

Forty-five minutes later, bundled in boots, hats, gloves, coats, and scarves, we venture down to the maintenance shed. We arrive in time to watch the farmers Presley hired, Pete and Ernie, hook up their giant palomino horses—Sunny and Shadow—to the farm's antique red sleigh.

"Where's Katherine?" I ask Presley. "I can't believe she's missing this."

Presley's eyebrows draw together. "She's still not feeling well. I'm worried about her, actually. She's been sick for a week."

"That's unlike Katherine," I say. "I bet she's pregnant."

Presley palms her forehead. "Why didn't I think of that? I wonder if she's taken a pregnancy test. Should we say anything to her?"

I shake my head. "She'll tell us when she's ready."

"I guess you're right."

Presley produces heavy wool blankets, and the three of us climb into the sleigh. Ernie and Pete guide the team down the hill past the new spa building, around the lake to the row of cottages under construction, and back up to the barn where a small crowd of guests sip hot chocolate while they wait their turn for a sleigh ride.

When they climb down from the sleigh, Jazz hugs Presley's waist. "Are you coming to my recital?"

"Yes, ma'am. And I'm bringing a surprise guest with me."

Jazz bounces on her toes. "Who?"

"Everett."

Jazz's grin spreads from ear to ear. "Yay. I can't wait to see him."

When Presley begins organizing the next group of sleigh riders, Jazz and I fill small Styrofoam cups with hot chocolate and trudge through the snow toward the cottage.

When we reach the terrace steps, Jazz says, "Can I go see the angel, Stella? Please!"

I reluctantly give in. "Fine. But only for a minute."

Inside the main building, I scan the faces of the guests for Naomi while Jazz stares up at the angel, the lights from the tree reflected in her golden eyes. After five minutes, I take her by the hand. "Okay, kiddo. Time to go." I lead Jazz back through reception to the rear entrance. "I picked up two new library books the other day. One is the story of Christmas, about Mary and Joseph, baby Jesus's birth, and the angel Gabriel. And the other is a book about Christmas angels."

"Oh goody. Let's hurry," she says and drags me back to the cottage.

Snuggled together beneath the warm blankets, Jazz insists I read the two new library books over and over until she finally dozes off. When she wakes around five thirty, we begin getting her ready for the recital. After a quick bath, I help her into her costume—a white flowing dress with lace at the hem and ruffled sleeves, a pale blue velvet sash, and white tights. I braid her hair with a thinner version of the same blue velvet ribbon and wind it into a high bun.

We're among the first to arrive at the high school auditorium where the recital is being held. When Jazz disappears down a long hallway with Tasha, I stake my claim to a row of seats near the front of the stage. As the auditorium begins filling up, Presley and Everett arrive, followed by Cecily, Opal, Brian, and Lucy.

At five minutes before showtime, the house is packed and only the aisle seat next to me, the one I'm saving for Jack, remains vacant. The lights are dimming when Naomi slides onto the seat, looking lovely as ever in a fake leopard-skin coat over a red silk dress.

"Sorry, Naomi. I'm saving that seat for Jack."

"I have no intention of staying. You know how opposed I am to this ballet nonsense. I'm here to make certain you received notification of the lawsuit."

I snort. "You won't win."

"Maybe. Maybe not. Are you willing to take that chance? I'm

here to offer you a deal. You give me half ownership in the inn, and I'll give you Jazz."

Even though I anticipated this move, I'm shocked at her audacity. For a nanosecond, I consider giving her what she wants. If for no other reason than to restore peace to my life. I could never stand being partners with Naomi, any more than Naomi could stand watching me be a mother to Jazz. Whether Naomi loves Jazz, she loved Billy. And Jazz is Billy's daughter. Once she's gotten her half of the inn, she'll marry her lawyer, become the ideal wife, and sue for custody of Jazz.

"Your missing some cards, Naomi."

Her red lips turn down. "What's that supposed to mean?"

I tap my head. "You're not playing with a full deck."

"Are you suggesting I have a mental problem?"

"Shoe fits," I say with a nonchalant shrug. "You need to leave now. Jack will be here momentarily."

"I'm going. But think about my offer. It would solve both of our problems." Naomi abandons the chair and disappears toward the back of the auditorium.

The curtain goes up and Tasha appears, welcoming the audience to the recital. As Jazz dances onto stage for the first act, Jack arrives with a bouquet of red roses.

The performance is a modified version of *The Nutcracker*, with younger dancers performing various aspects of the acts involving Clara while older ballerinas dance the Sugar Plum Fairy act. The recital is well choreographed, and all the dancers perform beautifully, most especially Jazz. And the audience rewards her with a standing ovation.

Afterward, we wait for Jazz in the lobby. "Sorry I was late getting here," Jack says. "The painters didn't leave until six thirty. They accomplished a lot today, though."

"Does that mean they will finish on time?"

Jack's expression is grim. "I'm not sure, sweetheart. We'll be

ASHLEY FARLEY

cutting it close. And we have an issue with one of the counter-tops. I've pushed the movers back until Christmas Eve. That's the best I can do."

I cup his cheek. "I'm sorry, Jack. You're working so hard. Tell me how I can help."

"You can hold your decorator off from installing Jazz's bedroom as long as possible. The house doesn't have to be perfect. I've instructed the painters to focus on finishing the bedrooms first. At least we'll be able to sleep there. We can live without a kitchen for a few days or a week if we have to."

"I'll sleep on the floor as long as the security system is working."

He cuts his eyes at me. "Is Naomi causing trouble again?"

"Unfortunately," I say, and update him about the lawsuit and Naomi's visit to the auditorium.

"Hang in there." Drawing me in for a half hug, he kisses my forehead. "We'll get through this somehow."

By the time Jazz emerges from the long hallway and we drive back to the inn, the reception is in full swing. Servers hand out flutes of champagne to adults and festive cupcakes to the kids. Jazz enjoys her moment of fame as her little ballerina friends gather around her to heap their praise.

I'm busy chatting with a group of parents and fail to notice when Naomi enters the solarium. Her words, loud and slurred, silence the room. "There's my baby girl. Come here and let me get a good look at you in your costume."

I excuse myself to the parents and cross the room to Naomi. Jack is at my side in an instant. "This is her big night," I say to Naomi in a low hissing voice. "Don't you dare cause a scene."

"Are you threatening me?" Naomi gets in my face, close enough for me to smell bourbon. "You're gonna get what's coming to you, Stella. You won't get away with stealing my daughter and my inheritance."

Jack appears at my side. Taking hold of Naomi's arm, he says, "Come on. Let's call you an Uber."

She jerks away from him and stumbles out of the room. Jack and I move to the doorway, watching Naomi's retreating back. When she reaches reception, she takes a left toward the main entrance.

"Should we have Martin go after her?" Jack asks.

I shake my head. "I'm tired of trying to save Naomi from herself."

We return to Jazz, who is hiding her tear-streaked face behind Presley. I kneel next to her. "I'm here, Jazzy. We won't let her spoil your big night."

Jazz throws her arms around my neck and plants her face in my chest. "I don't want my friends to see me cry."

"Okay then. Let's think of something pleasant to make the tears go away."

Presley tugs on Jazz's ruffled sleeve. "Guess what, Jazz? Everett's singing in Billy's Bar tonight. He wants you to come hear him." Presley's eyes meet mine. "If Stella will let you."

"Of course." I gently dig my chin into Jazz's head. "What say, Jazz? Wanna walk down to Billy's Bar?"

"Yes," Jazz says in a tiny voice. She sucks in a breath, wipes her face on my silk blouse, and pulls away.

As Jazz and I exit the solarium with Presley and Jack, I feel sympathetic eyes on us from kids and adults. Crossing through the reception hall, I sneak a peek at the front entrance. Much to my relief, Naomi is nowhere in sight. Later, when I get a free minute, I'll report the incident to Detective Sinclair. But for now, my primary concern is Jazz.

Inside Billy's Bar, we trail Jazz as she makes her way to the front of the crowd. When Everett sees her, he blows her a kiss, and she beams.

I normally wouldn't approve of a child's presence in an adult lounge, but tonight I make an exception. Jack secures a table off to the side, away from the partiers, and when the waiter arrives, we order a Shirley Temple for Jazz but no cocktails for the adults.

Everett's voice has an old-fashioned quality, but his melodies and lyrics are contemporary, like George Strait meets Kenny Chesney. The crowd loves him and begs for more after every song. For the first time all week, I'm able to relax. I lose track of time. I have no idea how long we listen, at least forty-five minutes. And I'm shocked to look up and see Detective Sinclair looming over our table.

Cupping her hands around her mouth, she leans in close to my ear. "I need to talk to you outside." Without waiting for my response, she turns and pushes her way back through the crowd to the lounge. With a sense of dread, I follow her. When I reach her, she directs me over to the windows.

"I wanted to deliver the news to you in person. Naomi was involved in a single car accident out on Old Mountain Road. We think she was headed to her boyfriend's cabin. Her car spun out on a patch of black ice, overturned, and crashed into a tree. She died on impact. The toxicology report will confirm it, but the odor of alcohol in the car was strong."

Guilt clenches my chest and steals my breath. A wave of dizziness crashes over me, and I lean against the window until it passes. "She was here earlier, threatening me and embarrassing Jazz. I knew she'd been drinking, but I did nothing about it."

"Don't go there, Stella. Naomi *was* living on the edge. Something bad was bound to happen to her eventually. We're fortunate she didn't kill someone. Another driver in another car or—"

"Jazz," I say. Tears spring to my eyes. What if Jazz had been in that car with her? Sinclair is right. Naomi was living on the edge. She was headed for disaster. My father knew what he was doing when he left me the inn. He sensed something like this might happen.

"Do you think you can identify the body?" Sinclair asks.

"I guess." I've never seen a dead body before. "Can you give me a few minutes? I need to get my purse and tell Jack where I'm going."

Leaving Sinclair by the windows, I head off toward my office. Out of habit, my eyes dart about, scanning the room for Naomi. I no longer have to worry about her. Jazz and I can rest easily. Naomi's out of our lives for good.

I remember my words to Brian from yesterday. *I just wish Naomi would go away for good.* Guilt of a different variety consumes me. I wished her away. And now she's dead.

16

PRESLEY

Naomi's death affects everyone at the inn. For Presley, the sudden turn of events is a reminder of the fragility of life. Her heart goes out to Jazz. Losing a parent is never easy at any age, even if that mother made the kid's life a living hell. Presley was Jazz's age when her father died of cancer. Presley had understood that something bad was happening to him, and when the time came, she said goodbye to him, which offered a modicum of closure to her six-year-old self. Her mother drank her way to a slow death, which gave Presley years to prepare. But Presley has never lost a friend or loved one to an overdose or car accident or suicide. She struggles to wrap her mind around what it's like to be living and breathing one minute and dead the next, zapped from the earthly world in the blink of an eye. Every minute of every day is precious, not to be taken for granted but to be lived to the fullest. Why, then, is she living in the mountains of Virginia, apart from the man she loves?

At quarter till eleven on Monday morning, Presley finds herself sandwiched between Everett and Lucy in the second row at Jefferson College's small chapel, awaiting the beginning of

Naomi's memorial service. "Where's Brian?" Presley asks Lucy. "Is he coming?"

"He got held up in court, but he's on his way."

Presley gives Lucy the once-over. She looks professionally somber in a navy pantsuit with a cream silk blouse. "I like your suit. Is it new?"

"Yes." Lucy smooths out a wrinkle on her pants. "Believe it or not, I finally went shopping. And you were right. Fiona's Fashions has clothes that are appropriately cute for women my age."

Presley suspects Lucy's rosy glow has something to do with the new man in her life. "I gather things are going well between you and Brian."

Lucy nods, her cheeks turning pink. "I forgot what it feels like to be in love."

Presley's brow shoots up. Love? Wow. It's only been nine days since their first date. "I'm happy for you, Lucy. Brian is a good man."

"That he is." Lucy lowers her voice. "Poor Jazz. She's so young. Hopefully, she won't remember how evil her mother was."

Presley cuts her eyes at Lucy. "Stella will make certain Jazz remembers only her mother's positive traits. And I'm sure there was plenty of good in Naomi. Remember the saying, Lucy. We shouldn't speak ill of the dead."

Lucy lets out a huff of irritation. "Is it always going to be this awkward between us? I was hoping we could forget about that ... *other matter*."

Presley tenses. "I can't just forget about that other matter, Lucy. Ever since I told you I'm your biological daughter, you've been jerking me around. You're nice to me one minute and practically hateful the next."

A wounded expression crosses Lucy's face.

Truth hurts.

Rita slides into the pew on the other side of Lucy. "Do you mind if I sit here?"

"Yes," Lucy snaps. "As a matter of fact, I do. I'm saving it for Brian."

Presley moves over, practically landing on Everett's lap to make room for Rita. "Come sit next to me, Rita."

"Thank you, Presley." As she's climbing over her sister, Rita steps on Lucy's foot.

"Ouch!" Lucy gives her sister a shove. "Watch out."

Rita winks at Presley as she takes her seat. "Oops. So sorry." She slips off her coat. "My heart goes out to Stella, Jazz, and Jack. Are you going through with the surprise wedding?"

"I'm not sure. Jack and I discussed it on the phone last night. He'll see how today goes and let me know this afternoon."

The low murmuring in the chapel ceases when Stella, Jazz, and Jack process down the aisle to the front pew. Reverend Malone emerges from a side door, taking her place at the pulpit. She reads several passages from the Bible before delivering a very brief and impersonal eulogy.

In her mid-thirties, Malone is attractive with shoulder-length brown hair. In four short days, if all goes as Presley has planned, Malone will administer the nuptials at Stella and Jack's surprise wedding. Thanks to Naomi, Stella's had enough heartache to last a lifetime. She deserves some happiness.

When the service ends, Lucy exits the pew without saying goodbye. Seemingly unfazed by her sister's rudeness, Rita asks, "Can I bum a ride back to the inn? Abigail borrowed my car today to go Christmas shopping. I rode over with Opal, but she's headed home afterward."

"Sure, as long as you're not in a hurry. Everett and I want to express our condolences."

"Not at all. I'd like to do the same." Rita's smile is warm, her hazel eyes kind, a stark contrast to her bitter sister.

As they approach the front of the church, Presley notices Jazz standing at the altar, staring up at a stained-glass window. When it's her turn to speak to Stella, she says, "Jazz is mesmerized by the stained-glass window."

Stella smiles over at her half sister. "Her recent obsession with angels is timely. It makes it easier to talk about her mommy going to live with the angels in heaven."

"She's such a sweet little girl." Presley shifts her gaze from Jazz back to Stella. "I know you have a lot on your plate right now. We have room for Jazz in the kids' camp this week if you need some time to yourself."

"Hm. Let me think about it. I could definitely use the time to help Jack get the manor house ready for Christmas. Can I text you later?"

"No need. I'll save her a space. Wait and see how she feels in the morning."

"Thank you," Stella says. "The diversion might do her some good."

Presley turns to Jack. "How're you holding up?"

"We're managing," he says and kisses her cheek.

Rita, Everett, and Presley exit the church together. Sensing Presley wants to talk to Rita about Lucy, Everett climbs into the back seat and stuffs earbuds in his ears, giving them privacy.

"I've tried, Rita, but I'm getting nowhere with your sister. She's hot and cold with me. But she's downright rude to you."

Rita presses her lips into a thin line. "I've found it's easiest just to ignore her. Lucy's life didn't turn out like she'd hoped, so she takes it out on the world."

"Did something happen between the two of you in the past that would better help me understand your relationship?"

Rita looks away, her breath fogging up the window as she stares out at the passing buildings on Main Street. When she speaks again, her voice is less angry. "We were close until a few years ago. She was once so vibrant and full of life. The cancer and divorce changed her. She was in such a dark place, and when she became desperate to find the child she gave up for adoption, I tried to help by reaching out to your adoptive parents. But Lucy is furious at me for it. I'm just sorry I dragged you into her problems."

Presley glances over at Rita. "You didn't drag me into anything. I came to Hope Springs on my own free will. I'm sorry it's not working out for Lucy and me, but I'm grateful to have found a friend in you."

Rita places her hand on Presley's arm. "I'm more than your friend, Presley. I'm your family. I imagine Christmas will be hard on you without your mother. And hectic with all these weddings. But Abigail, Emma, and I would very much like for you and Everett to join us for Christmas dinner on Christmas Day. I'm hosting this year. We usually eat around one o'clock. My parents will be there. They would very much like to meet you."

Warmth spreads throughout Presley's body. "You told them about me?"

"Of course. They know all about you. And, for what it's worth, Lucy is a fool. Any woman would be proud to have you for a daughter."

Presley makes a left-hand turn and drives up to the inn. "Thank you for saying that. I've been wondering what it is about me that turns Lucy off."

Rita shakes her head. "It's not you. It's Lucy."

Presley wishes she could believe her. If only she better understood what makes Lucy tick.

They separate in the parking lot. Everett goes to Billy's Bar to refresh his mixology skills, Rita returns to reception, and Presley walks on air to the barn. Rita has given her the best Christmas present ever. She knew none of her adoptive grandparents. All four of them died before she was born. And now she will get to meet her biological grandparents, her own flesh and blood.

Inside the barn, Emma is busy arranging art supplies on banquet tables covered in plastic tablecloths. With long blonde hair and blue eyes, she's beautiful enough to be a model, but she possesses the same kind-hearted, never-take-no-for-an-answer spirit as her mother.

When Emma sees Presley standing in the doorway, she says, "What's up cuz?"

Presley's jaw drops. "You mean, you know?"

Emma flashes her a mischievous grin. "Mom told me weeks ago."

"Why didn't you mention it during any of our many phone conversations?"

"Because I wanted to welcome you to the family in person." Emma comes over and gives her a quick hug. When she pulls away, she offers Presley a high five. "I'm so excited to have another cousin, especially a badass like you. Chris is cool, but we have nothing in common."

"I'm flattered," Presley says. "Thank you. And congratulations! I heard about your early acceptance to Cornell. You realize you can save your mom a lot of money on tuition if you skipped college and came straight to work for us after graduation."

"Ha ha. You're so funny." Emma play-punches her arm. "No way am I missing my chance to be a college student."

"That's the spirit. Enjoy every minute of it, because it goes by fast." Presley turns her attention to the art supplies—glue and construction paper, crayons and markers, and plastic vials of red, green, gold, and silver glitter. "You've been busy in here. This will easily keep the kids occupied for hours. Are you sure you don't want to be a schoolteacher?"

"No thanks. I'm sticking to event planning for now."

"Let's go over the schedule for the week." Presley removes

her iPad from her bag, and they sit down opposite each other at the table. "Tomorrow will be the warmest day. After that, it's supposed to be cold through New Year's with several chances of more snow. We'll do a nature hike in the morning, a scavenger hunt around the farm in the afternoon, and arts and crafts in between. Our gingerbread house contest is the main event for Wednesday morning. I'm waiting for a puppeteer to confirm for Wednesday afternoon."

Emma's baby blues grow wide. "A puppet show? Cool!"

Presley holds up her hand to show fingers crossed. She studies Emma closely. Presley doesn't know her young cousin well. But Emma doesn't seem like her normal bubbly self. "You seem sad. Are you okay?"

Emma's lanky frame slumps in the chair. "Chad and I broke up. It kinda sucks. But I'm dealing with it." She picks at the corner of a piece of red construction paper. "He got rejected from Cornell. He's going to Alabama. He's already found a new girlfriend. And guess where she's going to college."

"Alabama. What a jerk! I'm so sorry, sweetheart." Presley reaches across the table for her hand. "If he's that fickle, you're better off without him."

"I agree with you, but it doesn't make it hurt any less."

Presley squeezes her hand. "I'm sorry to say that only time will make it hurt less."

Emma straightens in her chair. "Don't worry about me, though. I promise not to let this interfere with my internship."

"I have faith in you, Emma. And we have our work cut out for us this week. Besides entertaining a packed house of guests for the holidays, I'm hosting my first weddings." Presley holds up two fingers. "Two weddings. Not one." She leans across the table conspiratorially. "Can you keep a secret?"

"Yes! I'm the best secret keeper ever."

Presley tells her about the plans for Stella's surprise wedding.

"Aww. That's so sweet. But will they still have the wedding? You know, with Naomi's accident and all."

"I hope so. Jack will let me know this afternoon." She pushes back from the table. "We need to go down to the maintenance shed to talk to Katherine about flowers."

Grabbing her coat, Emma says, "Do I get to help with the flowers?"

Presley holds the door open for her. "Katherine hasn't been feeling well lately. You and I may be in *charge* of the flowers."

17

STELLA

Reverend Malone's brown eyes grow wide behind tortoiseshell frames at the amount of my donation check. "Wow! Stella! Thank you. The college and chapel appreciate your generosity."

I wave away her praise. "It's the least I can do. This chapel and your friendship mean a lot to me in recent months."

Sliding the check in the pocket of her black robe, the minister removes the gray marble cremation urn from the altar and places it in my hands. The urn is heavy, more the marble than the ashes. Or so I imagine. Am I supposed to place it on the manor house fireplace mantel as a reminder of the pain and heartache Naomi caused us?

Melissa walks Jack, Jazz, and me to the front doors of the chapel. "This year will be different for all of you. But try to enjoy your holidays as best you can."

"Thank you." I kiss her cheek, and Jack wishes her a Merry Christmas.

Outside, on the steps of the chapel, Jazz casts a skeptical glance at the urn. "What's that, Stella?"

"It's called an urn. Go ahead. You can touch it."

She places her tiny palms on the marble. "It's so smooth and cold. Is something in there?"

I pause, thinking best how to explain cremation to a six-year-old. "Remember how we talked about your mommy being an angel now?"

"Yeah," Jazz says, her hands still on the urn.

"In this urn is the dust she left behind when she flew away to heaven. We refer to that dust as her remains. We have to decide what we want to do with those remains. Some people keep urns to help them remember their loved ones, and others scatter the remains in a special place, like over the mountains."

Jazz stands tall, chin high. "Let's do that. At our special place —the overlook. Can we go today?"

I lock eyes with Jack, who gives me a nod of approval. "I don't see why not."

"Can we eat lunch first?" Jazz asks. "I'm hungry."

I laugh. "I'm hungry too. Where would you like to eat?"

Without hesitation, Jazz says, "Lucky's!"

"I have a better idea," Jack says. "It's not so cold out today. Let's have a picnic at the overlook." Grabbing Jazz's hand, Jack swings her arm, lifting her slightly off the ground, as he walks toward the car.

My heart bursts with love for my fiancé. I'm not used to seeing him dressed up, and he looks handsome in his pressed khakis, blue sport coat, and striped tie. But as soon as he gets to the car, he tugs off his tie and changes from his sport coat to his Barbour.

When I call Cecily about a picnic, she is eager to assist. And when we stop by the inn fifteen minutes later, a large wicker picnic hamper is waiting for us at the valet stand under the portico.

On the way up the mountain, Jazz says, "When my friend

Sally's cat died, she cried for a week. I'm sad about Mommy too, but why don't I feel like crying?"

I shift in my seat so I can see her. "People handle grief in different ways. You may cry tomorrow or the next day. Or you may not cry for a month." I hold my hands out, as if to say who knows when it will happen. "One day, you may find tears on your cheeks and not even realize you're crying. There's no right or wrong way to express your sorrow when someone you love dies. But whenever it happens, it's okay to show those emotions."

"Do I get to live with you forever now, Stella?"

"At least until you go off to college." Grabbing her foot, I give her leg a shake. "Jack and I will always be here for you! Even after you graduate from college and get married and have children."

"Gosh. You'll be really, really old by then."

"Right!" I say with a laugh. "After Christmas, in January or February, Jack and I are going to get married, and the three of us will finally be a family. How do you feel about that?"

Her grin spreads from ear to ear. "That makes me sooooo happy." She drops her smile. "Is it okay to be happy?"

I stroke her leg through gray cable-knit tights. "Yes, Jack and I are happy too. I understand why that happiness confuses you when you're also sad about your mom. Sometimes feelings are like that. Promise me, you'll come to me or Jack if you're ever confused by your feelings."

"I promise." When Jack pulls into the overlook, she squeals, "We're here."

Jack grabs the picnic basket while I unbuckle Jazz from her car seat. She runs ahead of us to the wooden picnic table where we've eaten many meals together. "The table is wet," she calls back to us.

"I can fix that." Jack removes a roll of heavy plastic from the silver toolbox in the bed of his truck. With his pocketknife, he shears off three lengths for the benches and table. When we sit down at the table, Jazz throws open the lid of the picnic basket and inspects the contents.

"Soup," she says, placing a thermos on the table. One at a time, she removes plastic containers of assorted sandwiches, deviled eggs, potato salad, and fresh fruit.

I pick at an egg salad sandwich, but I have little of an appetite. I lift my face to the cloudless sky, letting the sun warm my skin. I feel alive and free again, after months of living with the constant threat of Naomi.

I leave the table and walk to the edge of the overlook. Below me is Hope Springs Farm, all seventy acres of sprawling lawn and woodlands, buildings and the lake. Opal brought me to the overlook for the first time on my second day in Hope Springs back in May, which now seems like decades ago.

"There's your farm down there," she'd said, and I still remember the impact of her words. My farm.

That was before I knew Opal was my grandmother and Jazz my half sister. Billy left me, the daughter he'd never met, the bulk of his estate while providing for Jazz with a small trust fund. He took a gamble on me. Not only was I his best hope for protecting his primary assets from Naomi, he also trusted me to restore the inn to its former glory. The inn is on its way, and I will continue to develop the rest of the farm until it reaches its full potential. If Jazz wants to pursue a career in ballet, I will support her in every way. But her half of the farm will be waiting for her when she returns.

Jack, with Jazz in tow and marble urn in his hands, joins me at the edge of the overlook. He removes the lid and holds the urn out for Jazz and me to take handfuls.

Jazz tosses hers in the air. "Fly away, Mommy dust." She rubs the ash residue off her hand onto her dress, and when

Jack offers her the urn again, she waves it away. "You do the rest."

Jack dumps out several handfuls of ash, and then tips the urn over, letting Naomi's remains billow outward. When the urn is empty, he sets it down on the ground.

Jazz tugs on my jacket sleeve. "Stella, is Mommy nice now that she's an angel?"

"I believe so. An angel's job is to spread God's love."

Seemingly satisfied, Jazz skips over to a large flat boulder and begins practicing her ballet moves.

"Be careful, Jazzy," I call.

Jack smiles as he watches her. "She's fine. If she falls, she'll land on the grass." He gives me a half hug and kisses my cheek. "You're amazing. You always know exactly what to say to her."

"I'm glad you think so. She asks some tough questions, sometimes."

He snorts. "Wait until she gets older. But you can handle it. You're gonna make a helluva mother to Jazz and our brood of other children. Did you mean what you said to Jazz about getting married in January or February?"

"The sooner the better, now that we no longer have the custody suit to worry about." I nestle into him, his body strong against mine. "I'm ready to be your wife, Jack. I'm just sorry it's taken so long."

"No worries." He gives me a squeeze. "You've had your share of distractions lately. You planned a lovely memorial for Naomi today. I know that wasn't easy given the circumstances."

"Selfishly, I wanted to get it over with as quickly as possible." I let out a deep sigh of relief. "I wasn't sure about spreading Naomi's ashes here. But it feels oddly appropriate. In her twisted way, Naomi loved this farm, as much as she could love anything or anyone."

Jack eyes the urn. "What do we do with that?"

"No clue. I'd rather not have it in my house. Do you think Jazz will ever want it for any reason?"

"I doubt it. Hopefully, she'll always remember today, the memorial service and picnic and spreading the ashes."

"Maybe we should ask her to be sure?" I call Jazz over, and she leaps across the muddy ground to us. "Do you have any thoughts on what we should do with the urn?"

Jazz taps her chin like I sometimes do. She appreciates being asked grown-up questions, and she always waits an ample amount of time before responding. "Why don't we leave it on the rock?" Jazz picks up the urn and carries it over to her rock. "Maybe it'll be here next time we come like a . . . um . . ."

"A memorial," I say. "I think that's a wonderful idea!"

We clean up our picnic, storing the empty containers in the basket, and pile into Jack's truck.

Jazz falls asleep within minutes, and I rest my head against the window.

"What're you thinking about over there?" Jack asks in a concerned tone.

"About how I'm supposed to act." I keep my voice low in case Jazz wakes up. "Should I pretend to be sad that a woman I despised is dead? I feel like people are watching me, waiting to see how I'll respond. I'm afraid to smile, for fear they'll think I'm celebrating a victory. My arch enemy is dead, and I got custody of my sister. I'm not gonna lie. I'm relieved Naomi's no longer a threat. That I no longer have to look over my shoulder. That I no longer have to think about shooting her with my gun."

"What?" Jack's head jerks toward me. "Since when do you own a gun?"

"I bought one last week. Detective Sinclair hooked me up with a woman at the shooting range who helped me pick out a handgun and taught me how to shoot it."

"Geez, Stella. I knew you were worried, but, except for the

night Naomi broke into the college, I never thought you were afraid. Why didn't you tell me?"

I sigh. "Because I didn't want to burden you. You've been so busy trying to finish the house in time for Christmas. And speaking of Christmas, do we cancel all our festivities and go into deep mourning? That seems hypocritical, and what point will it serve? Presley offered for Jazz to take part in the kids' Christmas camp this week. I could use the time to help you get the house set up and to make certain the inn is running smoothly, and my guests are properly taken care of. But is that wrong of me? To continue working as though nothing has happened?"

"Not at all. And we're not canceling anything." Jack reaches for my hand, bringing my fingers to his lips. "You and Jazz have suffered enough. I say we give her the best Christmas ever, to show her we are all in, that we are her family now and forever, no matter what lies ahead."

I think back a few weeks to the conversation I had with Jazz at the illumination party.

If there is a Santa, how will he find me?

He'll find you, sweetheart. That's part of the magic.

"You're right. Not only do we need to show her the magic, we need to make certain she believes."

18

PRESLEY

K atherine's white pickup is parked outside the maintenance shed, but she's neither in her office nor out back in her greenhouse.

"She's somewhere on the farm," Presley says. "We need to find her, to confirm that she's placed our flower order for the weddings."

As they wander the grounds down by the lake looking for Katherine, Presley quizzes Emma about her grandparents.

"Granddaddy is a trip," Emma says. "He tells off-colored jokes whenever my mother isn't listening. And Nana is the biggest socialite you've ever met. She's always hosting a party or playing bridge or tennis. I admit she looks hot in her tennis skirt for an old lady."

Presley nudges Emma with her elbow. "Sounds to me like a certain someone is just like her grandmother."

Emma tilts her head to the side. "I haven't thought about it, but you're right. I am a lot like Nana. But so are you. Which means you and I are a lot alike. Isn't it weird we're both event planners?" She doesn't give Presley a chance to respond. "I may have my grandmother's personality, but as far as looks, you're her twin. Considerably younger, of course. Wait until you meet her, Presley. You won't believe the similarities."

Presley has an empty feeling in the pit of her stomach. She's dreamed for so long of meeting a blood relative with whom she shares the same physical features. But what if her grandparents don't approve of her? What if they are disappointed like Lucy? "Will Lucy come for Christmas dinner?"

Emma rolls her eyes. "Who knows? Depends on her mood that day. Aunt Lucy is no fun anymore. When I was growing up, we came to Hope Springs for Christmas every year. Most of the time, we stayed with Aunt Lucy and Uncle Grant. They were always organizing holiday-related activities, baking cookies and going on tacky light tours."

Presley has a hard time imagining this Lucy of old.

With no sign of Katherine, Presley and Emma cut back across the lawn to the sidewalk, heading up the hill to the main building. "Are you close with your dad?"

"Not anymore," Emma says in a sad voice. "Abigail's closer to him than I am. She's going to Charlotte to visit him after Christmas. I know I'm not supposed to carry grudges, but I can't get over him cheating on my mom."

"I can see where that would be difficult. Did your father marry the woman he cheated with?"

Emma shakes her head. "He never loved her. Not like he loved my mom. He made a gigantic mess of his life. But he's doing better now. He's managing a five-star restaurant."

"I'm glad to hear it," Presley says. "Your mom seems happy in her new job."

Emma grips Presley's forearm. "Oh, my gosh! She *loves* it. Thanks for helping her get the job."

Presley smiles. "All I did was make the recommendation. Your mom did the rest. She has the perfect personality to be our guest services manager."

When they reach the stone terrace, Presley guides Emma across the veranda and through the french doors to the dining room. The lunch crowd has gone, and the waitstaff is setting up for dinner.

"When do I get to meet Everett?" Emma asks. "Mom says he's a dish, which means he's hot."

Presley laughs out loud. "Dish! I'll have to remember that one. You can meet Everett now, if you'd like."

"I'd like," Emma says, nodding her head vigorously.

Exiting the dining room, they enter Billy's Bar where Everett is pouring small amounts from liquor bottles into a cocktail shaker. As they approach the bar, he looks up from his work and smiles his kilowatt smile. "You must be Emma."

Emma responds with her most radiant smile. "What're you making?"

"I'm mixing signature drinks for the weddings. Cecily requested a cranberry martini. I added a secret ingredient to the traditional recipe. I'm calling it Mistletoe Martini." He holds up a cut crystal tumbler of pink liquid with cranberries floating on top.

"Ooh . . ." Emma says, eyeing the drink longingly. "Can I have a taste?"

Everett holds out his hand. "I'll need to see your ID."

She slaps his palm. "Seriously? I'm going to college next fall. Just a sip."

He pours a tiny amount in a glass and hands it to her. "Don't tell anyone. Stella could lose her liquor license for this."

Emma downs the drink in one gulp. "That's delicious," she says, licking her lips. "You're good at this." She peers over the bar. "Can I have a taste of what you're mixing up for Stella?"

Everett laughs. "A party girl in the making."

Emma sticks her tongue out at him. "For your information,

my mom says it's good to have a tolerance for alcohol when I go off to school."

Everett points a finger at her. "Before I go back to Nashville, you and I are going to have a talk about boys who take advantage of girls who drink too much."

Presley and Everett lock eyes and understanding passes between them. He was once that boy and she that girl.

Everett pours white liquid in her same glass. "I mixed my version of a White Russian for Stella. I'm calling it Snowball Fight."

This time Emma sips the drink. Her blue eyes pop. "That's seriously the best drink ever." She downs the rest. "I taste ginger, nutmeg, and cinnamon." She holds out her empty glass. "More! Please!"

"No way." Presley takes the glass from her and hands it back to Everett.

Emma sticks out her lower lip. "You're a buzzkill, Presley." Her pout is intended to elicit sympathy from Everett. Her cousin is a total tease.

"For the next two weeks, I'm your boss. And we're on a mission to find Katherine." Presley shifts her gaze to Everett. "Have you seen her?"

"Yes. A few minutes ago, headed toward the front with a bucket of branches."

Emma turns up her nose. "A bucket of branches?"

"He means greens, as in magnolia, pine, and holly." Presley takes Emma by the hand and drags her out of the bar.

When they encounter Jack in the lounge outside of Billy's Bar, Presley introduces him to her cousin. "How is Stella?" Presley asks.

"Confused. Exhausted. Relieved. But she admitted to me she's ready to get married, so the wedding is on!"

"Yes!" Presley offers him a high five. "You take care of Stella, and Emma and I will handle everything else."

Emma and Presley continue on through the lounge. They are nearing reception when Lucy steps off the elevator. Lucy flags Presley down. "Can I have a word with you?" Her gaze shifts to her niece. "Alone."

Emma glares at her. "Right. I'll go say hi to Mom."

Lucy leads Presley off to the side of the lounge. "I only have a minute, Lucy. I need to catch up with Katherine."

"I was thinking about what you said earlier in the chapel. And you're right. I have been sending you mixed signals. I was wondering . . . well, I'd like to start over with a clean slate. Are you free for dinner on Wednesday night?"

Presley mentally runs down her list of events for Wednesday. She has nothing that evening. While she's hesitant to set herself up for more heartache, Lucy is her biological mother, and she should give her one more chance. "I can make that work."

"Great. I have a wine tasting until six. Shall we say seven o'clock? And bring Everett," Lucy says in a manner that suggests she'd rather Everett not come.

"Thanks, but he has to work on Wednesday. I really must run, Lucy. I'll see you then if not before."

As she passes through reception, Presley motions for Emma to follow her outside when she's finished talking to Rita. Katherine is at the front entrance, assembling massive arrangements of Christmas greens and red velvet ribbon in matching stone urns.

"You look like you feel better," Presley says, despite Katherine's pale face and dark circles under her eyes.

"I'm trying." Katherine wipes her brow with the back of her gloved hand. "You might as well know. I'm pregnant. And I'm thrilled about it. But the morning sickness is bad. Some days are worse than others. I'm taking supplements and trying to eat the right foods. I'll help you as much as I can this week with the weddings. I ordered the most gorgeous red peonies. I know you said white flowers for Stella's wedding, but I couldn't resist."

Emma joins them. "Red peonies would be stunning in a bouquet with seeded eucalyptus and dusty miller."

Katherine nods at her and then does a double take. "You're awfully young to know about seeded eucalyptus and dusty miller."

Presley places a hand on Emma's shoulder. "This is my intern, Emma. She knows a lot about entertaining for someone so young."

Katherine smiles at her. "Welcome to the team."

When the inn's airport shuttle pulls under the portico, Presley glances at her watch. "That must be Cecily's parents. Right on time. Emma, why don't you help Katherine while I get them settled."

The van's back door opens, and two women pile out. There is no question but what they're sisters with round faces, curvy figures, and identical short haircuts that are wedged in the back and dyed yellow.

"Would you look at this place?" the woman with the blue-framed glasses says. "Our little Cecily's done got herself a good job."

Two men step out of the van, both average height and balding, one thin and one with a considerable beer gut. "Where's the bar?" Beer Gut asks.

His wife elbows him in the belly. "Shh! You promised to behave."

Presley makes her way over to them. "You must be Cecily's family. I'm Presley Ingram, event planner. Welcome to the Inn at Hope Springs Farm."

The woman without the glasses says, "I'm Cecily's mama, Winnifred Weber. But everyone calls me Winnie. And this here's my sister, Paulette Fisher." She gestures at the other woman and then the men one at a time. "The skinny man is my hubby, Mike, and the one with the gut is Paulette's worse half, Harold."

Presley shakes each of their hands.

"Mike, get our bags out of the van," Winnie demands in a tone that leaves little doubt that she wears the pants in their family.

When Mike moves toward the back of the van, Presley says, "Actually, Mr. Weber, leave the bags where they are for now. I'll help you get checked in, and then the van will drive you down to the carriage house where you'll be staying."

Winnie massages her turkey neck. "Carriage house? Where's that? Is my daughter stashing us in some remote building so we don't embarrass her?"

Presley fakes a laugh. "On the contrary. We reserve our carriage house for our VIP guests. There are two identical suites in the carriage house. Both suites have two king bedrooms, each with its own bath. You'll share a suite with your sister and have access to a lounge and kitchenette." She looks over at Mike. "We stocked the refrigerator with your favorite Pabst Blue Ribbon beer."

Harold rubs his trophy tummy. "I like the sound of that."

"If you'll come with me to reception . . ." Before Winnie can protest, Presley places a hand on her back, propelling her forward toward the double front doors. Paulette follows them inside while Mike and Harold remain with the van.

When Paulette tries to give her credit card to the guest services agent, Winnie snatches the card and hands it back to her sister. "No way! My treat."

"But you paid for our airline tickets," Paulette protests, but she accepts the card, anyway.

"And I'm happy to do it."

Winnie hands over her credit card, and the guest services

agent processes their paperwork and swipes room key cards through the machine.

"Where's my daughter?" Winnie asks while they wait. "I thought she'd be here to greet us."

"Cecily is overseeing preparations for dinner in Jameson's. She's extremely dedicated to her job. You should be proud of her." Presley thumbs a text on her phone. "I'm letting her know you're here. I imagine she'll come down to the carriage house soon to see you."

After they finish checking in, Presley rides with their guests in the van to the carriage house. When Mike and Harold go for the luggage, Presley says, "Let the bellhop get those while I show you around."

Mike and Harold head straight for the refrigerator in the kitchenette while Presley gives Winnie and Paulette a tour of the suite they will share upstairs.

"I ain't never stayed nowhere so fancy," Paulette says of the spa tub in the marble bathroom.

Presley smiles. "I'm glad you approve. Let me show you the rest of the house."

Downstairs in the small foyer, Winnie gestures at the stairs leading to the suite opposite hers. "Who's staying there? Do we have to share the lounge and kitchenette with them?"

"Those guests won't arrive until Christmas Eve," Presley explains.

"Our brother is coming in tomorrow with his family," Winnie says. "It'd be nice to have them stay here with us until Christmas Eve."

Presley hasn't considered the possibility, but it makes sense for the family to be together. "I'm not sure that's a good idea. The guests arriving on Christmas Eve specifically requested that suite," she says, stretching the truth.

"Aw, come on," Winnie says. "We've come a long way for this

wedding. We'd like to spend as much time together as possible. My brother will get out whenever you say."

"I would hate to inconvenience them by having them move on Christmas Eve," Presley says.

Winnie dismisses her concern with a flick of her wrist. "They won't mind one little bit."

Presley lets out a sigh. "As long as we have an understanding. Like yours, the suite is two bedrooms. We're booked to capacity on Christmas Eve. Every bed is spoken for."

An uneasy feeling overcomes Presley on the ride back to the main building. While she wants to accommodate Cecily's family, the other suite is reserved for Stella's parents. To avoid blowing the surprise, Presley must keep Stella's mothers out of sight until Christmas night. What if Winnie's brother refuses to change rooms? Presley can't let herself think about the possibility. What has she gotten herself into? Planning a surprise wedding is one thing. Seeing it to fruition is another. The enormity of the situation hits her like a snowball smack in the face.

19

CECILY

Cecily puts the finishing touches on her basket of edibles for her family. She saunters down to the carriage house, enjoying the warmth of the late afternoon sun on her face. She hasn't seen her family in two years, and she's dreading as much as she's looking forward to the reunion.

Winnie and Paulette greet her at the door, practically knocking her over when they come at her at with hugs and kisses.

"You're gonna make a beautiful bride," Paulette says.

"She's too skinny. You need to put some meat on your bones." Winnie has been complaining about Cecily's weight since she shed her baby fat in middle school.

Cecily holds up her basket. "I brought you some provisions." She moves past Winnie and Paulette into the lounge where her father and uncle are sprawled out on the couch, drinking beer and watching football as though they are in their own homes. Cecily has never understood how they enjoy reruns of games when they already know who won.

Harold waves at Cecily without getting up, but her father comes over and engulfs her in a bear hug. "Hard to believe my little princess is getting married. I'm looking forward to meeting your fella tonight."

Cecily softens. Her father is the only semi-sane one in the foursome. "And Lyle is looking forward to meeting you, Dad." She opens the lid on her basket and removes a bag of nuts. "I made those spiced pecans you like." She wags her finger at him. "But you have to share."

"Says who?" He flashes her a naughty grin and takes his pecans back to the sofa.

"What else is in there?" Winnie snatches the basket, sets it on a small round dining table, and digs through the contents. She looks up. "No Fritos and French onion dip?"

"Hope Springs Farm is a luxury resort, Mom. We don't serve Fritos and French onion dip here." Cecily hip-bumps her mom out of the way. "You have cinnamon pecan wheels and croissants for breakfast. And to snack on—cheese straws, nut mix, homemade hummus with pita chips, and pâté with toasted baguette slices."

Winnie turns up her nose. "Pâté? Who in this family eats pâté?"

Ignoring her mom, Cecily transfers the food items to the kitchen. It's a wonder neither of her parents has suffered a heart attack or stroke. Their poor eating habits are the reason Cecily pursued a culinary career. In high school, when she better understood the value of nutrition, she learned to cook her own meals to avoid her mom's greasy, starchy dinners.

Returning to the lounge, Cecily announces, "Our dinner reservations are at seven. I have to work until then. We'll meet Lyle and his parents at the front entrance at six forty-five and ride to the restaurant together. I trust you can fend for yourselves until then. If you feel like exploring, you can grab a drink in Billy's Bar, which is on the first floor in the main building just down from reception."

Winnie eyes her attire. "You're gonna change, aren't you? Surely, you're not gonna wear your chef's costume to meet your new in-laws?"

"Of course, I will change, Mom. I brought a dress to work with me. And this is not a costume. It's a uniform." Cecily turns her attention to her aunt. "You realize that neither Lyle nor I have met each other's parents. Which means this dinner will be super awkward. I wouldn't blame you if you'd rather eat here. I can reserve a table for you in Jameson's."

Paulette glances at her sister and then shifts her gaze downward. "Well . . . now that you mention it . . . that might be for the best."

Winnie loops her arm through Paulette's. "No way. You're coming with me."

Paulette shrugs. She's never been able to win against Winnie.

"Fine. But this is an important night for me, and I'm begging you, please talk to Lyle and his parents."

Winnie waves away Cecily's concern. "You ain't got a thing to worry about. We'll be our usual delightful selves."

That's exactly what I'm worried about, Cecily thinks. On the way back to the main building, she gives herself a firm talking to about doing whatever it takes to survive the week with her parents.

Passing through the kitchen, she enters her office and tosses the empty basket into the corner. When she turns to face her desk, she's shocked to see Alessandro in her chair, working at her computer.

"Alessandro! What're you doing in my office?" Going behind her desk, she spins the chair around, grabs a fistful of his chef's coat, and tries to pull him out of the chair.

He grips the armrests with both hands. "Give me a minute, Cecily. I'm almost finished. I'm placing my order for food for Friday night."

She lets go of his coat, and he turns back toward the computer. When she tries to look over his shoulder, he holds up his arm, blocking her view. He makes a final click and jumps up to face her. "It's all yours."

Cecily glares at him. "I can get a copy of that order from our supplier, you know."

"Go for it. But the food order won't tell you much about the event."

"This party has something to do with Stella's surprise, doesn't it?" She watches closely for his response, but his blank expression gives nothing away.

"I'm not confirming or denying that. You'll have to ask Presley." He pushes past her and exits her office.

She calls after him, "I'll remind you, Alessandro, that you work for me, not Presley."

He sticks his head back in the door. "Technically, I work for Stella. Paranoid is not a good look for you, Cecily. You can relax. I'm not after your job. I'm striving for bigger and better things."

At a loss for a smart comeback, Cecily says, "Whatever."

Closing the door in his face, she leans against it and squeezes her eyes tight, trying but failing to hold back the tears. Nothing has turned out the way she intended. She feels like an alien outsider when she's with her family. She loves Lyle. But she's not sure that's enough. Stella is supposed to be her best friend. Yet all of her other friends are excluding Cecily from their surprise. Her job is the only aspect of her life that feels right. She'll do whatever it takes to keep it. Alessandro is calling her bluff. He is totally after her job. He is waiting for her to let her guard down, before swooping in and pushing her aside.

She allows her imagination to run wild as she envisions the surprise party for Stella on Friday night. Cecily's not at the party, because she's on the dreaded fishing honeymoon. Alessandro outdoes himself with the food presentation. Stella is so blown away by his cuisine, she promotes Alessandro and fires Cecily.

Cecily pushes off the door. She will absolutely not let that happen. She wipes her eyes, steadies her breath, and marches out of the office. The kitchen is in full swing, preparing dinner for the early crowd. Cecily moves from one station to the next, assuring that every plate leaving the kitchen is presented in accordance with her high standards. The station chefs are her musicians, and Cecily is the conductor, making certain they perform in harmony.

It's six forty-five when she looks up at the clock. In her office, she strips off her work clothes and slips on her emerald silk dress. She slides her feet into her black suede booties and runs a tube of gloss across her lips. Grabbing her bag, Cecily takes off toward the main entrance.

Arriving out of breath in the entry hall, she takes in the scene in front of her. Mike and Harold occupy the center of the small room, laughing and cutting up as they drain the last of beer foam from their glasses. Winnie and Paulette, with their backs to their husbands, stand in front of the Christmas tree, admiring the ornaments. Lyle is with his parents at the door, the three of them looking as though they long to escape.

Albert Walsh wears an air of superiority that comes from years of career success. Margaret's complexion is free of wrinkles, and her platinum blonde hair cut with precision. They are handsomely dressed, he in a navy cashmere sport coat and gray flannel pants and his wife in a hot-pink taffeta top with slim-fitting black satin pants. Lyle has hinted that his parents are wealthy but seeing them in person is confirmation.

Cecily bypasses Mike and Harold and approaches her soon-to-be in-laws. When they see her, Lyle bursts out laughing, and his mother touches her fingers to her lips.

Cecily scrunches up her face. "What?"

Lyle eyes the space above her head. "You brought part of the kitchen with you."

"Oops." Cecily yanks off her chef's hat. "Things are a little hectic in the kitchen. I'm sorry I'm late."

"Cecily is always late," Lyle tells his parents. "Prepare yourselves. She'll probably be late to our wedding."

Cecily glares at her fiancé. Is he ganging up on her?

She sweeps her arm toward her parents. "Did you meet my family?"

"We met," Lyle says in a tone that lets Cecily know the meeting didn't go well.

"Okay then. Let's go to dinner." She moves past them to the door. "I'll drive my family, and you drive yours."

Cecily and Elmo have spent a lot of time and effort organizing tonight's menu, five courses balanced with seafood, beef, and vegetables plus options for dessert that include eggnog cake and chocolate peppermint cheesecake. Elmo, a boisterous, rotund man with a ruddy complexion, greets their party at the door and shows them to the private room at the back of the restaurant, overlooking a courtyard garden. The courtyard offers outdoor seating during milder months, but it currently showcases a multitude of different-sized Christmas trees decorated in thousands of mini white lights. In the center of a round table sits a creation of red roses and variegated holly, created and hand-delivered by Katherine earlier in the afternoon.

They stand around the table, seven pairs of eyes on Cecily, waiting for direction. Why didn't she think to make name cards? She gestures at the table. "Sit wherever you like, boy-girl."

The families divide, Cecily's to the far side with their backs facing the garden and the Walshes nearest the door. Cecily sits next to Lyle, who sits next to his mom, who is beside her husband. Mike takes the seat to Cecily's right, and since Winnie and Paulette can never be separated, Harold is stuck with Albert as a dinner companion.

Waiters appear with their first course—butternut squash ravioli—paired with a French Viognier. The combination of flavors explodes in Cecily's mouth, and she's momentarily rendered speechless. Elmo has upped his game since the last time she visited six months ago. Is the extra effort for her benefit? Or is he having to work harder to compete with Jameson's?

No one offers a toast or the blessing, and the table eats in silence for several excruciatingly long minutes. Cecily's family members gobble down their single ravioli and lick their lips, hungry for more, while Lyle's parents fork off small pieces, savoring every bite.

Margaret is the last to finish. She sets down her fork and dabs at her mouth with her linen napkin. "So, Cecily . . . I understand you and my son have a dilemma regarding your honeymoon." She leans across Lyle. "I can't say I blame you. I would be downright offended if Albert took me fishing on a romantic weekend." She straightens. "Which is why I'm treating the two of you to three nights at The Greenbrier, all expenses paid. I've made all the arrangements. You won't have to worry about a thing. The first day is for resting and romancing. On the second day, you, Cecily, will be pampered in the spa while Lyle goes fly-fishing with a guide."

Cecily waits for Lyle to object to his mother's interference in their lives. When he doesn't, Cecily says, "That's very generous of you, Mrs. Walsh, but we can't possibly accept. Didn't Lyle tell you? Come December thirty-first, if we don't find an apartment or house to rent before then, we'll be homeless." Cecily doesn't care if she sounds melodramatic. She's the only one who appears to understand the urgency of the situation.

"I forgot to tell you." Lyle flashes Cecily his guilty, naughty little boy grin, which may work on his mother, but it's no longer working on his bride-to-be. "I may have figured out our living situation. I found a house on campus. The guy's moving out on the thirtieth. He can show it to us tomorrow. I'm waiting for him to text me back with a time."

Under her breath, Cecily murmurs, "Are there any other important details regarding our marriage that you forgot to tell me?"

"No. Geez. Sorry, Cecily."

Cecily stews inwardly during the rest of dinner. Their housing problem is a convenient excuse for them to take their honeymoon later. If she leaves town now, there's a chance Alessandro will have stolen her job by the time she returns.

The two families exchange little conversation during the soup, salad, and main courses, and Cecily is relieved when dessert arrives. The servers pop corks on two bottles of champagne. She wishes she hadn't ordered it. Too late to take it back now. Maybe the toasting will provide the much-needed ice breaker.

Cecily waits until everyone has a flute in hand before lifting her glass. "Thank you all for coming such a long way. Lyle and I are honored to have you join us for this special occasion."

They all clink glasses and say, "Here, here."

Seven sets of eyes dart around the table, but no one offers another toast. Not Lyle, thanking Cecily for arranging the lovely dinner. Or Mike, offering a teary-eyed speech about how much he loves his daughter. Or Albert, cracking a joke about his son's sweaty socks now being Cecily's responsibility.

Cecily guzzles down her champagne. She and Lyle would've been better off eloping.

One waiter appears awkwardly in the doorway with a black

folder in his hand. She waits for Albert to signal for the check. When he doesn't, Cecily sends an elbow to Lyle's ribs.

"Ouch, Cecily! What was that for?"

"The check," she says out of the corner of her mouth.

He shakes his head as though confused. "What about the check?"

Did Lyle seriously forget to talk to his dad about the bill? Maybe his parents decided not to pay for dinner since they are sending them to The Greenbrier on their honeymoon. Or perhaps they're protesting, because Cecily's parents brought along two extra mouths to feed at over a hundred bucks a person.

Cecily flags down the waiter. Including tip, the total comes to nearly a thousand dollars, which will put a large dent in her savings account but won't break the bank. With a tight smile, she bids her future in-laws a pleasant evening, drops her family at the carriage house, and returns to her kitchen. Her domain. The one place in the world she's content. If she had access to a shower, she'd put a cot in the corner and live out of her office. She's not sure what this revelation tells her about her relationship with Lyle. Cecily is not sure about anything anymore.

20

CECILY

Cecily spends a restless night, tossing and turning and only catching a few winks of sleep. When the first rays of dawn creep through her blinds, she throws back the covers and dresses for work. She arrives at the inn to discover dirty pots and pans strewn about the kitchen, and Alessandro dancing to reggae music as he tends a cut of beef sizzling on the grill.

She kills the volume on his Bluetooth speaker. "What're you doing here so early?"

"Experimenting, *mia bella*."

"Your Italian charm won't work on me. What exactly are you *experimenting*?" She holds out her hand. "Never mind. Don't tell me. You're working on your menu for Stella's surprise party on Friday night."

"I'm not sure who the party is for." He hunches his shoulders, his arms out by his sides. He has a certain endearing quality about him.

She reminds herself that he's the enemy. "You're a liar. But whatever. Regardless of who the party is for, this is my domain, and I have final approval over every food item that leaves this kitchen. She holds out her hand. "Let me see the menu."

"I must clear it with Presley first."

She gets up close to his face. "For the millionth time. You. Do not work. For Presley."

"I'm sorry, Cecily. I mean no disrespect, but when it comes to this party, I take my orders from Presley."

"Ugh! Get this mess cleaned up immediately." Cecily storms off to her office where she spends the next few hours preparing for the days ahead.

Around eleven o'clock, as the early lunch crowd is trickling in, she receives a text from Lyle. *We have an appointment to see the house at one.* He follows with another text that includes the address. "Morning Glory Lane," Cecily reads out loud. Sounds like a cheerful place. Maybe this will be their new home.

Her enthusiasm grows when she pulls up to the curb in front of the house—a pale blue Cape Cod with darker blue shutters, cedar shingles, and dormer windows. She imagines planting flowers in the window boxes and placing rocking chairs on the front porch where Lyle is waiting for her.

As she approaches him, she holds up her crossed fingers. "Maybe this is our lucky day. This place is a dollhouse."

"Greg left the key under the mat." Lyle holds up a silver house key. "He had something come up, but he said for us to make ourselves at home."

"He's awfully trusting, letting strangers roam around his house, unchaperoned."

"I know the guy, Cecily. We play tennis together." He unlocks the door and steps aside so Cecily can enter.

Her excitement fades as she takes a quick tour. The interior is in shambles. There are multiple holes in the walls. Does Greg have an anger management problem? The upstairs bathroom is filthy, as though it hasn't been cleaned in years. Clothes are strewn all over both bedrooms upstairs, while dishes in the kitchen sink are piled high.

"This house is disgusting." She opens the refrigerator door and quickly slams it shut. "There is mold growing in there."

"You need to look past all that, Cecily. So, Greg is a slob. We'll hire a cleaning crew."

"The linoleum is yellowed and buckling." She's staring down at her feet, inspecting the linoleum, when something scurries across the floor. She screams, "A rat!" and throws herself on Lyle, arms around neck and legs gripping his waist. "Get me outta here."

He carries her through the living room and out the front door, setting her down on the porch. "Come on, Cecily. I can't believe you're afraid of a little mouse."

"That was no mouse, Lyle. That was a fat rat who probably has a nest of babies hidden somewhere in that house." She jabs her finger at the front door. "I refuse. To live. In a house. With a rat."

"Calm down, babe. We'll find something else."

"There is nothing else in this town." Cecily has reached her breaking point, but instead of crying, a sense of calm washes over her. "This is the final straw, Lyle. I can't do this."

"Do what, Cecily?"

"I can't marry you." She takes off her engagement ring and hands it to him. "You're not pulling your weight in this relationship. I planned a lovely dinner for our families last night, but did I get a single thank you from you? And you were supposed to talk to your dad about the bill I ended up paying. I tried to make conversation with your parents, which is more than I can say for you. As for our living arrangements, we could've rented Beverly's guest house, but no! You insisted on living on campus. We should never have pushed for a Christmas wedding. This engagement has been a disaster from the beginning."

Cecily turns away from his wounded face and runs to her car. As she speeds off, reality sets in and her hands shake. What has she done? Did she actually call off her wedding? Her parents are here. Her aunt and uncle. The rest of her family members are on airplanes headed here. She can't cancel the wedding. But can she marry an unsupportive man who will cause her a lifetime of angst?

Cecily drives aimlessly around town, checking her phone for missed calls or texts from Lyle every time she stops at a traffic light. After an hour, she gives up and returns to work. The sight of her favorite cousin, waiting for her in the kitchen, chatting and laughing with the station chefs, immediately boosts her spirits.

Cecily squeals and throws her arms around her. "Amelia! You're here." Holding hands, they dance a circle, Ring-Around-the-Rosie style, as though they are children reuniting after a long separation. Amelia's mother, Marion, is Cecily's father's sister. But Cecily's mother doesn't like Marion. And because Marion lives in New York state, the cousins rarely get to see one another.

They stop dancing, and Cecily holds Amelia at arm's length. "Look at you, girlfriend. You look amazing. I love the blonde streaks." She fingers a lock of Amelia's long hair.

Amelia's blue eyes go wide. "I highlighted my hair for the first time four years ago. Has it been that long since we've seen each other?"

"Apparently. Have you lost weight?" Her once plump cousin now has a killer body.

Amelia beams. "I discovered intermittent fasting last summer. Six years out of college and I finally shed the freshman fifteen."

Cecily gives her another hug. "I'm so excited you're here."

"Me too. I can't wait to meet my future cousin-in-law."

Cecily's face falls.

"Uh-oh. What's wrong?"

"Let's go out on the veranda. I have something to tell you."

"That doesn't sound good," Amelia says, trailing after Cecily through the restaurant to the porch.

Cecily turns on a propane heater, and they sit down at a small table by the edge of the veranda.

Amelia takes a deep breath, inhaling the crisp mountain air. "Cess, this place is fab. I bet you just love working here."

"I feel blessed to have found my dream job. Until an hour ago, I had my dream guy to go with it." Smiling a sad smile, Cecily tells her cousin about the problems she and Lyle have been having recently.

When she finishes her tale, Amelia says, "You're just having pre-wedding jitters."

"This is more than that." Cecily checks her phone again, but there's no word from her fiancé. "I guess Lyle realizes it too. We have some serious issues in our relationship. I made a mistake in pushing him to get married so soon."

Amelia places her hand on top of Cecily's. "Give him some time. He'll come around."

"I'm honestly not sure I want him to." Cecily falls back in her chair. "I feel bad making everyone come to Virginia, but even if Lyle and I make up, I don't think I can marry him right now."

"You shouldn't marry him until you're absolutely certain you're ready. As for us coming to Virginia, I'm thrilled to spend Christmas with my favorite cousin in a place that totally rocks." Amelia plants her hands on the table. "Wedding or no wedding, I'm staying. The only thing that could make it better is snow."

"You might get your wish." Cecily stares out at the mountains. "We've already had two storms this month, and I hear another is in the forecast for the end of the week."

Closing her eyes, Amelia tilts her face to the afternoon sun. "Hard to believe, as warm as it is today."

"Tell me about you," Cecily says. "Do you like your job? Do you have a significant other?"

Eyes still closed, her expression content, Amelia says, "Hate my job. No significant other."

Cecily laughs. "What's wrong with your job?"

Amelia opens her eyes and looks across the table at Cecily. "It's not the job. Being an administrative assistant for a high-profile politician has its perks. The problem is my boss. She's a bitch."

"You live in New York City. Can't you find another individual of such caliber to work for?"

"I'm looking. But don't say anything. I haven't told my parents yet. And I'm not limiting my search to New York. I don't love living in the city as much as I thought I would."

"Explore all your options. There are so many great places to live in this country. Take advantage of your freedom while you can."

Through the windows, a commotion inside the restaurant catches Cecily's attention. "What the heck?" Jumping to her feet, she hurries inside with Amelia on her heels.

Kids run wild throughout the dining room, crawling under tables and chasing one another in circles. "Make them stop," Cecily demands of Presley and Emma, who wear expressions of total bewilderment.

"We've been trying," Presley says, her voice raised above the screaming kids. "They don't listen."

Amelia finger whistles so loudly the kids all freeze in place. "Kids! Chill. No running or yelling allowed indoors."

"Who are these kids and what are they doing in my restaurant?" Cecily asks.

"They're guests," Presley says. "We organized a day camp to give their parents a break."

"We've just completed a scavenger hunt," Emma says. "We've

been all over the farm and throughout the main building, and they still have a ton of energy."

"The group would be fine, if not for the Tasmanian Trio," Presley says, and Cecily follows her gaze to three identical little boys with white-blonde hair, baby faces, and devilish smiles.

"Are they triplets?" Cecily asks.

"Yep," Emma says. "They're pure evil."

"Cecily!" Jazz rushes over and flings her arms around Cecily.

Cecily kneels down in front of the little girl. She hasn't spoken to her since her mother died. "I'm sorry about your mama, kiddo. Are you doing okay?"

"I'm fine." Cupping her hands around her mouth, Jazz whispers, "Those boys are really bad."

Cecily whispers back, "I can tell."

Presley shakes her head, as though at a loss. "We finished with our scavenger hunt early. We have an hour before their parents come for them at five o'clock. I have no clue how to occupy them until then."

"How about a game of Capture the Flag?" Amelia suggests.

Presley looks at Amelia. "I don't know who you are, or where you came from, but you are officially my new best friend."

Amelia laughs, a combination of a snort and a cackle that brings back fond childhood memories for Cecily. She introduces her cousin to the event planner and her intern.

When Emma mentions that she's been accepted early to Cornell, Amelia says, "Really? My brother, Ryan, is a junior in the engineering school." She pulls out her phone. "I'll text him to come hang out."

Presley turns to the kids. "Who's up for a game of Capture the Flag?"

The kids erupt in cheers.

"I could use some air." Amelia loops her arm through Cecily's. "What say, cousin? Wanna come with me?"

Cecily shakes her head. "I wish I could. I have to break the news to my parents that the wedding is off."

Presley spins on her heels to face Cecily. "Did you just say what I think you said?"

Cecily hangs her head. "Unfortunately. Lyle and I are having some issues."

"Any chance it's pre-wedding jitters?"

Cecily glares at her. "No, Presley. I know the difference between nerves and serious problems."

Presley gives her a sympathetic smile. "I know you're upset, and I hate to bring this up, but we've already ordered everything. Food. Flowers. Booze. We can cancel the DJ, but you'll lose your deposit."

"Let me talk to my parents. I'll let you know what we decide."

Cecily exits the french doors and crosses the veranda. Dreading the task ahead, she walks to the carriage house where she's relieved to find her parents alone in the lounge, working a jigsaw puzzle. She sits down at the table with them.

"Where are Paulette and Harold?"

"Taking a nap," Winnie says, fitting a cardboard piece into the puzzle. "Your uncle Buck and aunt Sheila just arrived with Jerry and Nicole. She has the cutest little baby bump. You should run up and see them. They are in the suite opposite ours."

"Maybe later. I need to talk to you guys about something."

Looking up from the puzzle, Winnie studies her face. "What's wrong?"

"Lyle and I broke up. The wedding is off. We made a mistake in rushing into marriage before we had the chance to really know one another."

Her dad narrows his brown eyes. "Are you sure it's not—"

"Yes, Dad! I'm sure it's not nerves. How do you want to

handle the situation? We've made deposits on the food and booze. We probably won't get much of our money back."

Winnie stares up at the ceiling while she considers what to do. "Since everyone is already here. And our family is large enough to have our own party. We'll have a family reunion. That way, if you and Lyle make up, you can still get married."

Tears prick Cecily's eyelids. "I wouldn't count on that happening."

"Oh, honey. I'm so sorry." Her mother scoots her chair closer to Cecily. "I admit, Lyle is not what I expected. I don't think he's right for you. He seems spoiled and immature."

"You don't even know him, Mom. He's not spoiled and immature. My career demands a lot of my time. And he's very patient."

Cecily pushes back from the table and flees the carriage house. She runs down to the lake and out onto the small pier. No longer able to hold back, the dam bursts and a torrent of tears flows down her cheeks. The Capture the Flag game is taking place off in the distance, over near the barn, far enough away they can't see her ugly cry.

Her mother is right. Lyle is spoiled and immature. But so what? That's part of his charm. Love is blind. And she loves his spoiled, immature self so much, her heart is ripping apart, and she can't catch her breath. What if he doesn't call? What if it's really over? Her dream job means nothing without him in her life.

21

PRESLEY

Capture the Flag is fun for all ages. It thrills the Tasmanian Trio when Amelia's brother joins the game. Ryan wrestles with them and chases them and lets them climb all over him. He's adorable, dark hair and bright blue eyes with Amelia's outgoing personality. Emma thinks so too, judging from the way she flirts with him. Knowing a hot frat boy when she goes to school next fall will serve her well.

When Presley's phone vibrates in her back pocket, she steps away from the game to accept the call from Stella's mother. "Presley! I'm so glad I caught you. We're bringing friends to the wedding, and I need to book an extra room."

Is this woman crazy? "There are no extra rooms, Hannah. We're booked solid."

"Please!" Hannah says in a sugary sweet tone. "Can't you work your magic? These guys are our oldest friends. When Marnie and I told them about the wedding, they insisted on coming. They've known Stella all her life. Don't hotels hold rooms back for emergencies?"

"I can talk to our reservations manager, to see if we've had any cancellations." Suddenly struck with an idea, Presley suggests, "However, I have you booked in a two-bedroom suite in the carriage house. Each of the king rooms has its own bath. Would you consider sharing your suite with your friends?"

"Yes! That's perfect. I stayed in that suite when I came back in July."

"We've remodeled it since then," Presley says. "I think you'll be pleased."

"I'm sure I will." After a brief pause, Hannah asks, "How are the wedding plans coming? I hope no one has spoiled the surprise."

Presley sighs. "Not yet. But that's my biggest fear."

"I heard about Naomi. Stella's been through so much. She deserves some special treatment. This is a wonderful thing you're doing for Stella and Jack."

Tingles of apprehension and excitement flitter across Presley's chest. "Let's hope Stella thinks so."

"Coincidentally, the flight Marnie and I originally booked is sold out. We changed to an early morning flight, so we can travel with our friends. We should arrive at the inn by noon."

"We'll be ready for you. Safe travels."

With a sense of dread, Presley ends the call. The room switchover is cutting it close for Christmas Eve. Checkout time is eleven. Hannah will arrive by noon, which could mean earlier. Presley explained the situation to Winnie's brother, Buck Blanford, when he checked in earlier, and he assured her they have no problem with moving to the main building on Christmas Eve. She will put housekeeping on standby. If all goes smoothly, they can turn the suite around quickly. Presley pockets her phone. Everything is going to work out as planned.

Presley waves across the lawn at Alessandro when he emerges from the carriage house with an empty room service cart. Loading the cart in the white service van, he walks over to Presley.

"What's with the worried expression?" he asks. "Is everything okay?"

"There are so many moving parts involved in this surprise wedding. I just got off the phone with Stella's mother. She's bringing extra guests with her."

"Not just any guests, Presley. Colton Cruse is coming with her."

"Who's . . ." Presley's mouth falls open. "You mean Colton Cruse from the cooking show?"

"The one and only. He also owns one of the hottest restaurants in Manhattan, Colton's Kitchen. I interviewed with him. He told me to come back after I had some experience, hence the reason I'm in Hopeless Springs, Virginia."

Presley shakes her head as though confused. "Wait. I thought you liked it here."

"Not hardly. I'm a city guy. Not a mountain man. But the opportunity was too good to pass up. Cecily's a genius." Alessandro cuts his eyes at Presley. "But don't you dare tell her I said that. She's making a name for herself. Being at the right hand of a rising star is the visibility I need."

Presley massages her temples. "You're giving me a migraine, Alessandro."

He lets out a deep breath. "Just promise me you won't tell Cecily about Colton Cruse. If she finds out he's here, she'll take over Stella's wedding and ruin my big chance."

"Don't worry about Cecily. She and Lyle will make up, and even if they don't go on a honeymoon, she'll at least take Christmas Day off."

"I wouldn't hold my breath, waiting for them to get back together. She's banging pots and pans around in the kitchen like she wants to beat someone with them." He glances nervously toward the main building. "I'd better get back before that someone is me."

He hurries to his van and drives off. She checks her watch for the time. Four forty-five. Fifteen more minutes before she can return the little devils to their parents. Mercifully, this day is almost over. She thanks Amelia and Ryan for their help and shepherds the kids to the barn.

The Tasmanian Trio's parents are waiting at the door. The mom is too thin and she appears wary, as though afraid of her own little boys. After spending the day with them, Presley doesn't blame her.

The dad asks, "What's on the agenda for tomorrow?"

"Indoor activities. Gingerbread house contest in the morning and pottery making in the afternoon." Presley looks down at the boys. "Maybe leave some of that energy in your hotel room tomorrow, guys."

The dad gives her a nod of assurance. "I'll talk to them."

After the other parents claim their children, Presley walks Jazz over to the caretaker's cottage where Opal is waiting in the swing on the front porch.

"Stella is running some last-minute Christmas errands," Opal explains. "She asked me to stay with Jazz until she gets back."

Jazz crawls onto the swing and curls up with her head resting in Opal's lap.

Opal strokes Jazz's hair. "Looks like someone had a big day."

Presley smiles at the child who can barely hold her eyes open. "Get some rest, Jazzy. We have a lot of fun planned for tomorrow."

Presley returns to the barn. Emma has left to go Christmas shopping with her sister, and she spends an hour tidying up. She's turning the lights out when Lucy appears with her iPad. "If you have a minute, I need to confirm the wine list for the weddings."

Presley motions Lucy to the table, and they sit down across

from each other. "We're down to one wedding." She explains about Cecily calling off her wedding. "I'm hoping it's only a case of the jitters, but Cecily left a message earlier, saying that the party will go on even if the wedding doesn't."

They spend a few minutes reviewing the wines for both events. Lucy snaps her iPad shut. "I have to cancel our dinner plans for tomorrow night. Grant had planned to take Chris to Colorado skiing for Christmas, but now he's come down with a severe case of the flu."

Presley slowly processes this information. Lucy invited Presley to dinner when she thought Chris would be in Colorado with his father. She doesn't want Presley around her son.

She levels her gaze on Lucy. "I had a wonderful mother in Renee. I'm not looking to replace her now that she's dead. I wanted to know more about my genetic lineage. You may find that difficult to understand, since your biological parents raised you, and you grew up knowing siblings with whom you share the same DNA."

Lucy pushes abruptly back from the table. "I don't have time to get into this now."

"Then make time," Presley says, jumping to her feet. "You once told me your parents made certain you received the proper care you needed, physically and mentally, during your pregnancy. Does that mean someone counseled you about the rape?"

Lucy looks down at the floor. "Not that it's any of your business, but I saw a therapist once. She wasn't helpful, and I never went back. Besides, it wasn't a real rape. He date-raped me."

"Rape comes in many forms, but it's still rape. When you found out you were pregnant, you hid out in your parents' house until the baby was born." Presley jabs her thumb at her chest. "Until I was born. You never even held me. Never knew whether I was a boy or a girl. You were eager to move on with your life, and you were successful in forgetting about the past. For a while.

For decades, even. When did that past start haunting you? Was it before I came to town? Was the rape partially responsible for your years of depression?"

Still staring at the floor, Lucy swipes at her eyes. "You don't know what you're talking about."

"Really? Then why not tell Chris about me? Why not tell Brian?" Presley asks, but doesn't wait for an answer. "Because, even though you were an innocent victim, you're ashamed of what happened to you. And I'm the product of that shame. I'm your dirty little secret."

Flinging her bag over her shoulder, Lucy spins around and flees the barn, leaving the door open on her way out.

Presley moves to the doorway and watches her march toward the main building. Proud of herself for standing up to Lucy, she's not sorry for the things she said. And she has a strong hunch they are true. Even so, a wave of melancholy washes over Presley at the loss of a friend. Ever since she met Lucy, Presley has been on an emotional roller coaster. She can't take it anymore. Unless Lucy gets the psychological help she needs, Presley wants nothing more to do with her.

As the last ounce of energy drains from her body, Presley locks up the barn and walks across the narrow road to the main building. Dodging tables on the veranda where guests enjoy the pleasant evening, she cuts through the dining room to Billy's Bar where a party is in full swing. Every table and barstool is occupied. The music is loud, the guests even louder. Presley's head begins to pound in earnest. Spotting Everett behind the bar, she gestures for him to follow her into the lounge.

"What's wrong, babe? You don't look like you feel well."

"I had a run-in with Lucy," she chokes out. "What time do you think you'll get off?"

"I can leave now. We're overstaffed. Everyone put in to work tonight, so they can have days off at the end of the week."

"Are you sure?"

"Positive." He kisses her cheek. "Stay right here while I tell Kristi I'm leaving."

He's back in less than a minute, and together they exit the inn through the main entrance, walking hand in hand down the drive toward Main Street.

"Did you hear Cecily called off her wedding?" Presley asks.

"Yep. News travels fast around here. I'm not surprised, though. I could tell she was having some doubts about marrying him."

"Do you think they were rushing into getting married?"

Everett hesitates before answering. "In their case, maybe. But when you love someone, and everything is right in your relationship, why wait?"

She takes hold of his arm. "Do you think our relationship is moving too fast?"

"Not at all. Being with you these past few days has felt so right, while the weeks we were apart felt so wrong."

She rests her head on his shoulder. "I'm glad to hear you say that. I feel the same way."

They walk the next block in silence. When they reach her apartment building, he asks, "Should we go home? Or should we grab an early dinner at Town Tavern?"

Presley weighs her options. Home seems too tranquil for the turmoil brewing inside of her. She needs to talk through what happened with Lucy. "Let's go to Town Tavern."

Presley loves the restaurant for its relaxed atmosphere and tavern-style decor—neon beer signs on exposed brick walls and booths with wooden tables. Pete, the bartender, is a friend. Normally, they'd sit at the bar with him, but tonight, Presley needs more privacy. They grab an empty booth in a quiet back corner, and when the waitress comes, they order burgers and non-alcoholic beers.

Presley takes a long pull off her bottle. "If someone put a tequila shot in front of me, I wouldn't hesitate to drink it," she says, and they both laugh thinking about the night they met. Her first night in town when she, as a guest at the inn, had found her way into Billy's Bar and ordered a tequila shot from Everett. She didn't drink the tequila that night, and despite the temptation to get blackout drunk, she won't go there now.

"Talk to me," Everett says. "What did Lucy do to you to make your beautiful face so sad?"

She recounts the scene with Lucy. "I don't regret anything I said to her. She needs help. She pushes everyone who's close to her away. She has a good thing going with Brian, but if she's not careful, she'll lose him too."

The waitress delivers their burgers, and they pause the conversation while they add condiments.

"Lucy's the reason you moved to Hope Springs. Are you ready to walk away from her?"

Presley stares at her burger without taking a bite. "For the sake of my emotional well-being, I have no choice but to walk away. Lucy's been jerking me around for weeks, and no matter how many times I tell myself it doesn't matter, her rejection cuts me deeply. When she looks at me, she sees the guy who raped her, and the revulsion is written all over her face."

"I'm sorry, babe. That's not fair to you. And it makes it hard when you work together."

"Tell me about it." Presley drags a french fry through her puddle of ketchup. "I've accomplished what I came here for. I now have Rita and the girls in my life. And I'm excited to meet my grandparents on Christmas Day. But I have no reason to stay in Hope Springs. I would leave with you after New Year's if not for my commitment to Stella."

Everett stops chewing. "Do you seriously mean that?"

"I do. I love my apartment and my job, but none of it feels

right when you're not here. I'm jealous you get to go back to Nashville. I'm homesick."

"Then start looking for someone to take your place."

"It's not that simple. I have to talk to Stella first. And I can't do that until after her wedding." As Presley stares down at her plate, tears blur her vision at the thought of having to stay in Hope Springs without Everett.

"Stella might surprise you. She's one of the most under-standing people I know. If she knew you were this miserable, she wouldn't hold you to your commitment."

"She's said as much to me. But I refuse to leave her in a lurch. Especially now with everything she has going on in her life. Naomi's death. Adjusting to being a parent to Jazz. New house and marriage." Presley dabs at her eyes with her napkin. "I can't stop thinking about Naomi. We all had issues with her, but it's hard to see someone so young die. Her death is a reminder. We never know what tomorrow will bring."

He takes her hands in his. "All the more reason to live every day to the fullest. I can only do that with you."

Half-eaten hamburgers forgotten, hungry now for each other, Presley and Everett pay the check and run across the street to her apartment where they make love until after midnight.

"I need fresh air," Presley says. "Let's go sit on the balcony."

Wrapped in blankets, they race to the living room window and throw open the sash. Everett straddles the low sill, with one foot inside the apartment and the other on the balcony. "Come here." He pulls Presley down in front of him. "You are a sex kitten tonight. What's gotten into you?"

She nestles close to him, her head under his chin. "I wanted to show you how much I love you."

"I got the picture." A horn sounds on the quiet street below. "Whether you realize it, you're gonna miss this town."

"Well . . . maybe. But probably not. I'm a city girl at heart. I knew that when I came here. But I don't regret my time in Hope Springs. For the past three years, while I was taking care of my sick mother, I had no life of my own. Being here has given me the opportunity to see my life from a fresh perspective, to decide what path I want for my future."

"I hope that future includes me," he says, blowing on her neck.

"I hope so too." She summons the nerve to ask the dreaded question that has been on her mind for weeks. "When do you go on tour?"

"Mid-January."

Her heart sinks. "Which means I probably won't see you again until June. Since there's nothing we can do about it, I might as well work out my six months. I have a twelve-month lease on this apartment, anyway."

He nibbles on her earlobe. "Don't give up so easily. Miracles have been known to happen at Christmastime."

It would take more than a Christmas miracle for all Presley's dreams to come true.

22

STELLA

O n Wednesday morning, after dropping Jazz at kids' camp, I grab a coffee from the main lobby and drive over to the manor house. Jack is waiting for me in the driveway. We have a full day ahead of us, preparing for the movers to arrive with his furniture tomorrow.

When my feet hit the pavement, he takes me by the hand and leads me to the passenger side of his truck. "You're coming with me. I have a surprise for you." He opens the door and lifts me up to the seat.

"Wait, Jack! Erma's coming to install Jazz's bedroom in a few minutes."

"She's already here. I explained that we will be gone until after lunch, and she assured me she's got everything under control."

When he tries to close the door, I block it with my booted foot. "But what about the kitchen? Are the appliance installers here yet?" I am so happy about all the plans and the work that's been done so far, especially the major miracle Jack's performed in getting the kitchen contractor to finish on time.

"They should be here momentarily. They know what to do.

Randy will supervise the installation." He slams the door and goes around to the driver's side.

When he climbs behind the wheel, I ask, "Where are you taking me until after lunch?"

"If I told you, it wouldn't be a surprise." He starts the engine and backs the truck through the grass, around my Wrangler, to the road.

"I don't have time for this, Jack. Christmas is in two days. And we have so much to do before then. I thought we were getting our Christmas tree this morning."

"Randy is doing that as we speak. The tree will be in the stand waiting for us to decorate when we return."

I toss my hands in the air. "Where's the fun in having your project manager pick out our tree? This is our first Christmas in our new house. Shouldn't we pick out our own tree?"

A smile tugs at his lips. "Trust me. This surprise will be worth it."

My curiosity eats away at my frustration. "At least give me a hint. The last time you surprised me, you gave me a house and a diamond ring. You set the bar high."

"I'll give you a hint. You're not getting a house or a diamond ring."

"Funny. Ha ha. Seriously. I'm going to jump out of this truck the next time you stop if you don't give me a real hint."

He pinches his bottom lip. "Hmm. Let's just say the surprise is as much for Jazz as it is for you."

I roll my eyes. "Like she needs anymore surprises. I have a surprise for you, too. But you'll have to wait until we get back to see it."

"Can I have a hint?"

I stick my tongue out at him. "Let's just say the surprise is not for Jazz."

"Touché," he says with a laugh.

When we exit the city limits, I ask "Are we going on a road trip?"

"Yep. We have about a forty-five-minute drive."

I settle into my seat and cross my legs. "How's the packing coming at your house?"

"They were in full swing when I left at eight. Randy will check on them while we're gone." Jack drums his fingers on the steering wheel. He's as keyed up as I am about the move and Christmas.

"Randy's having a busy day." I stroke Jack's forearm beneath his flannel shirt. "And you'll be too exhausted to attend Cecily's wedding tomorrow night."

Jack shakes his head. "Not me. My adrenaline will get me through Christmas. I'm sure I'll crash this weekend, though."

I laugh. "We both will. Let's hope Jazz adapts quickly to her new home, so we can get some rest."

"Don't worry. She will." Jack turns on his blinker and merges onto a two-lane highway. He fiddles with the radio, turning the volume low on his favorite country station. "Tell me about our plans for Christmas Day. Have you figured out how to get Jazz from the cottage to the manor house?"

"I have. With a lot of help from Katherine."

When I tell him my plan, a broad smile spreads across his face. "I absolutely love it!" And for the rest of the drive, we talk about the logistics of the move and getting everything in place before the big day.

We're in the middle of nowhere, on a long stretch of a wooded two-lane highway, when Jack makes a sudden right-hand turn onto a dirt road. After passing through a deep stand of pine trees, an attractive farmhouse comes into view. We follow the dirt road around the farmhouse to a large barn. In front of the barn is a sign that reads Allegheny Kennels.

"Kennels? As in dogs? Please tell me you're not giving Jazz a puppy." I think back to the illumination party, and how enamored Jazz was with the golden retriever puppy.

"Only with your blessing. But you need to see them before you say no." He turns off the engine and shifts in his seat toward me. "You can't go through life being neither a cat nor a dog person, Stella. At some point, you must declare your allegiance. Unless you discover you like both. Which would normally be fine, except that I'm highly allergic to cats."

I smack his gut with the back of my hand. "You are not."

"You're right. I'm not. I'm partial to dogs." Jack's expression turns serious. "I realize that now is not the most ideal time to get a puppy, but there's nothing like having a dog to love on when you're sad or lonely. I think Jazz could benefit from the love a pet will give her."

"I can't argue with that. We all need as much love as we can get right now. But aren't puppies a lot of work?"

He nods. "An enormous amount of work. But they are worth it. Not only do Bert and Amanda breed dogs, they train them as well. In a few months, when the puppy is a little older, we'll bring her back for boot camp."

"Her? Is this a done deal? Have you already picked out this puppy?"

"Not at all. We are under no obligation. Bert is an old friend. He's doing me a favor." Jack reaches for his door handle, and I reluctantly get out of the car. As we walk toward the barn, Jack explains, "Of the ten puppies in the litter, four of them are females, and they have sold all but one. We can have our pick, if we keep one. The others will go home with their new owners tomorrow."

The barn door bangs open and a middle-aged man dressed in jeans and a fleece emerges, his arms laden with four squirming white balls of fur. "Good to see you, Jack. Let's go out back, and I'll introduce you to my little friends."

We follow him around to the back of the barn to an area of grass sectioned off with knee-high gray fencing. Jack steps inside the fencing and plops down on the ground. Bert hands him the puppies one at a time, and he's as happy as I've ever seen him, a little boy again, as the puppies crawl all over him.

Jack motions for me to join him. "Come on, Stella. Don't be shy."

Careful not to land on a puppy, I step over the fence and lower myself to the ground. Jack drops a puppy in my lap. I pick up the warm furball and bring it to my chest. She smells sweet, like warm milk, and when I hold her in front of my face, she licks my nose.

Jack winks at me. "I think she likes you."

"We breed English golden retrievers," Bert explains. "They're known for their mellow temperaments and excellent health. This litter is exceptional. Healthiest puppies I've ever seen. You can't go wrong if you close your eyes and pick one. Then again, you may bond with one more than the others. I'll give you a few minutes alone. I'll be in the barn if you have any questions."

After he's gone, I set the first puppy down and pick up another. "Aww, Jack. They're so cute. How do you train them not to pee in the house?"

"You crate train them." He turns a puppy on her back and scratches her belly.

I frown. "You mean you lock them in a cage?"

Jack laughs. "Don't worry. Their crates are their safe places where they go when they need to be left alone. Which is important when you have a young child in the house. The process works, if you stick with it."

"You know a lot about dogs. How many have you had?"

"Six, since I was a boy. All golden retrievers. My last one died four years ago."

My heart swells as I watch Jack play with the puppies. I'm

lucky to have found such a kind soul. "Are you sure this surprise isn't really for you?"

He smiles. "I admit, I'm ready for another dog. But this surprise is for all of us. Dogs are the most loved members of the family. Does this mean we can get one?"

"You totally blindsided me, Jack Snyder. You knew that, once I saw them, I wouldn't be able to go home without one."

"Puppies usually have that effect on people. Now, which one is ours?"

We take turns cuddling with all four puppies. Their faces are nearly identical, although their body sizes vary. After fifteen minutes, when we still can't decide, we remove ourselves from the pack and watch them interact with one another. Jack and I agree on the smallest of the females who prefers to watch her sisters barrel over one another instead of taking part in the action. The way she quizzically tips her head to the side steals our hearts.

I wait in the car with the puppy while Jack takes care of the paperwork. In a few brief minutes, I fall head over heels in love with this creature. When Jack returns to the car, I say, "I've decided I'm a dog person. But you better watch out. I have a lot of making up to do. I've been missing out on the joy of pet ownership all my life."

Jack leans his head back and laughs out loud. "You may have as many dogs as you want."

As soon as we drive away from the farm, the puppy falls asleep in my lap. "Should we name her? No telling what Jazz will come up with if we give her the honor."

"It should be a family decision," Jack says. "But you and I will have ultimate veto power. We'll call her Puppy for now."

A family decision. I like the sound of that.

With Puppy asleep in my lap, I spend the drive home researching crate training on my phone. We stop by the pet supply store on the way into town to pick up the essentials. I carry Puppy in my arms while Jack fills a shopping cart with a wire crate, foam bed, puppy kibble, leash, collar, disposable waste bags, and bowls for food and water.

"We'll let Jazz help pick everything else out this weekend," Jack says on the way back to the truck.

We're pulling out of the pet store parking lot when Presley calls. "Stella, we have a situation."

My heart skips a beat. "Is it Jazz? Is she okay?"

"Jazz is fine. It's Cecily. She called off her wedding yesterday. I was hoping she and Lyle would work things out, but so far, that hasn't happened. Since you're her best friend, I thought maybe she told you about the breakup."

"I haven't heard from her. I've been so busy with the house. But I'll call her now and let you know what I find out." I end the call with Presley.

"What's up?" Jack asks, his eyes narrowed in concern.

"Cecily and Lyle broke up."

I click on Cecily's number. She answers on the third ring. "Cecily, you won't believe what Jack and I bought Jazz for Christmas. Can you come over to the manor house?"

"You mean right now?"

"Yes, now. Alessandro can hold down the fort for a few minutes."

"All right," Cecily says, reluctantly. "I'm on my way."

Jack smiles over at me. "We haven't even gotten that puppy home, and you're already exploiting her."

I shrug. "Sounds like Cecily needs some pet loving."

I wait in the yard for Cecily, encouraging Puppy to potty, while Jack takes the dog supplies inside and begins setting up the crate. She arrives twenty minutes later. "OMG, cutest puppy ever. Jazz will be thrilled." She scoops the puppy up and buries her face in her fur.

I wrap my sweater tighter around me. "It's getting cold out here. Wanna go inside?" I gesture at the house.

"I really can't stay," Cecily says. "Did you hear? I broke off my engagement."

"Presley told me. I would rather have heard it from you."

"You have enough going on without dealing with my problems."

"Not too much to talk to my best friend. What happened?"

"A lot of things, actually. Rushing the wedding was a bad idea." With Puppy nestled against her chest, Cecily quickly describes their housing situation, the disastrous dinner with their parents, and Lyle insisting they take a honeymoon.

"I don't understand. Why don't you want to go on a honeymoon?"

"I'm not comfortable being away from work right now. I'm pretty sure Alessandro is after my job." Still holding the puppy, Cecily starts off toward her car.

I run after her. "So what if he is? He won't get it." I grab her by the arm, spinning her around. "Alessandro has flair, Cecily, but he's not you. I'm blessed to have someone of your caliber on my staff. You have a job as head chef at Jameson's as long as you want it." I snatch the puppy away. "But you can't have the dog."

Cecily smiles, despite the tears welling in her eyes.

"The apartment above our garage is small, but you're welcome to it until you find something else. With or without Lyle."

A single tear streams down her cheek. "Thanks," she says, swiping at it.

"Have you heard from Lyle?"

"Not a word. I saw his parents checking out this morning. I assume that means he told them there's no reason for them to stay. He doesn't want to marry me. He's made that perfectly clear."

"Should you be the bigger person and call him?"

She bites her lip and shakes her head. "I can't. Not this time. Not until he apologizes about the dinner thing. He was in the wrong for not talking to his father about the bill. If he's not willing to pull his weight, I can't be in a relationship with him, no matter how much I love him."

"I'm so sorry, sweetie." With my free arm, I give her a hug, accidentally squeezing the puppy who lets out a yelp. "Are you sure you won't come inside where it's warm? We can send Jack out for coffee."

"Thanks, but I need to get back to work."

"How about if Jazz and I come to Jameson's for dinner tonight? We can talk then."

Cecily smiles a sad smile. "I'd like that."

I don't wait for her to drive away before hurrying inside. "The temperature is dropping by the minute," I say to Jack who is standing beside an enormous Fraser fir tree. "Wow, that's a lot of tree."

Jack rubs at his beard stubble. "I should have given Randy more direction. I told him to pick out a healthy tree. I didn't intend for him to get a sequoia. I have some ornaments, but not nearly enough."

"Don't worry about it. I'll make a Target run. Jazz won't notice as long as we have plenty of lights and the angel topper I found online."

Silence envelops us, the sounds of hammering and sawing noticeably absent. "Is everyone gone?"

"I think so." Jack turns to me, gently taking me in his arms so as not to smother the sleeping puppy. "For the first time since we closed on the house, we have it all to ourselves."

"Can we put her in her crate? I'd like to show you your surprise."

"Sure." Jack takes Puppy from me and gently places her on

the fleece-covered bed in her crate. She stirs, and I think she's waking up, but she curls into a tight ball and falls back asleep.

"Come on!" Taking Jack by the hand, I lead him upstairs to the second floor. We pause in the hallway outside of Jazz's lavender ballerina bedroom.

"You and Erma did an outstanding job in here," Jack says. "Jazz will love this."

"We still have to hang Opal's painting above her bed. She's bringing it over in the morning."

We continue down the hall, stopping short in the doorway of the master bedroom where I'm stunned speechless at the transformation. Warm shades of cream and champagne are on the wool carpet, satiny dust ruffle, and heavy linen drapes.

Jack steps tentatively across the threshold. "Whoa. This is more luxurious than your Presidential Suite at the inn."

I join him in the center of the room. "The mahogany chest on chest and rice bed belonged to my grandparents. I found them in one of our warehouses, along with several other priceless antiques I'm having brought over tomorrow." I lean into him. "Do you like it?"

"I love it. But when do I get to sleep in here with you?"

"After we're married. But we can do other things in here when Jazz isn't home." I push him down on the bed and fall on top of him. "How long do puppies sleep?"

"Not nearly long enough."

23

PRESLEY

P resley and Amelia are under the tent on the terrace, setting up for Cecily's wedding-turned-family-reunion when Presley receives a phone call from housekeeping. The woman is rapidly speaking broken English, but Presley understands enough to understand her worst nightmare has become a reality.

"I'll be there in a minute," Presley says and ends the call.

Amelia looks up from arranging small bouquets of red flowers for the tables. "Is something wrong?"

"I have VIP guests arriving today. They are booked in the carriage house, but Cecily's aunt, uncle, and cousin are refusing to vacate the suite. I don't understand why they're being so difficult. They agreed to this when they checked in."

"That's Cecily's mother's side of the family for you. Let me handle this." Amelia rubs her hands together. "Please! I've been waiting for an opportunity to tell them off for years."

"Sorry. I need to be tactful about the situation. Cecily and I are already on shaky ground." Presley laughs when Amelia's lower lip turns out in a pout. "All right. You can come with me."

She turns to Emma, who is placing enormous silver foil-wrapped poinsettias on the floor around the edges of the tent. "I'm going down to the carriage house for a minute. Are you okay here?"

"Sure." Emma stands back to admire her work. "I'm almost finished. I told Katherine I'd help her refresh greens. Should I meet you back here later?"

"Take your time," Presley says. "We're in good shape for now. The catering staff will set the tables later."

Grabbing their coats, Presley and Amelia hurry down the stone steps to the sidewalk. Amelia struggles to keep up with Presley's pace. "Who did you say these VIPs are?"

"I didn't. I'm not at liberty to tell you that, Amelia."

"Right," she says, a sly smile spreading across her lips.

Inside the carriage house, eight of Cecily's family members, including her parents, are crowded in the lounge, feasting on a tray of homemade doughnuts and talking at one another over the loud volume on the television. The local weatherman is broadcasting a white Christmas forecast, which Presley has heard rumors of but has not received confirmation of until now.

Presley claps her hands loudly. "Excuse me."

When they ignore her, Amelia finger whistles and the room immediately goes silent. She retrieves the remote from the coffee table and clicks off the television. She surveys the empty beer bottles and pizza boxes littering nearly every surface of the room. "We have other guests arriving any minute, and this place is a mess. Evidently, the party was here last night."

Presley sets her gaze on Winnie's brother. "We had an understanding, Buck. Your suite is booked for the weekend. You need to move to the main building right away."

"We would, if we had somewhere to go." Buck jabs a half-eaten chocolate doughnut at Presley. "I checked with your reservation department, and our rooms won't be available until later this afternoon. Do you expect us to hang out in the lobby until then?"

Presley inwardly groans. This is one detail she let slip. Why didn't she think to discuss the matter with Rita? "And that may very well be the case. I will speak to our guest services manager. If you're inconvenienced in any way, we will comp your rooms for tonight. But right now, I need you to vacate the suite upstairs."

When they hesitate, Amelia points at the ceiling. "Now. And let's get this lounge cleaned up."

Winnie cuts her eyes at Amelia. "Who do you think you are, bossing us around? Are you working here now?"

"Ha ha. No." Amelia glares back at her. "I'm embarrassed for you. I never knew you lived like a slob."

Buck and Sheila, trailed by their son and daughter-in-law, have no sooner marched in single file up the stairs to their suite when the front door swings open. A bellman ushers in four guests, two women and two men, one of whom is the unmistakable television personality—Chef Colton Cruse.

Amelia's jaw hits the floor. "That's . . ." Her phone is out, and she's thumbing off a text to Cecily before Presley can stop her. *Come to the carriage house now.* When Amelia lifts her phone to snap a pic, Presley snatches it out of her hand.

"He's our guest," Presley hisses. "It is our responsibility to keep his presence here a secret."

Abandoning Cecily's family in the lounge, Presley crosses the threshold into the foyer. "You must be Stella's parents. I'm Presley Ingram. So nice to finally meet you."

Hannah is movie-star glamorous, a willowy blonde with Stella's big round blue eyes. She introduces her wife, Marnie— an attractive petite woman with short dark hair and hazel eyes— and their friends, Colton and Marcos. Colton is pale-skinned and slightly balding, a stark contrast to his partner's dark good looks.

"The guests occupying the suite ahead of you are slow to check out," Presley explains.

"No worries," Hannah says. "Our flight was early. Good thing, too. They're predicting this snowstorm will bring a screeching halt to holiday travel starting later today."

"I'm glad you—" Presley is interrupted by a breathless Cecily, flying through the door.

Cecily appears more startled to see Stella's mother, whom she met last summer when Hannah came to the farm for a visit, than the famous chef. She gives Hannah a quick hug. "Stella didn't mention you were coming."

Hannah looks to Presley to explain. "Stella doesn't know they're coming," Presley says. "We're planning a surprise wedding for Stella and Jack."

Cecily lets out a squeal. "Get outta town! So, that's the big surprise. Wow! Planning a woman's wedding without her knowledge . . . That's gutsy of you, Presley."

Presley's plan is beyond gutsy. It's ludicrous. What was she even thinking? She wishes she could crawl in a hole and come out with the groundhog on February second. "I didn't tell you, because—"

"Because you thought I'd be on my honeymoon" says Cecily.

"And because I didn't want to steal your thunder," Presley says.

"Well, I've canceled my wedding, and I'm not going on a honeymoon, so I get to be a part of the surprise." Cecily does a little victory dance. This is the happiest Presley has seen her since before Thanksgiving.

Cecily offers her hand to Colton Cruse. "Cecily Weber. Head chef at the inn. I'm a huge fan."

Instead of shaking her hand, Colton kisses the backs of her

fingers. "I know who you are, my dear. And it's a pleasure to meet you. I look forward to talking shop with you."

Hannah digs a twenty-dollar bill out of her wallet and hands it to the bellman, who has been waiting patiently beside the door. "We'll take care of our luggage from here."

"Yes, ma'am," he says and hurries off.

Hannah turns back to Presley. "No need to worry about us, Presley. We'll keep ourselves occupied and out of sight. We thought we'd drive into the mountains and grab some lunch. It's Christmas Eve. We're gonna see what kind of trouble we can find. Brian has invited us for dinner tonight. He has a new girlfriend. I guess you know that. Apparently, she's the sommelier here. Colton is cooking, and the girlfriend is pouring wine."

Irritation crawls across Presley's skin. Why does she care that Lucy is entertaining Brian's sister and her friends?

"We're available to help tomorrow," Marnie volunteers. "Just tell us what you need."

"I will, as soon as I get my thoughts together. If you're okay with leaving your luggage here, I'll have a bellman carry it up as soon as your suite is ready."

"That'd be fine," Hannah says.

Cecily stays behind with her family when Presley and the others exit the carriage house. The four newcomers drive away in their rental car, and Presley walks with Amelia up the hill to the main building. In the reception hall, Amelia says, "I promised my brother I'd go shopping with him. Typical guy, he hasn't bought our parents anything for Christmas yet. If you'd like, I can come back this afternoon to help finish getting ready for the reunion."

"You've already been so generous with your time this week. You should rest up for the party. Or have your hair and nails done."

"I'd rather hang out with you. Your job is seriously cool."

Presley musters a smile. Her job is seriously stressful at the moment. "If you really want to help, text me when you get back from shopping and we'll assess what else we need to do for the party."

When Amelia heads toward the elevators, Presley goes in search of Rita in the reservation's office. "We have a situation," she says and explains about Buck Blanford's reluctance to leave the carriage house.

Rita's fingers fly across her keyboard like an expert. Has it been only three weeks since she started working here? "No problem. I have two available connecting king rooms on the third floor, which is what they'd originally booked. Should I call their suite and let them know?"

"That would be great. You're a lifesaver." Presley starts toward the door and then turns back around. "Are Lucy and Chris coming to your house for Christmas dinner?"

A flush creeps up Rita's neck to her cheeks. "I . . . well, I'm not sure. Lucy changes her mind with the wind."

"Tell me the truth, Rita. I understand if she's avoiding me."

Rita folds her hands on her desk. "She's hesitant to come. Not *because* of you, but because she hasn't told Chris about you yet. Don't let that bother you, Presley. Some years Lucy comes. And other years she doesn't. My parents are very much looking forward to meeting you. They will be disappointed if you don't come. As will Emma and Abigail and I."

"I'd like to meet your parents . . . my grandparents. I'm just not sure . . ."

Rita comes around from behind the desk. "I realize this is a big step for you. But you don't have to tell me now. You can even wait until the last minute to decide. Emma is cooking. She's planning a feast. There will be plenty to eat."

"Thanks. I'll let you know in the morning then." Near tears, Presley gives her a hug and hurries from the office to the lounge.

Her chest is tight, and she's practically hyperventilating by the time she reaches Billy's Bar. When she finds Kristi behind the bar, she chokes out, "Where's Everett?"

"He left a while ago. He said he had to run some errands."

She leaves the bar with chin lowered and tears blurring her vision. Outside in the lounge, she nearly crashes into Stella, who is emerging from Jameson's with a metal cart.

"Presley! Are you okay?" Alarmed at the sight of Presley's tears, Stella says, "What's wrong, honey?"

Presley shakes her head, unable to speak.

"You're coming with me. I have just the thing to cheer you up."

She considers objecting. She has much to do. But she needs to get away from work for a while.

Stella's gray Wrangler is waiting, engine idling, on the curb out front. "Lunch for the movers," Stella explains as they transfer large metal bins from the cart to the back of her Jeep.

Presley climbs in the passenger seat, and Stella pulls slowly away from the curb. "This must be hard for you, your first Christmas without your mom."

Presley nods, still not trusting her voice.

A large moving van is parked on the street in front of the manor house, and Stella adds her Wrangler to the line of trucks in the driveway. Stella opens her car door. "Come on in! Wait until you see what we got Jazz for Christmas."

Unloading the food bins from the back of the Jeep, they enter the house and pass through a mudroom to the kitchen where a group of four movers dressed in blue uniforms are unpacking boxes and storing the contents into cabinets.

"It'll take me a year to figure out where everything is," Stella says over her shoulder to Presley.

They set the food bins on the counter. "I brought in lunch

for you guys," Stella tells the movers. "Dig in whenever you're ready to take a break."

As they cross into the adjacent solarium, Stella yells down the wide center hallway to Jack, "Lunch is here." He's positioned himself by the front door so as to direct the movers as they enter the house with boxes and furniture.

In the far corner of the glass room, near an enormous Christmas tree with hundreds, perhaps thousands, of lights and few ornaments, is a dog crate. A sleeping fluffy puppy is curled up inside. Despite her plumpness, Presley can tell by her slim face that it's a girl.

Presley smiles, her mood softening. "Aww, so sweet. Is she a golden retriever?"

Stella nods.

"How is she sleeping in the middle of this chaos?" Presley asks.

The puppy stirs, looking up at them with one ear flipped over her head.

"She's exhausted," Stella says. "We just got her yesterday. Jack was up with her half the night."

"Poor baby misses her littermates."

Stella removes the puppy from the crate.

"Does she have to pee?" Presley asks.

"Probably. Wait here. I'll be right back."

While Stella's outside with the puppy, Presley looks around the downstairs. The house is slowly becoming a home. The Naomi chapter has closed, and Stella is finally getting her happily ever after. She has the love of her life. A baby sister she adores. A beautiful home. Dream job. Presley is delighted for her friend, but a tiny bit jealous at the same time. She wants so much to find her own happily ever after, yet can't imagine finding it in Hope Springs. She has to get out of this town before it smothers her.

When Stella returns, they sit on the hardwood floors near the tree while the puppy runs around, chasing a tiny bouncy ball.

"Jazz will flip when she sees this puppy," Presley says. "I remember how taken she was with that little boy's golden retriever the night of the illumination ceremony."

"That's what started it. Jack insisted on getting her this puppy. We never had pets when I was growing up, and I didn't understand what I've been missing."

"Puppies and kittens are the best. Aren't you, sweet little thing?" Presley holds the puppy up, kissing her nose. "Where is Jazz today?"

"With Opal. They're making cookies and wrapping presents. Opal has been a lifesaver this week. It's getting harder and harder to keep the house a secret from her."

Tell me about it. Presley thinks about all the different ways Stella's surprise could be ruined. Someone could have a slip of the tongue. Stella could pass Hannah and Marnie on the way in or out of the farm. Or she could wander over to the carriage house to check on Cecily's family. Only twenty-four hours left to keep up the charade. But a perilous twenty-four hours with Stella's parents in town and the transformation on the barn set to begin early tomorrow morning.

When the puppy returns to her crate, immediately falling asleep, Presley gets to her feet and walks over to the window, looking out across the expansive backyard.

Stella joins her at the window. "Why are you so sad, Presley? Is it Everett?"

Lucy's recent erratic behavior comes to mind, but Presley thinks it's inappropriate to mention that. "It's a lot of things," she says. "And Everett is part of it. Our long-distance relationship isn't working for me. The weeks we were apart were difficult. I can't help myself. I love him so much, I want to be with him all the time. But I love my job at the inn, too. And my new friends here."

Stella touches Presley's forearm. "I understand how important it is for us to be with the ones we love. If you need to resign, I will support your decision 100 percent. No one will ever replace you, but I'll eventually find someone for the job."

Presley angles her body toward Stella's. "I won't leave you in a bind. Besides, Everett is going on tour starting in January. Even if I move back to Nashville, I'll be alone. And I've been working on events for the spring and early summer. I'd like to see them through."

"Let's get through the holidays, and we'll sit down and have a serious talk."

"I'd like that." Presley turns her back to the window. "For now, I need to finish getting ready for Cecily's family reunion."

Stella gestures at the kitchen. "Don't you want some lunch?"

"I'm not hungry, but thanks."

Stella closes the door on the crate. "Then I'll drive you back."

"Don't be silly. I can walk." Presley crosses the room and Stella trails after her.

"But it's freezing out," Stella says.

"The fresh air will do me good."

"If you're sure." Jack has disappeared from the doorway, and no movers are in sight.

"I had a long talk with Cecily yesterday, but I haven't heard from her today," Stella says. "Did she make up with Lyle?"

Presley shakes her head. "Not as far as I know."

"Poor Cecily. This must be so hard for her."

"Are you going to her party tonight?"

"I don't think so. Cecily invited me, but I'd feel awkward at her family reunion. I think we'll have a low-key night with Jazz at the cottage."

She hugs Stella goodbye. "If I don't see you again, I hope you have a Merry Christmas."

Stella squeezes her in return. "Same to you, Presley. Try not to worry. Everything will work out."

With a final wave at Stella, Presley buttons her coat up against the cold and hurries down the sidewalk and across the road. She's relieved to hear Stella isn't going to Cecily's party. Someone could easily say the wrong thing and blow the surprise. Then again, Stella will be in her cottage, dangerously close to Hannah and Marnie in the carriage house. Presley should have paid more attention to the details. What's the worst that can happen if Stella finds out about the wedding? Stella could choose not to get married and disappoint all the people who helped make it happen. Presley's heart sinks, but her spirts are immediately lifted again at the thought of moving back to Nashville. She's taken the first step toward making that happen. While she's reluctant to leave her new friends and apprehensive about resigning from a job she enjoys, she knows deep down she's doing the right thing. A few sacrifices are worth it to be with Everett.

24

CECILY

Cecily waits at the carriage house to make certain her aunt, uncle, and her cousin and his wife clear out of the suite. She rides in the van with them up to the main building and introduces them to Rita, who promises to help them get settled into their new rooms. When Cecily returns to the kitchen, lunch is in full gear and her station chefs are hopping.

"We need to talk." She drags Alessandro into her office and closes the door. "I know about the surprise wedding. I just ran into Presley's parents at the carriage house. You won't believe who they brought with them."

"Colton Cruse," he says in a deadpan tone.

She eyes him suspiciously. "Are you saying you knew Colton Cruse was coming here?"

"Yes, I knew. And I'm warning you, Cecily. Stay away from him. Colton Cruse is all mine."

"Sorry to be the bearer of bad news, but Colton already belongs to someone far more handsome than you."

"I'm not interested in Colton romantically." Alessandro's hand flies to his chest. "My heart belongs to Mateo. I want Colton to hire me."

"Hire you? You mean for his New York restaurant?"

"*Esattamente.* I interviewed with him last summer. He told me to come back when I had some experience."

Cecily eyes narrow as the pieces of the puzzle fall into place. "So Colton Cruse is the reason you've been *experimenting* before dawn every morning this week."

"Sì. I've kept in touch with him, borderline harassing him. He called me on Monday night to tell me he's coming for Stella's wedding. He has an opening for a sous chef. Based on my performance at Stella's wedding, he'll consider me for the position."

Cecily thumbs her chest. "So, you're not after my job? This is the big kahuna job I heard you talking about on the phone your first week here?"

His heavy dark eyebrows become one. "I don't remember that, but yes. I never intended to stay in Hopeless Springs long. I couldn't tell you that. You wouldn't have hired me." Dropping to one knee, he presses his hands together under his chin. "Please, Cecily. Let me have this chance. Will you stay out of the kitchen tomorrow night?"

Cecily's mind spins. She sees how much this means to Alessandro. But how can she possibly pass up a golden opportunity to impress a world-famous chef like Colton Cruse? Then again, she could enjoy Stella's wedding without worrying about what's happening behind the scenes. "Fine. The kitchen is all yours tomorrow night. On one condition."

Alessandro kisses the back of her hand. "Name it."

"If Colton agrees and scheduling allows, I'd like to cook a private dinner for him and his guests on Saturday night."

"Fine by me. If I have my way about it, I'll be one of those guests and we'll be discussing the terms of my contract."

Cecily laughs, feeling a load lifted off her shoulders. "I'll be sure to put in a good word for you."

Late in the afternoon, Cecily sneaks away from the kitchen to check out the progress her catering staff is making in setting up for her family reunion. The tented terrace is just as she imagined. Although Presley warned her space would be tight with tables, chairs, and dance floor. It doesn't matter now, with only her family in attendance. Cecily feels guilty about the money her parents spent. She'll make it up to them by paying for the next wedding reception. If there is another wedding. She may end up a spinster, a lonely old chef married to her knives and sauté pans.

Cecily zigzags her way through the tables to the tent's clear vinyl sidewall overlooking the back lawn and mountains. The maintenance staff was to set up chairs on the dance floor for their guests to sit in during the nuptials. She'd envisioned saying her vows to Lyle with the twinkling white lights of the illuminated landscape as a backdrop. Tears spill from her eyelids, and she fingers them away.

Cecily doesn't hear Lyle's footsteps behind her until he places a hand on the small of her back. Whispering softly in her ear, he says, "We can still get married if you want."

She spins around and is stunned to see dark circles under his eyes and a thick beard stubble on his face. Cecily has never known Lyle to go a day without shaving. "You have some nerve showing up here two hours before we're supposed to get married, expecting everything to be okay between us."

He hangs his head. "That's not why I'm here. I came to apologize. I'm sorry for so many things. If you'll let me talk, I have a lot I need to say."

"Fine. But make it quick."

He pulls two chairs out from a nearby table, and they sit down facing each other. "Mom and Dad said to tell you goodbye.

My sister had her baby on Tuesday. A girl, born ten days early. My parents left immediately when Amy went into labor." Lyle removes a wad of cash from his coat pocket and presses it into Cecily's hand. "This is for the dinner. Dad was furious at me when I confessed that I forgot to talk to him about the bill ahead of time. He thought that, since you are a chef, you'd arranged a deal. He'd planned all along to pay for the dinner."

Cecily pockets the cash. This makes her feel a little better. At least, about his parents.

"My mom really likes you. She—"

"What're you talking about, Lyle? Your mom hates me."

He cocks his head sideways. "I thought you were going to let me talk."

Cecily drags her fingers across her lips, zipping them.

"Mom approves of the way you stood up to me. She said I was being selfish, insensitive, and immature. And she was right." Lyle takes hold of her hand. "I've done some serious soul-searching these past few days. I'm confused about some stuff, but there's one thing I'm absolutely certain of. I can't lose you, Cess. If you wanna get married, we'll get married."

"What, exactly, are you confused about?"

"I think we rushed into this wedding before either of us was ready to be married."

"I agree."

"My love for you isn't in question. But I think we have some issues to work out." Lyle takes her hands in his. "Remember that campus house we lost in the lottery?"

She nods. "What about it?"

"The guy who won the lottery doesn't want the house anymore. He's moving in with his girlfriend. The house is ours if we want it. What do you say, Cecily? Do you want to live together while we sort through our issues?"

Living together is the ideal solution, an opportunity to figure out if they are meant to be together forever. But she has no intention of letting him off the hook so easily. She gets up and goes to the tent window.

He comes to stand beside her. "I was on my way over here when the housing department called. I have to let them know today." He glances at his watch. "In twenty minutes."

"Wow. Twenty whole minutes to make such an important decision," Cecily says in a sarcastic tone.

"In fairness to them, they thought I'd jump at the chance to rent the house. If we don't take it, they need to contact the next person in line right away."

Staring ahead at the mountains, Cecily says, "My biggest concern, Lyle, is that you don't fully grasp the demands of my career. As long as I'm a chef, and I hope that's forever because I love my job, we will never have a nine-to-five schedule like other people. When we have children, you'll have to play a major role in taking care of them."

"I can deal with that." He flashes his little boy grin. "See! I'm becoming less selfish and more sensitive and mature already. The old Lyle would've made some sarcastic remark about not being ready to have kids yet."

Cecily has never been able to resist him. And she doesn't try now. "I like the idea of us living together. A lot, actually. Call the housing department. Tell them we'll take the house."

"Really?"

She cups his cheek. "Really."

He places the call, and she listens to his side of the conversation. They can start moving their things in right away. When he hangs up, he says, "I'll borrow my buddy's trailer. We can move in over the weekend."

"We'll have to wait until Sunday. I have a dinner thing Saturday night."

"Sunday it is." He leans over to kiss her.

"There's one more thing you have to do for me before I'm willing to forgive you," she says.

"Name it," he says in a soft voice, his lips close to hers.

"You have to be my date for the party tonight. Which, by the way, is now a family reunion. And I expect you to make a point of spending time with every single member of my family. They don't think very highly of you at the moment. You have a lot of making up to do."

"I can handle that. I deal with my players' angry parents all the time."

They stand together in silence, watching gray clouds build in from the west. "The view from here is incredible," Lyle says. "Maybe we can plan to get married this time next year."

Cecily vigorously shakes her head. "No way. Christmas is too hectic."

"Next summer, then?"

"That's awfully soon." Cecily wants plenty of time to make certain marriage is right for them. "Besides, the chance of thunderstorms is high in the summer."

"What about in the fall, when the autumn leaves are changing?"

She presses her body against his. "Fall could work. But let's not make any plans or put any pressure on each other. For now, I want to enjoy being together."

"I like the sound of that."

They turn away from the view. "Now, tell me about your niece," Cecily says.

He whips out his phone and scrolls through his pics until he finds one of a newborn with a scrunched-up face and misshapen head. "Her name is Meredith, and she's the prettiest thing ever. Amy tried to breastfeed, but that didn't go well. So Meredith is on the bottle, which she already loves."

Lyle talks on and on about Meredith as they walk together through the lounge. By the time they reach the kitchen, Cecily's faith in him is fully restored. Any man who loves his niece this much will make an excellent daddy.

25

PRESLEY

At almost midnight, Cecily's family reunion shows no signs of slowing down.

"Set up a self-serve bar for them, and let's get out of here," Presley says to Everett.

Ten minutes later, they leave the inn in separate cars, following each other to her building. In the hallway outside her apartment, Everett says, "Wait here. I have a surprise for you."

Presley's gray eyes widen. "A surprise for me?"

"Yes, you. Why should Stella have all the fun? Besides, it's officially Christmas." He gives her a peck on the lips and disappears into the apartment, returning a minute later with a red bandana. He ties the bandana around her head, covering her eyes.

"Seriously, Ev. Is this really necessary?"

"Stop complaining." Gripping her arm, he guides her into the living room. When he removes the bandana, she gasps at the Christmas tree in the corner—a perfectly shaped four-foot tall Fraser fir with colored lights and tinsel.

"So this is where you disappeared to today. I can't believe

you." Presley throws her arms around his neck. "I absolutely love it."

"A tree is a must-have on our first Christmas together." Everett gathers the pillows and blanket from the sofa and tosses them on the floor in front of the tree. Dropping to his knees, he pulls her down with him.

"You just made my Christmas, Ev." Tucking a pillow beneath her head, Presley stretches out on her back and stares up at the tree.

He nestles up beside her, draping the throw over their bodies. "Remember the night you moved into this apartment?"

Presley's mind travels back two months. "Mm-hmm. What part are you thinking about? When I bought you pizza for helping me unload my car, or when I told you about being adopted?"

He fingers a lock of her hair. "The part when I realized you were the girl for me. My soul mate."

"It seems like just yesterday. Oh wait, in the grand scheme of things, it was just yesterday."

He props himself on one elbow, looking down at her. "What's that supposed to mean?"

"Only that we haven't been together very long."

Everett rolls back over, his gaze on the ceiling. "Do you think Cecily and Lyle made the right decision not to get married tonight?"

"I definitely do. I had a chat with Cecily in the ladies' room. She wants to make certain Lyle understands how different their life will be because of her career. And I think Lyle still has some growing up to do."

"Do you think they rushed into this marriage?"

"Maybe. What's with all the questions?"

"I'm just thinking about our relationship," he says. "As you pointed out, we haven't known each other very long either. But that doesn't matter to me. I'd marry you tomorrow given the opportunity. Can you say the same?"

"Of course," Presley answers without hesitation. She doesn't have to think about it. She loves him. She wants to be with him, always and forever. She sits bolt upright. "Wait. Are you . . ."

"Asking you to marry me? Yes." He scrambles to his knees and crawls over to the Christmas tree, pulling a velvet ring box out from beneath the low-hanging branches. "I found this in an estate jewelry store. It's not the typical engagement ring, but it reminded me of you. When I make my first million, I will buy you the biggest diamond I can find."

Presley stares at the box, mouth agape. "I don't know what to say."

"You already said yes. No take backs." He holds the box out to her. "Go ahead. Open it."

She takes the ring box from him and slowly opens it. Inside is a gold ring set with three small stones—a velvety, royal-blue sapphire flanked by brilliant-cut diamonds. "It's stunning. I love it." She removes the ring and slides it onto her finger. "It's a perfect fit. How'd you know my ring size?"

"I borrowed a ring from your jewelry box. One I've seen you wear on that finger before."

"Remind me never to give you the spare key to my apartment again."

Pink spots appear on Everett's cheeks. "I promise I didn't go snooping around in your stuff."

"I'm teasing you, silly. You can have the spare key to my apartment anytime." Presley jumps on him, knocking him backward. Lying on top of him, she smothers his face with kisses.

"Soon, we'll each have a key to the home we share as man and wife," he says in a throaty voice.

She studies his face. "Are you saying you want to get married right away?"

"The sooner the better. Don't you?"

"More than anything. But my job—"

He kisses the tip of her nose. "Which brings us to surprise number three. I talked to Wade today. He wants to hire you to help organize my tour."

"What?" Presley pushes herself into a sitting position, straddling his midsection. "Wade Newman at Big Country Records, the man who is launching your career, wants to hire me to organize your tours?"

"Yep. Apparently, there are a ton of details involved with touring. According to Wade, they often hire people with your credentials for these positions."

"I don't know, Ev. That's an awful lot of togetherness." Suddenly overwhelmed, she slides down to the floor beside him and curls up close with her head resting on his chest.

He kisses her hair. "Look, babe. I'm throwing a lot at you at once. This whole tour thing is uncharted territory for both of us. We don't have to make any decisions tonight."

Presley yawns. "And we have a big day ahead of us tomorrow." She holds her hand out in front of her. "I love my ring, Ev. And I love you. I can't wait to spend the rest of my life in your arms."

Presley and Everett fall asleep on the floor. Forgetting to set her phone alarm, she doesn't wake until a few minutes after eight on Christmas morning. She shakes Everett awake. "We overslept. I should have been at the inn an hour ago. I need to shower." Clambering to her feet, she tugs her sweater over her head as she hurries toward the bedroom.

"Merry Christmas!" Everett calls after her.

She sticks her head back through the doorway. "Merry Christmas to you, Everett."

After a quick shower, with hair still wet, she throws on jeans and a gray cable-knit sweater. Cowboy boots in hand, she goes sock-footed to the kitchen where Everett is brewing a coffee for her to take with her.

He gives her the once-over. "You're wearing that to Christmas dinner with your new family?"

Tugging on her boots, she looks up at him. "I'm not sure I even want to go to this dinner."

"Why not? Because of Lucy? You don't even know if she'll be there. Besides, this isn't about her. It's about you meeting your grandparents. You want to meet them, don't you?"

She nods. "Very much."

"Then we're going." He spins her around, and with his hands on her shoulders, he marches her to the front door, helping her into her coat. "I'm right behind you as soon as I shower and shave. Text me the clothes you want me to bring you for dinner, and you can change at the inn."

Hooking an arm around his neck, she pulls his head down and kisses him long and hard on the mouth. "I can't wait to be your wife."

"And I can't wait to be your husband."

"We fell asleep before we could consummate our engagement," she says, her lips on his.

"That'll give us something to look forward to for tonight. After Stella's wedding."

Reluctantly, Presley leaves him standing in the doorway. She'd like to spend the day in bed with her new fiancé. But they'll have plenty of time together. Today is about Stella. As she hurries down the steps to her car, she imagines Stella's face when she sees her mothers, when she learns of her surprise.

On the way to work, Presley catches herself singing "I'm

Dreaming of a White Christmas." She's hurrying from the employee parking lot to the barn, texting Everett a description of the clothes she wants him to bring, when a weather alert appears on her screen. The several inches of snow predicted is now a blizzard.

Inside, the transformation from rustic barn to winter wonderland is in full swing. The maintenance staff erects groupings of artificial trees in the corners. Four lengths of white gauzy fabric fan out from the center of the peaked roof and down four wooden pillars to frame what will be the dance floor. Six-top tables draped in white linens surround the dance floor. One wreath—fashioned from Christmas greens and decorated with gold and white ornaments with dangling bead garlands—hangs from the ceiling. Katherine and Emma are working on the second while Amelia ties bells in pairs with thin red ribbon for guests to ring when the bride and groom arrive.

Presley approaches their worktable. "Merry Christmas, everyone. I'm sorry I'm late. I forgot to set my alarm."

In unison, the three women wish her a Merry Christmas.

"Have you noticed any activity next door at Stella's cottage?" Presley asks. "I have it on high authority that Jazz is getting a Christmas surprise of epic proportions."

"Oh, yeah!" Amelia says. "Katherine told us all about the house and the puppy."

"You missed it, Pres," Emma says. "Katherine arranged for a horse-drawn carriage to take Jazz over to the manor house. They were pulling out when we arrived around seven."

Alarmed, Presley says, "Stella didn't see you, did she?"

Katherine smiles at her. "We were careful to stay hidden until she left."

Presley peers over Amelia's shoulder. "I'm surprised to see you here so early. You were still dancing when I left around midnight."

Amelia cranes her neck to see Presley. "But I quit drinking early. Cecily, on the other hand, hit the tequila pretty hard." She snickers. "I don't imagine she's feeling so great right about now."

Presley takes a tour of the barn, admiring the decorations. "Y'all are doing a fabulous job. I'm excited to see my vision come to fruition."

Emma looks up from her work. "Whose dream wedding is this, Presley? Yours or Stella's?"

Presley makes a face at her cousin. "Ha ha. Aren't you the funny one. This is the first wedding I've planned. Naturally, it's special to me."

"Then you should copy it when you marry Everett." Emma's gaze shifts to Presley's left hand. "Hold on a minute. What is that on your finger? I've never seen you wear that ring before."

Presley admires her ring. "Everett proposed last night. I love it, even though it is unusual."

Emma drops a handful of greens as she reaches for Presley's hand. "That is beautiful. I love that it's different." She looks up at Presley. "Oh. My. God. You're getting married. That is so badass."

Presley laughs. "You think everything is badass."

When it's Katherine's turn to see the ring, Presley notices that the groundskeeper is practically green around the gills. "You don't feel well, do you?" she says in a low sympathetic tone.

She smiles. "I'm trying. I'm determined to make it to the wedding tonight. The ring is lovely, Presley. Congratulations. You and Everett are an adorable couple."

Amelia comes around to their side of the table. "Let me see!" She takes hold of Presley's hand. "Very pretty. Everett has excellent taste." She drops her hand. "So . . . does this mean you're leaving Hope Springs? Because, if you are, I might be interested in applying for your job."

Presley's jaw goes slack. "Are you serious, Amelia? You'd have to move to Hope Springs, which is a world away from New York."

Amelia considers this. "I think I might enjoy living in a small town. There's so much to do here, if you enjoy the outdoors. Which I do. I've been looking to make a change, anyway. I hate my boss. And I'd get to work with Cecily, who is like a sister to me. So, yes! I'm serious."

Presley's head spins. Everything is happening so fast. "This could work well for both of us. Are you staying in town through the weekend?"

Amelia bobs her head, her blonde ponytail bouncing up and down. "I'll be here until Sunday. But I can stay longer."

"I need to talk to Stella, and she'll want to meet with you. Obviously, that's not happening today. You should think this through, though, to be sure this is what you want. Maybe talk to Cecily about small town living."

"I'll do that." Amelia holds up two balled fists. "Yippee! I'm so excited."

"You have no idea." In a few brief hours, all the stars in Presley's universe have aligned. Everett proposing. Wade offering her a job. Amelia interested in taking over her position at the inn. Only the Lucy star remains out of line, but Presley won't let Lucy ruin her good mood. Not today. Not on Christmas.

26

PRESLEY

Everyone pitches in to prepare for the wedding reception. Everett hauls rolling clothes racks over from the main building to use for the coat check and sets up the bar on the far side of the barn, near the temporary divider that sections off the makeshift kitchen for the catering staff. Emma helps Presley create bouquets of white roses with silvery greens for the tables while Amelia ties bunches of mistletoe with creamy satin ribbon on the backs of gold Chiavari chairs. Presley designates Katherine the honor of designing the bridal bouquet—a stunning display of red peonies, white roses, and anemones—along with a crown of baby's breath with white ribbon streamers for Jazz.

At eleven thirty, after one last walk-through in the barn, Presley hurries to the main building to change into her red knit dress, tall black boots, and gray cashmere fur-lined wrap before heading to Rita's for Christmas dinner.

On the way over, Presley admires the sight of Everett at the wheel of her Volvo. He is handsome in a navy sport coat and gray flannel pants. "You clean up well. I think I'll keep you."

He smiles over at her. "Good thing since you already said yes."

"No take backs," they say in unison and laugh.

"I'm setting a reminder." Presley thumbs the reminder into her phone. "But you can't let me forget to stop at my apartment for Stella's dress on the way back."

"The wedding dress is key. How could you forget it?"

They arrive at Rita's house as Lucy's navy sedan is speeding away from the curb. Presley glimpses a shock of auburn hair over the top of the passenger's headrest. *Chris.*

"Wonder what that's about," Everett ponders out loud.

"I know what it's about. Lucy found out I was coming."

Rita is waiting for them at the door. "Emma is beside herself about your engagement. I'm thrilled for you both." She gives them each a hug. "Let me see the ring."

Presley holds out her hand, and Rita fingers the ring. "It's lovely. Emma was right. It is very you, Presley." She turns to Everett. "Excellent choice."

Everett beams. "Thank you."

Rita shivers. "Brr. It's freezing out here. Come on in." She motions them inside.

"These are for you and the girls," Presley says, handing Rita a shopping bag of gifts. "And a little something for your parents."

"That is so thoughtful. Thank you. We have gifts for you, as well." Rita takes the shopping bag from Presley and places it on the floor at the foot of the stairs. "Emma's in the kitchen. She'll be right out. My parents are running a few minutes late, and Abigail drove to Charlotte ahead of the storm to see her dad. She left early this morning. She just texted to let me know she got there safely."

"Please tell her we missed her," Presley says. "We saw Lucy

and Chris just now. They sure left in a hurry. Is something wrong?"

Rita lets out a sigh. "Lucy's not herself today. She and Brian broke up last night."

Presley narrows her eyes. "What? Weren't they hosting a dinner for Stella's parents and Colton Cruse?"

"They had a fight after the guests left," Rita explains.

"About what?" Presley asks, and when Rita looks away, she adds, "Did it have something to do with me?"

Rita sighs. "Lucy apparently had too much to drink. She confessed to Brian that you are her biological daughter and that she's been pushing you away. Brian asked Lucy what she could possibly have against a nice girl like you. Lucy told him she couldn't be with someone who didn't have her back."

"Did Lucy tell you all this?" Presley asks.

Rita shakes her head. "Brian called me first thing this morning. He was worried about her. Lucy left his house in an Uber. He'd been trying all night to get her on the phone, to make certain she made it home safely."

Presley's eyes narrow. "So, instead of answering his calls, she let him worry?"

Emma emerges from the kitchen, wearing an apron over a gray wool dress. "Aunt Lucy's being a royal bitch today."

Rita scolds, "Emma! Language. Please."

"Well, it's true," Emma says. "I feel sorry for Chris. He wanted to stay. But Lucy wouldn't let him because . . ." She bites down on her lip.

"Because I was coming," says Presley,

"That's her problem," Emma says. "We will not let Aunt Lucy ruin our Christmas."

The front door swings open and a female voice calls, "Yoohoo." Presley and Everett stand back while Rita and Emma welcome Presley's grandparents with kisses and hugs.

Rita and Emma move out of the way, and Presley's breath hitches when she sets her eyes on her grandmother for the first time. Presley is in a time warp—fifty years into the future, and she's looking at her own reflection in the mirror. Carolyn Townsend has aged well and is stylishly dressed in slim-fitting black pants and a long gray cowl-necked sweater.

Everett whispers in Presley's ear, "I hope you look that hot when you're eighty."

Presley elbows him in the ribs.

"My dear." Carolyn moves toward Presley with outstretched arms. "The resemblance is uncanny."

Presley's throat swells and she's unable to speak.

Samuel appears at his wife's side. "Holy smokes. I've just traveled back five decades. You truly are the spitting image of Carolyn at your age." His genuine smile sets Presley at ease.

Extending her hand, she manages a weak, "I'm Presley. Nice to finally meet you." She introduces Everett as her fiancé, and they congratulate her on her engagement.

Rita collects everyone's coats. "Let's sit in the living room by the tree."

When they migrate into the adjacent room, Carolyn and Samuel make a beeline for the sofa. "Come. Sit next to me," Carolyn says to Presley, patting the space beside her.

Presley lowers herself to the sofa, and Everett claims the wingback next to her with Rita in the matching chair opposite him.

"You outdid yourself with the tree, Rita." Carolyn's gaze shifts to her granddaughter, who is standing beside her mother's chair. With a smirk tugging at her lips, she adds, "Or did Emma decorate it?"

Emma pats Rita on the head. "The tree was all Mom. She did a good job."

Rita smiles up at her daughter. "That's a compliment coming from you."

Emma leans against the chair, crossing her legs as though she's planning to stay awhile. "There are so many trees at the inn, Nana. You should come see them. Presley, tell Nana and Pops about the surprise wedding you're planning. It's amazing. You wouldn't believe it." Emma goes on to describe the winter wonderland wedding theme in vivid detail. "What'd I miss, Presley?"

Presley laughs. "I think you covered it."

"Presley planned her own dream wedding for Stella," Emma says. "I told her she should copy the theme when she and Everett get married."

"I would have a hard time finding a venue in Nashville with the same charm as the barn at the farm," Presley says.

Emma's eyes go wide, as though a thought has suddenly occurred to her. "Excuse me while I check on things in the kitchen. You need to help me future cuz-in-law." She pulls Everett out of his chair and drags him out of the living room.

Shaking her head, Rita watches them go. "I'm sorry. My daughter is awfully full of herself today."

Carolyn smiles at Presley. "Because she's so taken with her new cousin."

"I feel the same way about her. Emma has been a lifesaver at work this week." Presley tells her new grandparents about all the goings-on at Hope Springs Farm.

Everett and Emma return from the kitchen looking like cats who swallowed canaries. Presley suspects they're up to something, but she doesn't have time to quiz Everett before they move to the dining room to eat. Carolyn and Sam sit down on either side of Presley at a round table set with linens and crystal. Emma distributes dinner plates rimmed with a holly and ribbon design and loaded with wedges of crab quiche, slices of succulent honey baked ham and a salad of tender baby greens, dried cranberries, blue cheese crumbles, and walnut vinaigrette.

During dinner, her grandparents grill Presley about every aspect of her life, from her earliest memories until now. As they talk, it dawns on Presley that Lucy never once asked about her adoptive parents, their home life, or where she went to college.

Presley has an unobstructed view of the window from where she's sitting at the table, and while they're eating bread pudding for dessert, a light snow falls. They linger over coffee, and when Presley pushes back from the table around two o'clock, the light snow has become heavy.

"I hate to leave," Presley says. "I've had such a wonderful time. But we need to get back to the inn to figure out how this weather will affect the wedding."

Emma gets to her feet and begins gathering dessert plates. "I'll be there in a few. After I help Mom clean up."

Removing her phone from her bag, Presley sees a string of texts from Jack. "I would offer to help clean up, but Jack is texting me. I'm sure he's worried about the weather."

"You need to go," Rita says. "We'll have this cleaned up in no time."

Presley hugs each of her grandparents. "I loved meeting you. I hope I see you again soon."

"We'll make certain of it." Sam's warm smile tells Presley he means it.

Carolyn takes Presley's face in her hands. "You're a darling girl, and I'm thrilled to know you. As for Lucy, she can be difficult but she has a genuine heart. Life has dealt her blows that have made her overly cautious and less trusting. She will eventually come around. My grandson, Chris, is a good boy. I'm certain he will be open to having a half sibling, especially a young woman as pretty and lively as you. I hope you get a chance to meet him soon."

Presley's eyes fill with tears. "We've already met, although briefly. I'd like to get to know him better."

Carolyn drops her hands from Presley's face. "I want to stay in touch." Retrieving her small purse from the living room, she digs a card out and presses it in Presley's hand. "Here are my numbers. Please text me so I'll have yours."

Presley stares down at the card, a watercolor of a blue hydrangea with Carolyn's name, address, and numbers printed on it. A modern-day calling card. Her grandmother has swag.

Presley and Everett make a dash for the car. Everett scrapes the snow from the windows, and they drive slowly toward the inn. His eyes on the road, wipers going at full speed, Everett asks, "*If you had the chance, would you marry me today?*"

"I've already told you I don't want to wait," she says absentmindedly as she scrolls through her text messages. "Jack thinks we should move the ceremony from the chapel to the barn because of the weather. He's worried Stella will overhear him and wants me to call the minister."

She clicks on the number Jack provided, and a woman's voice answers on the third ring. Presley introduces herself and explains the situation. Reverend Malone says, "I think you're smart to move the ceremony to the farm. What time should I be there?"

"Around five thirty," Presley says. "We'll start the ceremony as close to six thirty as possible. Do you need someone to come get you?"

"That won't be necessary," Malone says. "I have a four-wheel drive."

"Okay then. Be careful. It's nasty out."

When Presley hangs up, Everett says, "You have a very nice family, Presley. So what if your biological mother has some issues? You have an aunt, cousins, and grandparents who adore you. Will it be hard for you to leave them?"

"Yes. But it won't stop me from moving to Nashville. We can always come back for visits. I would love to stay at the inn as guests."

Everett smiles. "Maybe we can come back next Christmas."

Presley hopes they are married by then. She thinks back to Everett's question. *If you had the chance, would you marry me today?* She would marry him in a heartbeat. She closes her eyes and says a silent prayer that Stella feels the same way about Jack.

They are approaching the inn when Presley's phone pings with a reminder. "Darn. You forgot to remind me to stop by my apartment for Stella's dress. I need to check on a few things here. Do you mind going back for it?"

"Not at all. Tell me what to get." He navigates the Volvo around a group of guests under the portico and parks on the curb.

"Stella's dress is the one with the sheer sleeves. If you're not sure, FaceTime me. Be careful when you take it off the mannequin. The garment bag is on the shelf in my closet. Try not to wrinkle it."

"I can handle it. My mom does alterations for a living, remember? I grew up helping her in her sewing room."

"Seriously? Do you know how to sew on buttons? Because I'm terrible at it."

"Buttons are my specialty. I'm good at hemming as well."

"Your skills will come in handy when we have children." Presley smooths her red dress over her knees. "I guess I'll just wear this to the wedding. While you're at my apartment, will you please grab my silver sandals out of my closet and my pearl drop earrings and pearl choker out of my jewelry box? Since you're already so familiar with my jewelry box," she says with a smirk on her lips.

"Ha ha. I didn't realize that being married to you meant being your personal valet."

She play-punches his arm. "You're the rising country music star. If I take Wade's job, I'll be *your* handler."

"*When* you take the job,"—Everett leans across the console to kiss her—"I'll be all yours for the handling."

27

STELLA

Exhausted from the day's festivities, I curl up on the sofa with my new UGG throw blanket, one of my many gifts from Jack. Less than a minute later, Jazz and Puppy climb under the blanket with me. Jazz has christened Puppy many names today. Kringle and Holly among them. Much to my relief, none of them have stuck.

I'm drifting off to sleep when Jazz taps my cheek. "Hey, Stella? Do we get to live in this house forever?"

I open my heavy eyelids. "Would you like that?"

"Yes! Can I sleep in my ballerina bedroom tonight?"

"Fine by me. I'll be in the room right next to you." I lock eyes with Jack, who is gathering up wrapping paper and stuffing it in black trash bags, and he winks at me. Goal accomplished. After months of bunking with me in my tiny bedroom in the cottage, Jazz wants to sleep in her own bedroom.

"Can Puppy sleep with me?"

"Absolutely not," I say. "Puppy will be happier down here in her crate."

"Well, now. Let's think about this for a minute." Jack ties the trash bag, tosses it with the others by the french door, and comes to stand by the sofa. "Maybe we can put the crate in Jazz's room for a few nights until Puppy adjusts to her new home."

I understand where he's coming from. Jack has spent two sleepless nights with the puppy. "You're the animal expert. I'm willing to try it, but only for a few days. This will not be a permanent situation, Jazz. Do you understand?"

"Yes'm." Confusion crosses her face. "Where will you sleep, Jack?"

"In one of the other bedrooms for now. Until Stella and I get married. Then she and I will sleep together in the bedroom next to you."

"Why don't you get married today?" Jazz suggests.

Wouldn't that be nice? I look up at Jack. I cannot wait to be his wife and to chart our future together. "I'm sorry, kiddo. Weddings take months to plan. But it'll happen soon enough."

"Aw," Jazz moans. "I want us to be a family."

"We already are a family," Jack says. "In every way that counts. We love each other like family, and we're living together like one." He kisses us both on the forehead before taking the bags of trash out to the garage.

Once he's gone, Jazz asks, "Stella, will you have a baby when you get married?"

"I hope so. Would you like to have a little brother or sister?"

Jazz furrows her brow. "But the baby won't really be my brother or sister, will it?"

"Technically, the baby will be your niece or nephew." I reposition myself on the sofa so I can see her better. "But Jack and I have been talking, and we'd like to legally adopt you. You'll always be my half sister, but I'd like to raise you as my child. If that's okay with you."

She nods. "I'd like that. A lot. But what will I call you?"

"Whatever you want to call me."

"I think I'll keep calling you Stella for now."

I smile. "Stella is fine with me."

I pull Jazz and the sleeping puppy close. I shut my eyes, and the next thing I know it's three o'clock, and Jack is gently shaking me. "Time to get up. We have to get ready for your family dinner."

I rub my eyes with balled fists. "Seriously? Why are we meeting Opal and Brian so early?"

"It's Christmas. They want to see you."

I nestle deeper beneath the blanket. "Why don't they come here first? We can exchange gifts and have a drink before going over to the inn."

"I'll text them." Jack disappears into the kitchen. I've fallen back asleep when he returns ten minutes later with a coffee for me.

"Brian and Opal are already at the inn, sitting by the fire in the lounge. They'll come see the house after dinner."

"All right." Throwing back the blanket, I lift Jazz onto my lap and swing my legs over the sofa. "I need to check on my guests, anyway."

With the threat of a snowstorm, I had the foresight to pack a bag for Jazz and me with enough clothes to get us through the weekend. On Monday, I'll begin moving our things over from the cottage. Flutters of excitement bounce around in my belly at the thought of living in the manor house. My dream has finally become a reality. Once I marry Jack, sooner rather than later I hope, I'll have everything I've ever wanted. It all seems too good to be true. I say a silent prayer, thanking God for my many blessings and promising to be my best self for all the people I care about, including my many guests.

At Jazz's insistence, Jack and I reluctantly agree to allow Puppy to accompany us to the inn. We pack a canvas tote with kibble, treats, and toys, and place the puppy in her travel crate for the short trip. Jack has a hard time seeing the road through the thick snow. Even the wipers set at full speed help little. When we reach the portico, Jack has a word with the valet attendant while I help Jazz get Puppy out of the crate.

"I know you want to show your puppy off to Opal and Brian," I say. "And it's okay if she comes inside with us now, but she'll stay in her crate at the cottage while we're at dinner. Understood?"

"Aww," Jazz says and stomps her foot.

"Jasmine. Don't you dare give me a hard time. You've had a wonderful Christmas."

Jazz buries her face in the puppy's fur. "I'm sorry, Stella."

Jack opens the front door, and Jazz and I step inside. The small crowd gathered in the entryway yells *surprise* in chorus. I'm startled and confused, and I take a minute to comprehend that all these people are my family members and friends. Opal and Brian. Presley and Cecily. Emma and Rita. And what's the surprise? It's not my birthday. Or Jazz's or Jack's.

Presley and Cecily move out of the way, and my mothers step forward. Behind them, I see the tops of Colton's and Marcos's heads.

My hand flies to my mouth. "What're you doing here?" I look up at Jack, who is now holding Jazz and the puppy. "What's going on?"

"Your friends and family have planned a surprise wedding for us. We're getting married today."

My thoughts become jumbled. "But how is that possible? I don't even have a dress."

"Yes, you do," Hannah says. "We bought you the dress you fell in love with in Richmond."

"What about a marriage license? Don't you need a blood test?"

"Not in Virginia," Brian says. "Only a valid photo ID is required. The clerk of court is a friend. He's doing me a favor in exchange for dinner on the house in Jameson's. He should be here any minute." Brian flashes his phone. "I was just getting ready to call him, to make certain he's not stuck in the snow."

"And what about a minister?"

"Reverend Malone is waiting in your office," Brian says.

Flutters of excitement bounce around in my tummy. "Sounds like you've thought of everything."

"Please, tell me you're okay with this," Jack says in a low voice intended only for me.

"I'm more than okay with this. I'm ecstatic." And I am. I'm blissfully happy about the prospect of becoming Jack's wife today.

Jazz's chin quivers. "I don't understand, Stella. What's happening?"

"Remember earlier, when you asked why we don't get married today?"

Jazz bobs her head.

"Well . . . we're getting married today!"

Her grin spreads from cheek to cheek. "Yay!"

I turn my attention back to the group. "I don't know what to say. I'm flattered you would go to such trouble for me. I'm overjoyed to be marrying Jack today. And thrilled to have you all here with us to celebrate."

I move toward my mothers, hugging them both at once. "I've missed you both so much. I hope you can stay awhile."

"Colton and Marcos are leaving on Sunday, but we're here until Tuesday."

"Perfect. We can have a nice long visit."

Colton engulfs me in a hug. "Marcos and I booked our

flights immediately when we found out about the surprise wedding.

"You always were an unconventional one, Stella Boor," Marcos says.

I say to Marcos under my breath, "This is one time when I would have preferred a little convention."

Hannah hooks an arm around me. "We've transformed your cottage into a beauty salon. Marnie's flat iron is heating up as we speak. Whenever you're finished up here, come on down, and we'll help you get ready."

The group disperses at once. Opal leaves with Marnie and Hannah for the cottage. Brian walks down the hall to call the clerk of court. Colton and Marcos head off toward the bar. Jack sets Jazz down, and they go over to look at the tree. Poor Jazz. In all the excitement, no one is paying attention to Puppy.

"I can't believe you all did this for me," I say to the remaining three—Presley, Emma, and Everett.

"It was mostly Presley," Emma says.

Presley shakes her head. "Not true. It was a group effort. There is one thing we couldn't decide for you. Who do you want to give you away?"

I've often wondered about this myself. I could never choose one of my mothers over the other. In the small chapel, having three of us walk down the narrow aisle would be awkward. "Since the ceremony is in the barn, and there's not really an aisle, I'll have Hannah and Marnie stand near me on the dance floor and give me away."

"That works," Presley says.

"Guess what, Stella? Presley and Everett got engaged last night." Grabbing Presley's hand, Emma lifts it up for me to see her engagement ring.

"That's gorgeous. I love sapphires. I'm so excited for you both."

"They're getting married as soon as possible so they can be together. Isn't that so romantic?" Emma bounces from one foot to the next. "Wait until you see the barn, Stella. We've transformed it into a winter wonderland. The theme was Presley's idea. It's her dream wedding."

Presley shoots Emma a death glare. "Shush, Emma, please. Stella doesn't want to hear about this right now. Today is her day."

"Today is our day, Presley. You did all the work." The idea comes to me out of the blue, but it makes perfect sense. "If only you had a dress, we could have a double wedding."

Everett places his hand on Presley's back. "She has a dress. A debutante dress that carries special memories of her mother."

I turn to her, taking hold of her forearms. "Seriously, Presley. Let's do it. Let's have a double wedding."

Presley vehemently shakes her head. "No way! This is your surprise, Stella."

"A surprise I'd be more than happy to share with you. Please say yes!"

Everett leans in close to Presley. "In the car earlier, when I asked if you'd marry me today given the chance, you said you would. Will you?"

"I thought you were speaking figuratively." Presley's lips form an O. "Wait a minute? You set me up." Her eyes travel from Everett to Emma and back. "I smell rats, Stella. These two have manipulated us into considering a double wedding."

"Because it's a brilliant idea." I let go of Presley's arms. "All I really care about is being married to Jack. And I'll be forever grateful to you for making that happen for me. You just got engaged last night. This may be too soon for you. But if Everett wants this, and you want this, I say we go for it."

Presley shifts her gaze slightly to the right of me. "What

about Jack? I'm not sure he'll want to share his wedding with us."

"I'll go talk to him. While I do, I'm sure Jazz would love to show you her puppy."

We move as a foursome across the entryway to them. Jazz's face lights up when Everett, Emma, and Presley ask to see her puppy.

I pull Jack aside. "How do you feel about sharing our wedding with Everett and Presley?" I explain about their engagement and interest in getting married quickly.

Jack hunches his shoulders. "Fine by me. Presley came up with the idea, and she worked so hard to make the surprise happen. Why not give her something in return?"

"I feel the same way. But isn't this all a little . . . crazy?"

Jack takes me in his arms. "My life has been nothing but crazy since I met you. And I wouldn't have it any other way. This day has been one for the record books. A surprise wedding. A raging blizzard. Jazz got a house and a puppy for Christmas. By the way, the puppy's new name is Angel."

I look up at the angel on top of the tree. Jazz believes her mommy is now an angel. The day we spread Naomi's ashes at the overlook, I told Jazz that an angel's job is to spread God's love. The little animal is certainly spreading a lot of love. "I think Angel is lovely. Let's make sure this name sticks."

28

CECILY

C ecily slips unnoticed away from the group. No one will miss her. She has no role in the wedding. When she tried to check on things in the kitchen, Alessandro kicked her out. She wanted to be here, to see Stella's face when they announced the surprise. In all the confusion, she doubts Stella even noticed she was there. She should've stayed at home until the ceremony. She could've used the time to pack in preparation for her move. Lyle is playing basketball with friends and won't arrive for at least another hour. She might as well get a drink from Billy's Bar. She could use some hair of the dog after all the tequila she drank last night.

Cecily takes a seat on a stool at the bar and orders a glass of champagne from Kristi. She's taking her first sip when Colton and Marcos sit down on either side of her.

"Taking the night off from the kitchen?" Colton asks.

"Not willingly. Alessandro won't let me in the kitchen. He's too busy trying to impress you."

"Alessandro." Colton shakes his head and snickers. "He could ruin every item on the menu tonight, and I will still hire him. I wanted him when he interviewed with me weeks ago, but

ASHLEY FARLEY

my kitchen was full. I like his style. And his Italian heritage intrigues me. I'm sorry to say, you may be looking for his replacement come Monday."

"Who am I to stand in the way of Alessandro's dreams? I will miss him, though. He has been a valuable asset during his brief time here. He has enormous potential and a strong work ethic. He will not disappoint you."

"I sensed that about him," Colton says. "But I'm glad to have you confirm it."

Kristi places flutes of champagne in front of Colton and Marcos, and the threesome toasts the bride- and groom-to-be.

"I hope you'll give me the honor of cooking for you tomorrow night," Cecily says.

"How about if we cook together," Colton suggests. "Like you, I have a difficult time being away from the kitchen for too long. Do you have any VIPs you need to impress?"

"Let me think about it. We're booked solid for reservations, but we keep the community table open for first come, first served. I'll reserve it and talk to Stella. She may want to invite her family and a few friends for a post-wedding dinner."

"You're making quite a name for yourself down here, Cecily. A lot of eyes are watching you. If you decide you want to get out of this small town and spread your wings, the world is your oyster."

"That means a lot coming from you, Colton. But Stella and I are just getting started. I fully expect the wellness center to put us on the map. And then the world will come to me, and I can stay right here in this charming little town."

"I love a gal who knows what she wants."

And Cecily knows exactly what she wants. She wouldn't trade her life in Hope Springs for a career at an illustrious establishment in New York or Charleston or New Orleans. She can have everything she wants right here. If she plays her cards right, she'll make enough money to hire a team of nannies to help with her children. So what if Lyle never grows up? She hopes he never changes. He has many redeeming qualities, and she loves him just the way he is.

As for not being included in Stella's wedding plans . . . Presley was doing Cecily a favor by keeping her in the dark about the surprise. She didn't want Cecily to think her wedding any less important than Stella's.

But Cecily is Stella's best friend, and she wants to be a part of her big day. She drains the rest of her champagne. "Excuse me, gentlemen. I need to attend to the bride."

Exiting the main building, Cecily hurries through the snow across the terrace to the cottage where she finds a flurry of activity. While Opal steams the wedding gown in the kitchen, Hannah and Marnie give Stella and Jazz makeovers in the bedroom. Presley, seemingly oblivious to the activity around her, sits alone on the sofa in the living room wearing a red knit dress and a wide-eyed expression.

Cecily plops down beside her. "What's up? You look like a deer in the headlights."

Presley's eyes remain fixed on an unidentified object on the bookshelf. "Emma and Everett have coerced me into having a double wedding with Stella."

Cecily grasps her arm. "Back up a second. When did you and Everett get engaged?"

Presley shows Cecily her engagement ring. "Last night."

Cecily gawks. "And you're getting married today? That's the shortest engagement in history."

Presley looks at Cecily for the first time. "Except for those people who get married on a whim in Las Vegas. But I know what you mean. My mother always taught me to be methodical when it comes to making decisions, to weigh the pros and cons of all my options. I've made exactly two impulsive decisions in my life, both of them after Mom died. One in coming to Virginia. And the other taking the job here at the inn. Those choices led me to Everett."

"I'm not judging you, Presley. I'm the poster child for impulsive decisions. But how does Stella feel about sharing her wedding?"

Presley shrugs. "It was her idea, and she seems fine with it. I wouldn't consider this crazy scheme otherwise. I'm disappointed Everett's mom isn't here, but he's already called her, and she's thrilled for us."

"Something's holding you back. Otherwise you wouldn't be sitting here, looking like you lost your best friend. Take it from someone who called off her wedding at the last minute. If that little voice inside of you is telling you you're not ready to be married, you should listen to it."

Presley shifts on the couch to face Cecily. "That's the thing, though. That voice is telling me I *am* ready. And I trust my intuitions. I have this ability to sense certain things about people. I call it my people reader. It rarely fails me. Even when Everett and I first started seeing each other, and he was keeping secrets about his past, I had a gut feeling that he was a genuine soul, tormented by the choices he'd made. And I was right. We are meant to be together. I feel it in my core like I've never felt anything before." When she exhales a deep breath, her body slumps against the back of the sofa. "On the other hand, as you pointed out, we've been engaged less than twenty-four hours."

"So . . . let me get this straight. You're saying you're worried because you're not worried?"

Presley nods. "Pretty much. Yep."

Cecily jumps to her feet. "Then stop worrying and marry the man. Everett is a great guy, and he obviously adores you." She pulls Presley off the sofa. "Now. Do you have a dress? You could borrow mine."

"I'm going to wear my debutante dress." She gestures at a black garment bag draped over a nearby chair.

"Show me."

Presley unzips the garment bag to reveal a satin off-shoulder dress. Cecily lifts the dress out of the garment bag. "It's pretty. But simple. It makes a lovely wedding dress and a veil would complement it beautifully. I'd love to lend you mine. But I want it back."

"Would you mind? Everett brought your veil over by accident. He thought it was Stella's. It's in the bedroom."

"Awesome! But we need to style your hair. The veil is designed for an updo."

With wedding dress draped over arm, Cecily follows Presley into Stella's bedroom. Jazz is twirling around in front of the full-length mirror while the puppy nips at the hem of her ivory tea-length frock.

"Wow! You look amazing, kiddo," Cecily says to Jazz. "I love your dress."

Jazz spins around again. "Thanks! Opal picked it out for me."

"Does your puppy have a name?"

Jazz scoops up the dog. "Angel. Santa brought her to me."

"Santa went overboard this year." Cecily gives the puppy's head a rub. "Angel is adorable."

Cecily turns her attention to Stella who is seated in a chair on the other side of the bed near the bathroom. Marnie is brushing her curls while Hannah applies makeup. Cecily presses her lips together to keep from laughing. Stella hates being fussed over. She's tolerating being pampered only for the sake of her parents.

Stella smiles at Cecily. "I'm glad you're here. I was just getting ready to text you."

"Were you surprised?" Cecily asks.

When Stella nods, Marnie yanks her hair. "Hold still."

Stella slaps the brush away. "Seriously, Marnie. What're you trying to do? I don't have enough hair to put it up."

"Wait! I almost forgot." Presley leaves the room and returns with her tote. "Ginger, at the bridal salon, thought this would be perfect with your dress," she says, presenting Stella with a rhinestone embellished headband.

"Ooh. I love it." Stella takes the headband and hands it to Marnie. "Be gentle, please."

Marnie grunts. "Since when are you so tender-headed?"

Stella ignores her. "So, Cecily, I was wondering if you would be my maid of honor. I understand if it's too soon after calling off your wedding."

"Not at all. Lyle and I made the right decision to live together for now. We couldn't be happier. And I'd love to be your maid of honor, except . . ."—Cecily stares down at her silver metallic ruched-fitted dress—"this dress shows too much cleavage for a bridesmaid."

"I was thinking you could wear the bridesmaid dress I bought for your wedding. The one you picked out. It should fit. You and I are about the same size." Stella gestures at the closet. "Get it out and let's see."

Cecily removes the gray velvet dress from the closet. "Seriously? This is so blah."

Presley and Stella look at each other and laugh. "We tried to tell you the green was a prettier color," Presley says.

Cecily shakes her head. "I really haven't been myself lately." She takes the dress into the bathroom and emerges five minutes later. "At least it fits."

Stella cranes her neck to see Cecily. "It looks much better on you."

Hannah powders Stella's nose one last time, and Marnie gives her hair a final shot of spray.

"Can I get up now?" Stella stands without waiting for

permission. "Your turn, Presley." She gestures at the chair. "Marnie is a whiz at updos."

Cecily sits down on the bed to watch Marnie style Presley's hair. "Did y'all know Presley has a special ability to read people? She calls it her people reader."

Presley sticks up her nose at Cecily. "Go ahead. Make fun of me."

"I'm not making fun of you," Cecily says. "I'm curious what your people reader told you about me when we first met."

Presley doesn't hesitate. "You often let your drive to succeed cloud your judgment. When you want something, you go after it, no matter the cost."

"Like when I decided to get married at Christmas and turned into a bridezilla." Cecily's eyes are on Presley. "I've been a real pill lately, and you've taken the brunt of it. I owe you an apology. I hope you can forgive me."

"Of course I forgive you." Presley grimaces when Marnie jabs her with a bobby pin. "Your determination is one of your best attributes. You're a true friend at heart, and that's what's important."

"What about me?" Stella holds out her hand, palm up. "Read my fortune."

"I don't read palms," Presley says. "Everything I sensed about you the first time we met turned out to be true. You always put other people first, hence your willingness to share your wedding with me. You always give others a chance, regardless of whether they deserve it. And you're a total badass."

"What about me?" Jazz asks, climbing onto the bed beside Cecily.

Presley smiles at Jazz. "I don't need special powers to know you're the sweetest, most talented little ballerina ever."

"Who's gonna be your flower girl, Presley?"

Presley shrugs. "I guess I won't have one. A maid of honor either for that matter."

"I'll be your flower girl," Jazz offers, and Cecily adds, "And I'd be honored to be your bridesmaid, if you'll have me."

Presley locks eyes with Stella. "Do you mind sharing your attendants? You're already sharing so much."

Stella smiles. "This is *our* wedding. It's only fitting for us to share attendants."

Emma appears in the bedroom doorway, a dusting of snow in her hair, two bottles of champagne in her hands, and the professional photographer in tow. "Brides! Let's get dressed. Thirty minutes until showtime."

When Cecily notices the puppy sniffing around near the corner, she scoops her up. "Jazz, I think Angel needs to go potty."

"Okay." Jazz takes the puppy from Cecily. "Will you go with me?"

"Sure!" Cecily grabs their coats and follows Jazz outside to the front porch.

Jazz sets Angel down on the porch, and even though the snow has lightened considerably, the puppy balks at the white landscape and scampers behind the child's legs. Cecily and Jazz dance about on the porch, leaping from one foot to the other, blowing warm breath into cold hands, until Angel finally relieves herself on the wooden floor.

Back inside, Stella is dressed and waiting for Cecily in the living room with two flutes of champagne. Cecily takes one of the flutes and holds it out to Stella. "To you, Jack, and Jazz. May all your days be merry and bright."

"What a lovely thing to say, Cecily. Thank you." Instead of clinking her glass, Stella gives her a hug.

They ignore the photographer who circles them, snapping photographs from every angle.

Pulling away, Stella runs her finger under both eyes. "No more toasts. Hannah will kill me if I mess up my makeup."

"I can't believe Presley pulled this off," Cecily says, and takes a sip of champagne.

"Right? She's amazing. She got the idea after our shopping trip to Richmond."

Cecily points at her gown. "After she saw you in that dress. You're stunning, Stella. Jack's teeth are gonna fall out when he sees you."

Stella laughs out loud. "Let's hope not." She grows serious again. "Are you really okay, Cecily?"

"I'm better than okay. Lyle and I love each other. We just realized we aren't ready to get married. We had unrealistic expectations of each other. We're working on realigning those expectations to see if we can make our relationship work."

Stella clinks her glass. "I have no doubt but what you will."

Cecily has no doubts either. But she's glad she's bought herself more time. She wants to be settled when she marries Lyle, not scurrying around looking for somewhere to live and feeling insecure about her job. And she'd like to be able to take time off for her honeymoon without feeling guilty. Whenever that day comes, she'll glide down the aisle, looking every bit as relaxed and beautiful as Presley and Stella do today, when she meets her man at the altar.

29

PRESLEY

B y six thirty, the worst of the snowstorm has come and gone. Brides, grooms, and their attendants pile into the horse-drawn sleigh for the short ride. Guests ring bells as the wedding party enters the barn in single file with Jazz leading the procession to the dance floor. Everett and Presley stand off to the side while Stella and Jack approach a robe-clad Reverend Malone.

Malone raises her hand to silence the crowd. "Welcome family and friends to this most unusual of weddings."

The crowd chuckles.

Jazz stands between Stella and Jack, staring up at them as they exchange their nuptials. When Malone pronounces them husband and wife, Mr. and Mrs. Jack Snyder, Jack hooks an arm around her waist and dips Stella slightly backward when he kisses her. The guests cheer and ring bells.

Jack scoops Jazz into his arms, and the new family moves out of the way so Everett and Presley can have their turn.

If she'd planned her wedding from scratch, Presley would inevitably have purchased a new dress. But she's glad she didn't. Memories of her mother are at the forefront of her mind as she stands in front of the minister. She can almost feel Renee's arms around her, supporting her as she begins the next chapter of her life.

Katherine somehow managed to find the flowers to duplicate Stella's bouquet for Presley, which Presley hands off to Cecily when she turns to face Everett. He looks amazing in a dark gray suit she's never seen him wear, didn't even know he owned. There's much they don't know about each other. But they know the important stuff. Their love is deep. Their commitment to being together forever is solid.

Everett leans down and whispers, "Have you been drinking?"

Presley blushes. "Just a teensy bit. I'm just so happy, Everett."

"I promise to make you even happier when you're my wife." When he moves to kiss her, the minister clears her throat.

"Kissing comes after." Reverend Malone smiles, and Presley giggles.

The ceremony is brief. Everett and Presley say their vows. Reverend Malone pronounces them Mr. and Mrs. Everett Baldwin, and when she gives him permission to kiss his bride, Everett plants one on Presley's lips that elicits more cheers and bell ringing from the guests.

With no fathers in attendance, Stella and Presley agree to forego the traditional round of dancing. Instead, Stella and Jack, when the lights dim, take to the dance floor first. Through the band's speakers comes Billy Jameson's rich voice as he sings Stella's favorite of his songs, "You and Me, Always and Forever." According to Stella, her father wrote this song for her mother. And the tears streaming down Hannah's face are confirmation.

Everett and Presley are up next. Presley chooses Louis Armstrong to serenade them for their first official dance as man and wife. She has vague memories of dancing on her father's feet to "What a Wonderful World" in their living room on

Christmas Eve with the lights from the tree twinkling in the background.

Presley relaxes in Everett's arms. This is where she's meant to spend the rest of her life. "I don't want this night to end," she says.

"Who says it has to end?" Everett's breath is warm near her ear. "I've booked us a room. Actually, Stella insisted on comping us a room."

"Great! So we can make the walk of shame home tomorrow in our wedding attire?"

"I'm one step ahead of you. I packed a bag for us when I went to your apartment for the wedding dresses. I made sure to throw in that black negligee I found in your drawer."

She smacks his chest. "That's it! No more snooping around in my things." He laughs and she adds, "I'm serious, Everett. I don't like that."

"I know, babe. And I promise I won't do it again. I just thought you might like something naughty to spice up our wedding night."

She rests her head on his shoulder. "I should be angry at you and Emma for scheming this whole thing up."

"But you're not. We both got what we wanted. We're married. We can move on with our lives together." He hugs her close. "Did I tell you how amazing you look?"

"Mm-hmm. But tell me again."

And he does, over and over while they dance.

The crowd goes wild for the bluegrass band, and they are soon surrounded on the dance floor where they remain through the first set. Everett heads off to the bar for liquid refreshments while Presley meanders over to the banquet table. Alessandro has hit it out of the park, and she loads up her plate with a variety of delectables, each created to perfection with his unique flair.

Presley looks up from grazing a charcuterie board to find Chris hovering nearby. She's momentarily thrown off guard. His name was definitely not on the invitation list. "Hey there. Are you enjoying the wedding?"

He hunches his bony shoulders. "Not really. I wasn't invited, and I don't know anyone here. Mom wouldn't let me stay at home alone in the storm."

"Well, I'm glad you came," Presley says.

Chris steps closer to her. "That day, after you left our house, I asked my mom if we were related. Even though I'm a boy and you're a girl, you can't deny that we look alike. Mom ignored my question, which I take to mean *yes*."

An awkward silence falls over them as they study each other. While Chris is still a boy, he will soon be a young man. And he's right, the resemblance is undeniable.

Presley is the first to break the silence. "Where *is* your mom?" She's seen Lucy from a distance, but Lucy hasn't tried to approach her. Not to even offer her congratulations.

Chris's eyes travel to the dance floor where Lucy and Brian are dancing a slow song.

"I take it they made up," Presley says.

"I guess." Chris sounds like he could care less about his mom's love life. "I've been watching you all night. The way you carry yourself reminds me of my grandmother. You're way too young to be Nana's daughter. You're what? Twenty-eight, twenty-nine?"

"Thirty." Presley considers explaining the situation, but she'd rather him come to his own conclusion.

"So, you could be any of Nana's daughters' children. Probably not Aunt Anna's though, since she's gay."

This is news to Presley. Neither Rita nor Lucy speaks often of their older sister who lives out west.

"Who is your biological mother, Presley? Rita or Lucy?"

"It's not my place to tell you." Presley stares down at her feet. Or *is it* her place to tell him? He's her half brother. Genetics don't lie. Why should she deny herself the chance to know her only sibling because her biological mother is too stubborn or bitter or selfish or whatever Lucy's problem is? She looks up at Chris. "But I think you have a right to know." Setting her untouched plate on a tray stand, she guides him away from the crowd to the side of the barn.

"To answer your question, Lucy is my biological mother."

Presley sees the wheels in his mind go into motion. "You're thirty years old. And Mom's fifty. That means she was twenty when you were born. My dad dated my mom in high school and college."

"But they broke up after their freshman year. I'm your half sister, Chris."

"Then who's your father?" he asks, in a tone bordering on accusatory.

"Some random guy—" Presley stops herself. Is she really gonna lie to her brother? "This is a little . . . sensitive. But again, I think you have a right to know. I tried to get Lucy to tell you herself, but she's embarrassed by what happened, even though it was not at all her fault. Her sophomore year in college, your mom went to a fraternity formal with a guy who drugged her drink and date-raped her."

"Whoa." Chris falls back against the wall, raking his hands through his hair as this information sinks in.

Presley inhales a deep breath. She might as well tell him the whole story. "Your mom was a virgin. She didn't remember the rape and had no reason to suspect she might be pregnant until it was too late to . . . to have an abortion. Not that she would've. We haven't talked about the what-ifs. Your mom made great sacrifices to have me. And she gave me up for adoption so I could have a better life."

"I can't believe there was such a thing as date-rape back then."

"I'm not that old, Chris. Your mom worried how you might react, since you're only a few years younger than she was at the time."

He scowls. "Right. She doesn't like to talk about the birds and bees. I go to my dad with all my questions."

"Maybe one day Lucy will talk to you about her experience. Knowing the truth about what happened might make you more respectful of the girls you date."

He stares down at the floor without responding.

Presley notices Emma watching them with a concerned look from over near the bar. "I know this is a lot to process. Do you think it would help for you to talk it over with Emma?"

Looking up, Chris follows her gaze to Emma. "I'm fine. Who's that guy she's with, anyway?"

"Ryan. He's Cecily's cousin." When Chris's eyes narrow in confusion, Presley adds, "Cecily is our head chef."

"Oh. Right." Chris gives his cousin a thumbs-up before returning his attention to Presley. "My mom hasn't been very nice to you, has she?"

"She's struggling with some issues. But Rita and the girls have made up for it. I met your . . . our grandparents today. They're pretty awesome." She laughs. "Was that today? It seems like a week ago."

They stand for a few minutes, watching the crowd without saying anything. When Chris speaks again, his mood appears to have lightened. "So. Wow. Wait until I tell my friends I have this hot, thirty-year-old chick for a sister." His smile fades. "Sorry if that sounded weird. I'm an only child. I don't know the proper protocol when discussing one's sister."

"That's make two of us. I don't have any siblings either."

His eyes light up. "But we're not only children anymore, are we? We're half sister and brother. Will you buy beer for me?"

Presley cuts her eyes at him. "Not on your life."

"That's fair," Chris says with a shrug, as though it was worth a try. "I heard someone say you're moving to Nashville. Is that true?"

Presley nods. "But Everett and I will definitely be back to visit."

Chris shuffles his feet. "I'm thinking about applying to Vanderbilt. My college counselor says I have a good shot if I keep up my grades."

"Good for you, smart boy. You can stay with Everett and me when you come for a college visit. I'll show you the town."

"Yes!" He punches the air.

"I'll be in Hope Springs for at least another week, if you maybe wanna grab lunch or something."

"That'd be cool! Can Everett come? I've never met a country music star."

Presley laughs out loud. "He's not a star yet. But yes, he can come. I don't have my phone with me. How about if I give you my number and you text me?"

Removing his phone from the pocket of his blue blazer, he taps in her number as she recites it.

When Amelia summons her for cake cutting, Presley waves, signaling she'll be there in a minute. "I hope you'll stick around for a while. Everett is going to sing." She brings her finger to her lips. "But don't tell anyone. It's supposed to be a surprise."

"No way! That's awesome. Maybe I'll get to dance with the bride."

"Which one?" Presley says, and they both laugh.

Presley starts off and then turns back around. "I'll look for you later to dance. And by the way, I think you're pretty hot too."

The guests go wild when Everett opens with the song he wrote about Presley. He follows with the one he wrote about himself at a particularly vulnerable stage of his life. Even after all these years, Everett's emotions are raw as he sings "Show Me the Way." The crowd loves him, and every time one song ends, they beg him for more.

Presley stands near the front of the small stage. When she feels a hand on her bare shoulder, Presley cranes her neck to see Lucy standing behind her.

"Can we talk?" Lucy asks, and while Presley resents the intrusion, she allows Lucy to lead her to a quiet corner across the barn.

"The wedding was sudden," Lucy says in a tone of disapproval or suspicion—Presley is not sure which.

"I'm not pregnant, if that's what you're wondering."

"The thought never crossed my mind."

Of course the thought crossed Lucy's mind. The thought crossed the minds of every single guest in attendance tonight. Having spent the past two months vying for Lucy's attention, Presley suddenly doesn't care if she never sees her again.

"When did you get engaged?"

Presley doesn't show her the ring. "Everett asked me last night. What can I say? I'm trying to be more spontaneous."

Lucy's fingers graze the fabric of Presley's sleeve. "Your dress is nice. Did you have to borrow it from someone?"

Presley steps backward, away from Lucy's touch. "This is my debutante dress. My mother presented me when I made my debut. The dress reminds me of her. Wearing it is the next best thing to having her here with me." She's being intentionally cruel by bringing up her adoptive mother, but Lucy doesn't even flinch. She didn't suddenly have a change of heart about Presley. She wants something.

"What did you say to my son?"

Right. Just as Presley suspected. "I told him the truth. About everything. And he was okay with it, as I knew he'd be."

The muscles in Lucy's face tighten, as though she's struggling to maintain her composure. "I assume you'll be leaving town now."

Anger pulses through Presley's body. "Yep. After New Year's. Your dirty little secret is going back into hiding."

Lucy's eyes dart around the barn. Is she looking for an escape? Or for Brian to save her? "I promised Brian I would try to make my relationship with you work. But I can't do it. Not if you're going to be so hostile."

"I'm being hostile?" Presley says, her voice now raised. "What do you think you've been to me these past weeks?"

"I was confused about a lot of things. Mostly what happened back in college."

"So you confessed to Brian and suddenly everything is fine? I stand by my original assessment—you need psychiatric help."

Presley spins away from Lucy. As she crosses the dance floor, Everett steps down off the stage and walks toward her. Presley's racing heart slows and a sense of calm overcomes her. One door is closing, but another is opening. Everett is her future. Presley is finally ready to accept that Lucy was never meant to be a part of her life.

30

THE DAY AFTER

The day after Christmas, Cecily and Lyle stay in bed until almost noon, dozing and making love. Lyle makes breakfast in bed for Cecily—rubbery eggs and soggy bacon. Grateful for the pampering, she doesn't complain about his mediocre cooking. He sips coffee while he watches her eat. "We need more mornings like this. What's gotten into you today?"

"I'm using the snowstorm as an excuse to play hooky from work." She doesn't admit it to Lyle, but she can relax knowing Alessandro isn't plotting to steal her job. She sets the tray aside and sinks deeper beneath the covers, pulling him with her. "But I agree. More mornings like this are definitely in our future."

The snowplows work overtime and the roads are cleared when she heads off to work around two o'clock. As she drives to the inn, the words to "It's a Wonderful Life" are on her lips and the courses for the night's dinner with Colton on her mind. When she arrives, the station chefs are busy preparing food for the late lunch crowd. Ten minutes later, Colton and Alessandro file into the kitchen through the back door.

"Colton offered me the job," Alessandro announces, his grin wide and arms spread in a Victory V above his head.

"Congratulations," Cecily says, giving Alessandro a high five. "Please tell me you're not leaving until after New Year's."

"Nope. I told Colton I couldn't start until mid-January. That should give you plenty of time to find my replacement."

Cecily is acutely aware of the eager faces of her station chefs watching her. "We'll probably promote from within. But it's nice to have the additional time, anyway."

Colton smacks Alessandro on the back. "Have you forgotten, old buddy? We had a deal. I give you a job, you fix me—"

"My famous hangover cure. I'm on it." Alessandro shrugs off his parka and hangs it on a peg beside the back door. "Cecily? Would you like one?"

"Sure! I could use an infusion of nutrients."

"I'll be right back," Alessandro says and disappears through the swinging doors to the dining room.

Cecily and Colton move to the corner of the kitchen, out of the way of the staff. "Are you still up for a cook-a-thon?"

"Bring it on," he says in a deep voice.

"I've been texting with Stella this morning. She's inviting her family and a few close friends to dinner. As of now, we have fifteen, including you and me and our significant others."

"Excellent. Your resident fishing guide brought in some gorgeous mountain trout earlier. I confess I've been perusing your impressive collection of cookbooks. I'm itching to try out one of the recipes I found." Colton goes to her office and returns with a worn leather journal of handwritten recipes. "I dined here once, when I was a boy in my early teens. Hugo Perez was the resident head chef at the time. He made a great impact on my life. He's the reason I pursued a culinary career."

Cecily's jaw goes slack. "You're kidding me? What a small world. Does Stella know this?"

"She does now," Colton says. "When Hannah told me Stella

was down in Virginia managing a historic inn, we put two and two together."

"Some of Hugo's recipes are quite complicated," Cecily says. "I've been brave enough to try only a few. What do you think about designing our entire menu from his journal?"

Colton runs his hand lovingly across the leather cover. "I would consider it an honor."

"And I consider it an honor to learn from you."

Alessandro enters the kitchen with three tall Bloody Marys.

Cecily eyes the drinks suspiciously. "This is your famous hangover cure? A Bloody Mary?"

Alessandro hands each of them a drink. "My Bloodies are special. I have a secret ingredient."

Cecily and Colton take simultaneous sips, their eyes growing wide at the same time.

"That's amazing," Colton says.

"What's the secret ingredient?" Cecily asks.

Alessandro purses his mouth in a smirk. "Wouldn't you like to know?" He bumps her shoulder. "Maybe, if you're super nice to me for the next few weeks, I'll tell you before I leave."

She returns the shoulder-bump. "Or, maybe, I can figure it out on my own if I drink more than one. Mix us up a pitcher. We have a lot of work to do to get ready for this dinner tonight."

Colton and Cecily cook and sip their way through the afternoon and early evening. They follow Hugo's recipes to the letter, and every dish turns out perfectly.

They are awaiting the arrival of their guests a few minutes before eight when Colton asks Cecily, "How would you like to appear on my television show? I'll have to check the schedule, but I'm hoping we can fit it in while Alessandro is still here."

Cecily manages to appear calm despite her heart racing in her chest. "How would that work? Would I have to travel to New York?"

"Actually, I was thinking of bringing a crew down here. We would cook side-by-side like we did today, minus the Bloody Marys. We would highlight Jameson's and bring Stella in to talk about the history of the inn."

Cecily beams. "What an amazing offer, Colton. Thank you. On behalf of Jameson's, I accept. I know Stella will be thrilled."

"We'll work on the menu together, but it might be fun to feature Chef Hugo."

Cecily taps her chin. "Or maybe I can adapt a few of his traditional dishes to something with a more contemporary flair."

Colton gives her the nod. "Even better."

Cecily's phone dings in her pocket with a call from Lyle. "Excuse me a minute," she says and takes the call in her office.

"Hey babe," Lyle says when she answers. "Do you mind if I skip the dinner tonight? I'm working on a surprise for you."

She drums her fingers on the desk, trying not to let her irritation show. "You'll have to tell me the surprise before I'll let you off the hook."

"You drive a hard bargain, Cecily Weber."

Her lips pressed in a thin line, she says, "Damn right, I do. What's the surprise?"

"I'm moving your furniture into the new house. A couple of my buddies are helping me. We're on a roll. If all goes as planned, we can spend our first night together in our new home."

Warmth spreads throughout her body. This is the Lyle she fell in love with. "That's awesome, babe. You're the best."

"Damn right, I am," he says, and she imagines him smiling his goofy smile through the phone.

"I'll help you move your kitchen stuff and clothes over whenever you're ready next week."

"Thank you," she says. "I love you."

"And I love you. Bring me home some leftovers."

Presley leaves Stella and Amelia in Stella's office to discuss the terms of Amelia's employment. She feels ten pounds lighter as she crosses through reception into the lounge. Not only did Amelia accept the job offer, she also agreed to take over the lease on Presley's apartment. If all goes well, Presley can return to Nashville with Everett at the beginning of the year.

As she passes by Billy's, she sees that Everett is busy behind the bar. She sits down on one of the love seats near the entrance to Jameson's to wait. She's thumbing through the December issue of *Virginia Living* magazine a minute later when Katherine drops down next to her on the love seat.

"I need to sit a minute while Dean is in the restroom," she says, her complexion pale and a bead of perspiration on her brow.

Presley closes the magazine. "Are you still not feeling any better?"

"It comes and goes. A wave of nausea hit me just now." Katherine studies Presley closely. "The wedding was lovely, Presley. I can see how happy you are. You're wearing the glow of a well-loved woman."

"I never knew I could be so happy in love." If only she could be happy in other areas of her life. While she's thrilled to have bonded with her half brother, she feels guilty about the things she said to Lucy last night. Even if those words needed to be said.

Dean emerges from the restroom, and Katherine gets to her feet. She gestures at the dining room. "Is it okay to go on in?"

"Please. Make yourselves at home. I'm just waiting for Everett. We're at the community table. We had mostly early reservations tonight. Hopefully, the guests will clear out shortly, and we'll have Jameson's to ourselves."

Dean gingerly takes hold of his wife's arm, as though she's a fragile object that might easily break, and ushers her into the dining room. How exciting for them to be planning for the birth of their first child. Presley and Everett are nowhere near ready for children, but she suspects when the time comes, Everett will be every bit as patient and doting as Dean.

Before Presley can sit back down, Brian and Opal arrive with Hannah and Marnie. Brian gives her a half hug. "I want to thank you again for last night. Stella was thrilled, and I'm glad things worked out for you and Everett as well." Brian's voice is flat, and his smile doesn't meet his eyes. And why isn't Lucy with him?

"Thank you, Brian. It was a special evening."

"My dear." Opal takes Presley's hands in hers. "I owe you a debt of gratitude. My daughter and I have not been on good terms in some time. But your surprise wedding was the ice breaker we needed to get back on track." She drops Presley's hands and latches onto Hannah's arm, as though afraid of losing her. "Because of you, our family is on the mend."

Presley's face warms. "You give me too much credit, Opal. I came up with the idea. But we were all instrumental in pulling it off." She hugs Opal, Hannah, and Marnie in turn. "I'm so happy for you all."

"Where's Stella?" Brian asks, his eyes scanning the lobby.

"She's finishing up with Amelia. She'll be right down. Please, go ahead in and get a drink," Presley says, motioning them to the community table.

They've no sooner entered Jameson's when Rita, Emma, and Chris appear with somber faces. Now Presley knows something is wrong. There's no reason Stella would've invited Chris to her family dinner. The dial on her people reader is spinning out of control. "Where's Lucy?" she asks and braces herself for the answer.

"She's . . ." Emma looks to her mother for permission to continue.

The hairs on the back of Presley's neck stand to attention. Emma never waits for her mother's permission for anything.

Rita nods for her to continue.

"She checked herself into rehab this morning," Emma blurts.

"What?" Presley stumbles backward, and Chris grabs her, preventing her from crashing into the lamp table beside the sofa.

"It's not as bad as Emma makes it sound," he says.

"Let's sit down." Rita lowers herself to the love seat, pulling Presley down with her. Chris and Emma drag chairs up close to them. "Lucy had a meltdown when she got home from the wedding last night. She scared poor Brian half to death. He may never be the same again."

Presley's eyes meet her half brother's. "I'm so sorry. This is all my fault. I never should've told you about me."

He shakes his head. "I disagree. I have a right to know. Anyway, I started it by asking how we are related."

Rita says, "No one's at fault here except Lucy. She should've told Chris the truth a long time ago."

"But I point-blank told her she needed psychiatric help," Presley says, her tone raised and panicked.

"Because she does." Rita strokes Presley's thigh. "I've told my sister that many times myself. She's been mentally unstable and depressed for years. But now we know why. We found out last night that she's addicted to prescription pain killers. In hindsight, I think maybe she began using them when she had cancer. None of us ever suspected a thing."

Chris hangs his head. "I did. I've seen her take the pills before. But I had no idea she was abusing them. She threatened to take the whole bottle last night." His gray eyes swim with tears. "If Brian hadn't been there . . ."

Presley can only imagine the scene that took place. Poor Chris. He may never be the same either. "How's she been getting the meds?"

"She stole one of Uncle Grant's prescription pads," Emma interjects.

"Let's think positively about the situation." Rita looks at each of them in turn. "We now understand the problem. And we can make certain she gets the help she needs. I, for one, am relieved to know the pills are the source of her erratic behavior. Once she gets clean, our old Lucy will come back."

Chris's lips part in a soft smile. "I hope so."

"Does Stella know?" Presley asks.

Rita nods. "She and I talked about it for a long time earlier this afternoon."

"I understand enough about wine to cover for Lucy while she's in rehab," Presley volunteers. As the words leave her lips, Presley's heart tumbles to the floor. She's ready to move back to Nashville and begin her married life with Everett. But her heart bounces back into her chest where it belongs. These people—Rita, Emma, and Chris—are her family. And they've come to mean a lot to her. They need her. And she won't let them down. And Lucy . . . well, Lucy gave Presley life. And Lucy's been through so much. Rape. Cancer. Divorce. She deserves some happiness. And Presley is in a position to help make that happen.

Rita tucks a strand of Presley's hair behind her ear. "You're going home to Nashville with Everett. Stella's not worried. Between the two of us, we can cover the wine shop."

"We'll see," Presley says. "We don't have to make any decisions about anything tonight."

When Rita gets to her feet, the others follow her lead.

Presley wraps her arms around her half brother. "Are you okay? You're welcome to stay with me this week."

Chris stiffens, and Presley realizes he's not used to having young women hug him, even if she is his sister. "Thanks, but my dad is finally getting over the flu. Although, when the time comes, I'll take you up on that offer to show me around Nashville."

Presley musses his hair. "Deal." She turns to the others. "Y'all go on in. I'm going to wait here for Everett."

Truth be told, Presley needs a minute to herself. She moves over to the window, staring out across the landscape of lights. Her heart aches for Lucy for what she's going through. At the same time, Lucy's addiction to prescription pain killers is something tangible she can work toward overcoming. Presley closes her eyes and says a silent prayer for Lucy's full recovery. She would like to know the real Lucy, the confident woman Presley saw glimpses of when they were still friends. The woman Emma remembers fondly from Christmases past. The woman Rita claims was once so vibrant and full of life. The woman Lucy was before bitterness began eating away at her soul.

Stella taps her champagne glass with her knife to get everyone's attention. When the table grows silent, she says, "I know you all are hungry. I promise we'll get to the food in a minute."

"Where's Jazz tonight?" Cecily asks, the question on everyone's mind.

Stella smiles. "At home with a babysitter. When I left, she was cuddled up on the sofa with Angel, eating pizza straight out of the box while watching her new favorite movie, *Homeward Bound*. A week ago, I would never have left Jazz with a babysitter. A week ago, she would've refused to stay with one. It helps that said babysitter is Liz, our guest services agent from the morning shift."

Several guests chuckle.

"Jazz feels safe now. That's in part because of you. Because of your kindness toward her. You've coddled her without making her feel like an outcast. She sends her love to all of you."

Stella's eyes travel the table, pausing briefly at each one of her guests. "It's hard to believe only a few weeks have passed since many of us last gathered at this table for Friendsgiving. So much has happened, so much water over the damn.

"I'd like to extend my deepest gratitude to all of you for the surprise wedding. A lot of time and effort went into planning the event, and I am overwhelmed by your generosity. The evening was beyond special. Having my mothers here." Her gaze shifts from Hannah and Marnie to Brian and Opal. "And my new family." She spreads her arms wide. "And all my new friends. It was a fairytale ending to a chapter in my life I'm relieved to see come to a close."

Stella dabs at her eyes with her napkin. "I'm the luckiest woman alive today to be Mrs. Jack Snyder." She lifts her glass to Jack. "To my amazing husband for his never-ending patience and for standing by me these past months. We've struggled through our share of thick. I pray for thin in the years ahead."

Stella clinks Jack's glass and then turns to Presley and Everett. "I'd like to propose a toast to the other newlyweds. I'm honored to have been able to share my wedding with you. I wish you all the happiness in the years ahead."

"Here! Here!" everyone calls out in unison.

Stella takes a sip of champagne. "Soon, we'll be saying goodbye to a few of our friends. Alessandro. Presley. Everett. Your time here has been brief, but your impact on our lives has been great. We will miss you, but you always have a place here at

Hope Springs Farm. I hope you will carry the friendships that you've made here in your hearts forever."

There is not a dry eye at the table as they toast their futures. Waiters pour more champagne and serve the first course, the beginning of a celebration of family and friendship that will long be remembered by all.

Scottie's Adventures

Breaking the Story

Merry Mary

ACKNOWLEDGMENTS

I'm grateful to many people for helping make this novel possible. Foremost, to my editor, Patricia Peters, for her patience and advice and for making my work stronger without changing my voice. A great big heartfelt thank-you to my trusted beta readers —Alison Fauls, Kathy Sinclair, Anne Wolters, Laura Glenn, Tammy Underhill, Kate Rock, and Mamie Farley. And to my behind-the-scenes go-to girl, Kate Rock, for all the many things you do to manage my social media so effectively.

I am blessed to have many supportive people in my life who offer the encouragement I need to continue the pursuit of my writing career. I owe an enormous debt of gratitude to my advanced review team, the lovely ladies of Georgia's Porch, for their enthusiasm for and commitment to my work. To Leslie Rising at Levy's for being my local bookshop. Love and thanks to my family—my mother, Joanne; my husband, Ted; and the best children in the world, Cameron and Ned.

Most of all, I'm grateful to my wonderful readers for their love of women's fiction. I love hearing from you. Feel free to shoot me an email at ashleyhfarley@gmail.com or stop by my website at ashleyfarley.com for more information about my characters and upcoming releases. Don't forget to sign up for my newsletter. Your subscription will grant you exclusive content, sneak previews, and special giveaways.

ABOUT THE AUTHOR

Ashley Farley writes books about women for women. Her characters are mothers, daughters, sisters, and wives facing real-life issues. Her bestselling Sweeney Sisters series has touched the lives of many.

Ashley is a wife and mother of two young adult children. While she's lived in Richmond, Virginia for the past 21 years, a piece of her heart remains in the salty marshes of the South Carolina Lowcountry, where she still calls home. Through the eyes of her characters, she captures the moss-draped trees, delectable cuisine, and kindhearted folk with lazy drawls that make the area so unique.

Ashley loves to hear from her readers. Visit Ashley's Website @ashleyfarley.com

Get free exclusive content by signing up for her newsletter @ ashleyfarley.com/newsletter-signup/

facebook.com/ashleywfarley

twitter.com/AshleyWFarley

instagram.com/ashleyfarleyauthor

CPSIA information can be obtained
at www.ICGtesting.com
Printed in the USA
LVHW091401261020
669842LV00006B/430

9 781735 521213